Arabian Nights, 1914

Arabian Nights, 1914

A Novel About Kaiser Wilhelm II

Eric Koch

mosaic press

National Library of Canada Cataloguing in Publication Data

Koch, Eric, 1919-
 Arabian nights, 1914 : a novel about Kaiser Wilhelm II/ Eric Koch.

ISBN 0-88962-800-9

1. William II, German Emperor, 1859-1941—Fiction. I. Title.

PS8521.O23A77 2003   C813'.54   C2003-900937-8
PR9199.3.K6A77 2003

No part of this book may be reproduced or transmitted in any form, by any means, electronic or mechanical, including photocopying and recording, information storage and retrieval systems, without permission in writing from the publisher, except by a reviewer who may quote brief passages in a review.

Published by Mosaic Press, offices and warehouse at 1252 Speers Road, Units 1 and 2, Oakville, Ontario, L6L 5N9, Canada and Mosaic Press, PMB 145, 4500 Witmer Industrial Estates, Niagara Falls, NY, 14305-1386, U.S.A.

Mosaic Press acknowledges the assistance of the Canada Council and the Department of Canadian Heritage, Government of Canada for their support of our publishing programme.

Copyright © 2003, Eric Koch
Printed and Bound in Canada.
ISBN 0-88962-800-9

Mosaic Press in Canada:
1252 Speers Road, Units 1 & 2,
Oakville, Ontario
L6L 5N9
Phone/Fax: 905-825-2130
mosaicpress@on.aibn.com

Mosaic Press in U.S.A.:
4500 Witmer Industrial Estates
PMB 145, Niagara Falls, NY
14305-1386
Phone/Fax: 1-800-387-8992
mosaicpress@on.aibn.com

Le Conseil des Arts du Canada   The Canada Council for the Arts

www.mosaic-press.com

Other Books by Eric Koch

FICTION

THE FRENCH KISS
McCelland & Stewart, Toronto, 1969

THE LEISURE RIOTS
Tundra Books, Montreal, 1973
German paperback version, Die Freizei Revoluzzer, Heyne Verlag, Munich

THE LAST THING YOU'D WANT TO KNOW
Tundra Books, Montreal, 1976
German paperback version, Die Spanne Leben, Heyne Verlag, Munich
(Both German versions were reissued together in 1987 under the title C.R.U.P.P.)

GOODNIGHT, LITTLE SPY
Virgo Press, Toronto and Ram Publishing Company, London, 1979

KASSANDRUS
Heyne Verlag, Munich, 1988

LIEBE UND MORD AUF XANANTA EICHBORN
Verlag, Frankfurt, 1992

ICON IN LOVE: A NOVEL ABOUT GOETHE
Mosaic Press, Oakville, 1998
Noblepreis fur Goethe, Fischer Tachenbuch 14536, Frankfurt, 1999

THE MAN WHO KNEW CHARLIE CHAPLIN
Mosaic Press, Oakville, 2000

EARRINGS
Mosaic Press, Oakville, 2002

NON-FICTION

DEEMED SUSPECT
Methuen of Canada, Toronto, 1980

INSIDE SEVEN DAYS
Prentice Hall of Canada, Toronto, 1986

HILMAR AND ODETTE
McCelland & Stewart, Toronto, 1996

THE BROTHERS HAMBOURG
Robin Brass, Toronto, 1997

Table of Contents

Premise xi

Introduction: Portrait of a Modern Monarch . xiv

Chapter 1: Monday, July 6 1
    Wedding in Berlin

Chapter 2: Tuesday, July 7 13
    The First Alois Penner Monologue
    The Debut

Chapter 3: Wednesday, July 8 . . . 25
    The Ottoman Locomotive

Chapter 4: Tuesday, July 14 34
    The First Alphonse Picard Monologue
    The Court Preacher

Chapter 5: Friday, July 17 49
    Mayerling

Chapter 6: Sunday, July 19 62
    The First Jonathan Lind Monologue
    The Friend

Chapter 7: Monday, July 20 76
    An Act of True Courage

Chapter 8: Thursday, July 23 . . . 86
    The Pilgrim

Chapter 9: Friday, July 24 105
    The Second Alois Penner Monologue
    The Almost-Alliance.

Chapter 10: Sunday, July 26 . . . 117
    The Second Alphonse Picard Monologue
    How to Attack America

Chapter 11: Monday, July 27 . . . 133
    Two Cousins at Sea

Chapter 12: Monday, July 27 (continued) . 143
    The Second Jonathan Lind Monologue
    The Nephew

Chapter 13: Tuesday, July 28 . . . 156
    The Interview

Chapter 14: Tuesday, July 28 (First Continuation) 170
    Holy War - Made in Germany?

Chapter 15: Tuesday, July 28 (Second Continuation) 180
    The Dance

Chapter 16: Wednesday, July 29 . . 192
    How to handle the British

Chapter 17: Wednesday, July 29 (continued) . 203
    The Gypsy

Chapter 18: Thursday, July 30 . . 212
    Why was His Majesty in such a good mood?

Chapter 19: Friday, July 31 . . . 226

Chapter 20: Saturday, August 1 . . 239

Author's Note

I have tried not to take too many liberties with the facts as reported in the textbooks. But once I reached the last chapter I went berserk and unrestrained, wildly wishful thinking took over.

The portraits of the historical characters correspond closely to those drawn by their contemporaries. Other characters I invented.

The books I came across that inspired me most were those written by John C.G. Röhl, Isabel Hull and Nicholas Sombart. I am grateful to them for giving me many rewarding ideas.

Premise

Ouda was an imaginary desert kingdom not far from Mesopotamia. It was so small, so sleepy, so poor, so hopelessly stuck in the Middle Ages, and so strategically uninteresting, that by 1914 neither Russia nor England, nor France, nor even the moribund Ottoman Empire, had bothered to swallow it up. The world knew it primarily as the land of the magnificent King Shahriyar, who in better days, a millennium ago, on his way to visit his brother in a neighbouring desert kingdom, suddenly remembered that he had forgotten the golden cup he was to bring as a present. Returning to his palace to retrieve it, the King discovered his beloved wife in the arms of a slave. He was beside himself with rage and promptly ordered his Grand Vizier to cut off both their heads. After recovering from his grief, he decided never to marry again because — so we are told — he was convinced that there was not a single chaste woman on the entire face of the earth. (Woman, in this sense, did not include the inhabitants of his harem who were, in effect, slaves.) Instead, to save himself in future from the wickedness and cunning of women, he would take to his bed a different beauty every night. In the morning, by which time there was no longer any doubt about the lady's lack of chastity, he would have the Grand Vizier cut off her head. This went on for some time. There arose a clamour in the land. The fathers and mothers of the slain women called the plague upon King Shahriyar's head and called on Allah for help.

At last the Grand Vizier's beautiful daughter, Sharazad, also known as Sheherazade, responded to Allah's call. To her father's horror, she volunteered for service in the King's bed. The Grand Vizier could do nothing to stop her. After their lovemaking, she told the King a magnificent story, open-ended so as to leave him in suspense. In the morning he spared her life in order to hear what happened next. This went on for one thousand and one nights.

Zade, Sheherazade's literary descendant and the heroine of this novel, was irresistible. Her rare beauty, charm and intelligence had enriched the lives of many men. Unlike her mother, who still wore the traditional scarf over her head, ears and shoulders and a simple brown dress that concealed the shape of her body and therefore protected her from the impudent glances of men, Zade wore colourful and daring western dresses. Like the Young Turks who were now running the Ottoman Empire, she thought of herself as a modern Muslim. Zade had inherited from the original Sheherazade a realistic, sober, unromantic attitude towards love. Like her, she considered herself exempt from Islam's rigid laws against adultery. But she bestowed her favours only on those she considered worthy of Allah's and her benevolence. Her king's name was also, of course, King Shahriyar. He observed the ritual of postponing her decapitation every morning only as a courtesy to her.

Being close to the sources of Ouda's revenues, Zade's father, the Grand Vizier, was considerably richer than his impoverished king and, unlike him, could afford to send his daughters to expensive foreign schools. Zade had learned Turkish, English, French and German at the best institutions in Cairo and Constantinople.

She was progressive and far-sighted. Her reason for sharing King Shahriyar's bed was political. She wanted to convince him that, in order to enable Ouda to survive in the twentieth century, he had to lead his country into the modern world, educate his people, have everybody participate in decision-making about public matters, industrialize and make the desert bloom. Otherwise, he would lose his throne. This would certainly happen if there was a war in the region. In that case, Ouda would most undoubtedly be swallowed up by one empire or another.

Zade advised him to follow the model of Kaiser Wilhelm II of Germany. He was the essence of the modern monarch and represented the wave of the future. Germany had only recently united. But under the Kaiser's inspired leadership it had spectacularly surpassed the older powers in political, economic and scientific progress. By now — the year was 1914 — Germany's steel production was equal to that of Britain, France and Russia combined, she told King Shahriyar. Population, production, exports were soaring. German universities were the envy of the world. Clearly, Allah was on the Kaiser's side.

The Kaiser was the subject of all the stories Zade told King Shahriyar every night. They were based on newspaper clippings, magazine articles, memoirs that Ali Hassan, one of her former lovers, sent to her. He was now, thanks to her influence on the King, Ouda's Ambassador to Germany.

Introduction

Portrait of a Modern Monarch

If Kaiser Wilhelm was not himself an infidel, Zade told King Shahriyar after they made love for the first time, he would be a worthy successor to the Prophet Himself. Wilhelm never doubts for a minute that he is a direct instrument of God and that his word is God's word. He has himself said, "Remember that we Germans are the chosen people of God. On me, as German Emperor, the spirit of God has descended. I am His weapon, His sword and His vice-regent. Woe to the disobedient! Death to cowards and unbelievers!"

This, my glorious King, is indeed the Prophet's language. The Kaiser has thought deeply about the divine origin of his kingship and finds constant reassurance and inspiration for it in his archaeological studies of treasures of Hittite, Babylonian and Assyrian cultures, all close to Ouda.

The world has always understood that Wilhelm takes his role seriously and admires him for it. When his visited Rome shortly after he ascended the throne, the Italian press greeted the young monarch as il nuovo Cesare [the new Caesar]. On that occasion he made a speech in which he said he believed he had a mission to crush the Gauls, just like Julius Caesar. And he saw nothing inconsistent with the spirit of the new age when he wrote in the Munich Town Hall Album for Distinguished Guests, on September 8, 1891, suprema lex regis voluntas [the will of the king is the supreme law]. No wonder the Viennese said he wanted to be the stag at every hunt, the bride at every wedding and the corpse at every funeral. Though many people laugh at his constant play-acting, he is immensely popular, and in his style of government he undoubtedly represents the Germany of today. Without the people's happy consent, he could not survive for a single day.

> Unification of Germany: 1871
> Occasion: Defeat of France in Franco-Prussian War.
>
> Unifier: Chancellor Otto von Bismarck. ("Not by fine speeches or majority votes are the government's issues of the day decided but by blood and iron.")
>
> Monarch: Kaiser Wilhelm I, King of Prussia, grandfather of Wilhelm II who succeeded him in 1888, at the age of twenty-nine.

According to the constitution that Bismarck had devised, the monarch alone runs the government. He chooses the Chancellor, all the ministers and all the higher officials of state, both civil and military. They are responsible only to him, not to the Reichstag [the parliament]. Today, more so than in Bismarck's time, leaders of industry and finance are also welcome to serve, not only Prussian Junkers, as in the old days. The Reich is a loose federation of twenty-five states. All except the two city-states of Hamburg and Bremen have their own rulers. The president of the Bundesrat, the upper chamber, has to be a Prussian, to show which of the members of the federation is the dominant one.

Being the grandson of Queen Victoria is as important to Wilhelm as being Kaiser of Germany. No blood is bluer than his. But none of her descendants, many of them also crowned heads, is as modern as he is. The Kaiser delivers speeches on matters of high policy. The others only make old-fashioned ritual addresses on ceremonial occasions.

What a vast contrast between him and the other infidel monarchs who brutally, and evidently unaware of their shameless blasphemy, rule over men of the true faith in their respective empires — the Tsar, the King of England and the President of the godless French republic! It is true that Wilhelm rules over a few colonies in Africa and Asia, and there is no doubt a small number of Muslims among his subjects. But compare that to half of the world's three hundred million Muslims who live under British rule and the fifty million Muslims brutalized by the Tsar, not to mention those languishing under the French yoke!

Just as Allah, the Lord of Creation, is at the centre of the heart of every Muslim, so Kaiser Wilhelm, the All Highest, as all Germans call him, is at the core of German life. He gives it its style, and I would not be at all surprised if in future years his period will be called Wilhelminian, just as his uncle Edward VII's is already being called Edwardian. Pictures of him are everywhere — a truly beautiful, glowing man with his clear blue eyes and a boldly defiant, proudly pomaded upturned mustache, shaped like a W. No wonder every normal, healthy-minded German woman, young and old, virginal or non-virginal, dreams of being embraced by him. He employs twenty court photographers. To be photographed with him lifts a person far above the ranks of ordinary mortals. For the last six years, he has also appeared in a new kind of photographs, not yet seen in Ouda, pictures that move in time with the way we move. And since the souls of infidels yearn more for glittering uniforms than our souls for the simple cloth of the servants of Allah, he has three hundred German regimental uniforms, in addition to many Austro-Hungarian regimental uniforms and countless British, Russian and Portuguese admiral uniforms, and field marshals' and colonels' uniforms from who knows where. He spends many hours every day changing them and wears ribbons and decorations from all over the world. He requires the help of countless servants to dress. In a suit and tie he would seem to be in disguise.

Of course, one must never forget that in the Kaiser's Germany senior civilian state officials would never dream of attending an important social of official function except in uniform. Mind you, the Kaiser does not really like civilians, especially diplomats. He prefers schneidige or zackige soldiers, even brainless schneidige or zackige ones, and the worst term in his vocabulary is to be schlapp [slack]. That is a quality reserved for civilians.

Kaiser Wilhelm is constantly on the move, turning up suddenly at unexpected, surprising places. There is a joke in Berlin that he has no time to rule. Restlessness and speed are the essence of his personality and his régime. He even gobbles his food like a starving man. Some well-meaning journalists have remarked that the I.R. he puts after his signature — Imperator

Rex — really means Immer Reisefertig — always ready to travel.

That, honoured friend, is what it means to be modern. Wilhelm der Plötzliche, Wilhelm the Sudden, his people call him lovingly. Others say he is an "exercise in perpetual motion." He travels not only in imperial trains but also in exciting new motorcars. Two hundred days out of every year he is not in his castles in Potsdam or Berlin, or in any other of his sixty-seven castles. He is somewhere else. His court is twice as expensive as the British court. The day may not be too far off when he will fly in the air in one of those new machines the Germans are building. He finds them exciting, just as he does all new things his inventors and scientists dream up.

He is bursting with energy, just like his country. Fortunately, he is helped by an above-average intelligence, a splendid memory, a quick understanding of complicated issues and remarkable oratorical gifts. In fact, he loves talking. His versatility is extraordinary, especially considering that his education was mainly military. He did some perfunctory law and economic studies for four terms at the university in Bonn, but no one ever claimed that he learned very much there. (His cousins King George V of England and Tsar Nicolas II of Russia are no better educated.) Occasionally, he sees himself as another Frederick the Great, the most revered of Prussian kings. On other occasions, he models his conduct on our own kindly caliph of Baghdad Haroun-al-Rashid with whom Charlemagne had such amicable relations. He was the hero of many stories in the original Thousand and One Nights. It was in that generous role that the Kaiser forgave the wealthy and influential Prussian minister of finance, Johannes von Miquel, for having been a friend of a man called Karl Marx — apparently some sort of unpleasant revolutionary — fifty years ago. When this was brought up in the Reichstag, Miquel offered his resignation. Wilhelm wouldn't hear of it.

Harun-al-Rashid was in a much better position than Wilhelm — he did not have to worry about any constitution. Once Wilhelm has appointed a chancellor, he is bound by the constitution to ask him to countersign all his major orders; otherwise they don't count. Harun-al-Rashid had no such obligations. For any law, and for the budget to go through, the Kaiser needs a majority vote in the Reichstag, which is elected by universal suffrage So, unless a majority in the Reichstag gives the Kaiser the money for arms and for battleships, he can't make war, nor can he declare war without the consent of the Upper House.

On the other hand, the chancellor can't do anything important without the Kaiser's consent. In that respect, the Kaiser's absolute authority is not so very different from that of Harun-al-Rashid, or from the Sultan in the Ottoman Empire.

Back to Wilhelm's lifestyle. Germans don't seem to mind that the Kaiser's hectic speed doesn't give him much time for reflection, or that he has absolutely no Sitzfleisch, the German word for the ability to persevere in necessary but unpleasant tasks. They don't seem to mind that he prefers parades and ceremonies and — above all — making speeches to hard work. They do the hard work; that is not something they expect of the monarch. He gets up late in the morning, has three warm courses for breakfast, has an engagement or two, has lunch, sleeps again, after which he has further duties to perform, all of which usually require speech-making and story-telling. Then he gets ready for the evening's banquet.

Some people say that he suffers from caesaromania and cannot take criticism. I don't think that is true at all. It all depends on the way criticism is presented. All that is required is to couple criticism with praise for something for which in his own eyes he deserves praise. That is all. Then invariably he is grateful for it.

The Kaiser had a dreadful childhood. When he was small boy, he was forced to endure excruciating, agonizing exercises and treatments, including electric shocks, to overcome the handicap of his crippled left arm, which eventually was about fifteen centimetres too short. This handicap was the result of an injury he suffered at birth, which was unusually difficult, when his arm was wrenched out of its socket and some of the muscle tissue was torn. The other day he told somebody that at times his younger brother Heinrich "howled with pain when compelled to witness the martyrdom of my youth." He was forced to ride a horse. Whenever he was thrown off, he was made to mount it again and again and again. To a lesser person, such experiences would no doubt have done permanent harm. But not to him. He recovered from these sufferings triumphantly. Now his right hand compensates for the defects of the left. His grip is equal to that of the world champion boxer John Sullivan. And he occasionally finds it amusing to turn his rings inwards and then squeezing the hand of eminent visitors until tears come to their eyes.

Of course, Germany is not Ouda and Ouda is not Germany. True, on the surface the two countries may not have much in common. But if you, oh mighty King Shahriyar, provide the leadership to our people that Kaiser Wilhelm gives to his, it may be revealed that the Prophet's Message of Peace will inspire you and him in equal measure.

Chapter 1

Monday, July 6

Archduke Franz Ferdinand and his wife were assassinated in Sarajevo on June 28, 1914. To judge by Kaiser Wilhelm's responses to previous crises, Zade understood that it would ultimately be up to him to decide whether or not this event would lead to what everybody was talking about — a possible world war. Such a war would be the end of Ouda.

1905:	First Morocco Crisis
1911:	Second Morocco Crisis
1912–13:	First Balkan War
1913:	Second Balkan War

On June 29, Zade wrote this letter to Ali Hassan, Ouda's ambassador in Berlin.

> Dearest Ali,
> I have decided to go to Berlin.
> The information about Kaiser Wilhelm you sent me has, as you know, been eminently useful in my systematic attempt to bring our king into the twentieth century. May I thank you again. I now think I know him well.
> I am convinced I can prevent him from setting the world on fire. I know you will do your best to arrange at least one encounter between me and him — alone.
> It will be good to see you again.
> Zade.

Zade arrived at the Anhalter Bahnhof in Berlin at eleven sixteen on the morning of Monday, July 6, 1914. The weather was hot and humid. Throughout the spring and early summer there had been more thunderstorms than usual.

Zade's dark-blue travel costume, with its long skirt, fashionably tight in the corseted hips, had been made for her by a Parisian couturière especially imported for the occasion from Athens, and she wore spectacular silver earrings and bracelets. The serene, classical beauty of her oval face, with its brilliantly clear, dark eyes, unusually expressive curved eyebrows, eloquent mouth, proud chin and olive-coloured skin may well have reminded the ladies on the train of those depicted on vases in the collection of ancient Islamic art in Berlin's National Gallery.

Looking out of the window, the German landscape appeared to her as exotic as Ouda's would appear to a German traveller. She had said her morning prayers while the train approached Leipzig. Though on alien territory among alien people, she knew that her ability to achieve her mission depended not only on luck, in other words on Allah's help, but also on Ali Hassan's diplomatic skill in arranging the intimate encounter with the Kaiser that she had requested.

As for Ali, he had experienced her power first-hand. She had reversed the seemingly hopeless downward curve of his life in Ouda. Ali had been a congenital gambler and speculator before he accepted her invitation to make love to her. He never gambled or speculated again. She did not have a doubt in her mind that the same invitation would have a similar salutary effect on the Kaiser.

Ali was at the station. Genuinely delighted to see each other, they joyfully embraced. He wore a black suit, a stiff collar, a dark blue tie. A handsome man with a quick, easy smile, not quite as tall as Zade, he usually looked slightly unshaven. Because of his sharp wit and quick repartee, Berliners often thought he was Jewish. This did not please him particularly because he had noticed that many non-Jewish Germans did not seem to like Jews. To him, of course, Jews and Christians, both being infidels, were, in moral and cultural terms, equally remote. But since Berlin Jews often had a family-likeness to the inhabitants of Ouda, he sometimes imagined he had more in common with them than with the Christians.

Ali summoned a porter who loaded Zade's heavy trunk on a wagon while she held on to a leather briefcase containing carefully chosen and bound excerpts from her Tales of Thousand and One Nights: The 1914 Version, which she had translated into German and had printed in Alexandria. She intended to ask Ali to send them to the Kaiser through diplomatic channels.

The porter pushed the wagon towards the horse-drawn Droschke Ali had parked on the Askanischer Platz near the station's bustling main entrance.

Population of Berlin in 1910:	3 million
Number of automobiles in 1905:	2,000
Number of automobiles in 1907:	2,400

Source: Ruth Glatzer, Das Wilhelmische Berlin, Siedler 1993, p. 87.

"So you came anyway," he said, as the Droschke made its way along the Königgrätzerstrasse towards the Ouda embassy near the Wilhelmstrasse, where a room was waiting for her.

Zade did not grasp his meaning.

"Did you not receive my telegram?"

"No."

"Oh, that's terrible! I don't know what could have gone wrong. This is not the first time. I said that on July 8 — that is on Wednesday — the Kaiser will leave once again for his annual cruise in the Baltic. He heard the news about Sarajevo while on board and rushed back home. Now he is leaving again. I suggested you postpone your trip."

"You mean he has left Berlin? I don't believe it!"

"He wanted to stay but the Chancellor insisted he go. It would have a calming effect on everybody, he said. Of course, both knew perfectly well that the Austrians would use the assassination to provoke a war with the Serbians. They had planned to have one all along. So this ploy — summer holidays for everybody as though nothing had happened — would be a very useful deception."

"You mean the Germans were secretly encouraging them?"

"Of course. And the generals, too, wanted the Kaiser to go. So he wouldn't be in their hair."

"But surely he can send telegrams from his cruise ship?"

"Of course. And he does."

Zade mulled this over.

"When do you think he's coming back?"

"He usually goes for four to six weeks. But he can come home at a moment's notice."

She looked out of the window at the horse-dawn carriages, the tramways and a few motorcars. She did not miss the camels. The traffic here was far more orderly than in chaotic Cairo and Constantinople.

"What will I do while I wait for him?"

"Don't worry," Ali said. "A lot is about to happen. Not everybody has left Berlin."

They were passing the Ministry of War at the corner of the Leipzigerstrasse and the Wilhelmstrasse.

"We will have to figure out our strategy," he went on. "It won't be easy. I have only few connections at court. Berlin is big. Ouda is small. Ever since I arrived I have been working hard to catch the Kaiser's eye. I want to tell him that we can be useful to him in many ways. As you know, he is extremely interested in our part of the world. But he has not noticed me yet."

Zade held up her leather briefcase and told him about her stories. "It's obvious he likes to be flattered," she said. "I thought these might help things along."

"Good idea. I will send them to the palace tomorrow morning. I will ask them to forward them by diplomatic courier to Bergen, in Norway. I'm sure they will do that for me. There somebody will pick them up. I will add a note saying that the author is in Berlin and can be reached through the Ouda embassy."

They turned into the Wilhelmstrasse.

"Does he have a mistress?" she asked.

"No. If he did, everybody would know." Ali gave a little laugh. "This town loves gossip. But there has been no one since he came on the throne — and that was twenty-six years ago. There is no evidence that he has any interest whatsoever in women other than his wife. One assumes many have tried. None has succeeded. As I say, our task is very, very difficult. All we can do is pray."

At last they arrived at Luisenstrasse 16, around the corner from the German Foreign Office. The Ouda embassy occupied three small rooms in the north-east corner of the third floor, next to the embassy of Oranda. On the second floor were the offices of three journalists, Alois Penner, bureau chief of the Austrian Double Eagle, Alphonse Picard of the Mériot agency, and Jonathan Lind of the English Talbot News Agency. All three were friends of Ali Hassan.

"Is there a mosque in Berlin?" Zade asked Ali, after the coachman had brought up her trunk and deposited it in her room.

"Yes, in Neukölln. And they are building a new one in Münsdorf."

He knew she could not pray together with men.

"We need Allah's help. I'll go with you tomorrow morning and wait outside."

Arabian Nights, 1914

❈ Wedding in Berlin ❈

Let me describe to you, o happy King, the scene of the handsome, virile, twenty-two-year-old Prince Wilhelm's wedding. The date was February 27, 1881. Wilhelm was far from being a modern monarch, not yet even Crown Prince. The bride, a picture of robust health but no great beauty, was Princess Augusta Victoria Frederica Louisa Feodora Jenny of Schleswig-Holstein-Sonderburg-Augustenberg, universally known as Dona. They were in love.

After a short service, the guests moved to the White Hall of the Schloss where the silver and white decorations formed the perfect background to the bright and colourful dresses and uniforms. They filed past Wilhelm's grandfather, the eighty-four-year-old Kaiser Wilhelm I, and the Kaiserin Augusta, the granddaughter of Goethe's patron, Duke Karl August of Saxe-Weimar, bowing to each in turn. The guests included Wilhelm's uncle, the Prince of Wales, later Edward VII, whom he already detested, and representatives of most royal houses of Europe. Even the venerable, awesome Prince Otto von Bismarck was there, famous for avoiding royal functions whenever he could, usually on the grounds of bad health. But in this case the delicate relationship with the future monarch was at stake. So he thought he had better go, especially since the young man was a great admirer of his, unlike Vicky, the Prince's mother, Queen Victoria's eldest daughter, and his father, Crown Prince Friedrich, both of whom loathed and detested Bismarck.

In the centre of the floor was a polished inlay of the crowned Prussian eagle. Everyone avoided stepping on it because it was as slippery as glass. It was important to keep this in mind since, according to an ancient Prussian tradition, the guests were expected to participate in the ceremonial pageant that was about to begin. The lights were extinguished, the band of the Garde de Corps began playing solemn, festive music and the Marshall of the Court, carrying his wand of office, led into the room twenty-four pages each carrying a resin torch. Everyone proceeded to walk slowly past the Kaiser and the Kaiserin, seated on their thrones, and past Wilhelm and Dona on their gilded chairs, with decorations, jewels and sword hilts glistening in the flickering lights. The twenty-four torches yielded a sweet aroma of resin.

Now, my noble lord, Your Majesty may have noticed that all this was a little different from your own wedding, and from the way we do things in Ouda generally. Dona's hands and feet were not painted with elaborate designs of henna, including the name of her husband-to-be, nor, as far I know, had the married women of her circle shared with her, the night before the wedding, the secrets of married life. Whether or not they did, the secrets must have been revealed to her at some time. The couple subsequently produced six sons and one daughter.

I said when they were married they were in love, which was fortunate but by no means necessary, since marriages in royal families among infidels are almost invariably arranged, as all ours are. Non-royal infidels are supposed to marry for love only, in these modern days. Vicky had gone to considerable trouble to create conditions to facilitate her oldest son choosing Dona. However, it would never have occurred to Wilhelm in any case to marry a lady outside the circle of eligible and politically acceptable princesses. That he loved her helped.

His mother favoured the marriage because she was close to Dona's family, even though Vicky's mother, Queen Victoria, was unenthusiastic about the union. At first, Vicky tried to like Dona, but Dona was shy and frightened of her, and made a number of gaffes, which Vicky quickly pointed out to her. This did not make for a very good relationship. Soon Dona found her mother-in-law patronizing and domineering. Vicky hoped that conjugal life would calm Wilhelm down and make him a little more manageable. The truth was that he had been a problem to his parents, especially to his mother, from the moment he was born. In this case, Wilhelm had happily done what his mother wanted, namely marry Dona. Soon after he was married, he sided with his bride against Vicky's attempts at bullying her.

He had been in love before, not long ago, with a cousin of his, Princess Elisabeth — Ella — of Hesse-Darmstadt, the sister of Alix, the future wife of Tsar Nicholas II. Ella rejected him. Incidentally, Dona was also related to Wilhelm, but far more remotely. Her grandmother was a half-sister of Wilhelm's grandmother Queen Victoria and a cousin of Wilhelm's grandfather. It seems that Vicky had opposed the match with Ella, quite justifiably as it turned out, not because of the blood relationship, which was the only reason for her opposition, but because there was hemophilia in the Hesse-Darmstadt family.

Wilhelm had been in love with Dona since their first meeting, two and half years before the wedding. Why then the long delay? The answer — there were serious obstacles. The old Kaiser, the Head of the House of Hohenzollern, who had never heard of Dona, had to give his consent, and so did the Chancellor, Bismarck. The first obstacle, apart from Wilhelm's youth, was the unresolved question of Dona's rank in the nobility. Was it high enough to make her worthy of one day becoming the Kaiserin of Germany? Perhaps not. There was talk that in the House of Schleswig-Holstein-Sonderburg-Augustenberg there had been a number of irregular marriages. One of Dona's grandmothers was said to be a mere Danish countess, perhaps even the illegitimate daughter of a Danish king. There was also talk of an aunt being married to a commoner, Professor Johannes Esmarch, a surgeon in Kiel. This made some members of the court observe sardonically that this connection might one day be useful. The happy couple might obtain the surgeon's obstetrical services inexpensively.

Furthermore, it was asked whether other candidates might not be more suitable. But what candidates? The English princesses were too young and too closely related. Catholic or Greek Orthodox princesses were out of the question. And Wilhelm knew all the eligible Protestant princesses and found them ugly, sickly or dimwitted.

But by far the most serious, and at first seemingly insuperable, obstacle was that Dona's father still had claims on the duchies of Schleswig and Holstein, which the Prussians insisted belonged to Prussia by law. The Duke of Schleswig-Holstein-Sonderburg-Augustenberg would have to renounce these claims formally if the marriage could ever be considered. But would he do hat? Not very likely. Moreover, he had opposed Prussian policies ever since the Prussian-Danish war in 1864.

In July 1879, Dona softened the old Kaiser's heart a little when she visited him with her sister in Bad Ems, but not enough to enable him to initiate negotiations with her father, the Duke. First, the Kaiser requested Bismarck to compose a formal memorandum on the political aspects of the proposed union. Bismarck was unenthusiastic about the "Augustenbergers." So he procrastinated, an art he mastered.

During their long wait, Wilhelm and Dona were not allowed to write to each other, let alone meet. First, Bismarck said he was unable to write the memorandum requested from him because his wrist hurt too much, he would have to take the cure in Bad Kissingen to alleviate the pain. This elicited from Wilhelm's father, the liberal Crown Prince and inveterate adversary of the conservative Chancellor, the wry observation that "certainly, if one slaughters three ministers at one time and introduces protective tariffs to raise the price of foodstuffs one does not have much time and energy left for other things!" In the end, discussions dragged on and face-saving formulas were endlessly examined, among others the possibility, if the Duke really refused to renounce his claims to the duchies, of demanding from him a guarantee not ever to raise the matter.

At last — Allah intervened. On January 14, 1880, the Duke died suddenly in an inn near Wiesbaden. The road to marital bliss was clear.

·

On the day before the wedding, February 26, 1881, freezing but happy crowds welcomed Dona to Berlin. The flags were out on Unter den Linden. The Princess's unheated carriage was drawn by eight black horses wearing heavy red brass-studded harnesses. It swayed from side to side like a ship at sea, warming her up a little but no doubt making her feel quite nauseous, in her tight corset and uncomfortable formal dress with its long train. Fortunately, the ride did not take very long. Perhaps she was cheered up by the float advertising Singer sewing machines just ahead of her. (One day I will explain to Your Majesty what they are.) At the head of the procession, as custom prescribed, rode the master butchers of Berlin, in their top hats and frock coats. White doves were released from the Brandenburg Gate. On reaching the Schloss, the mayor of Berlin made an inaudible speech and Dona gave an inaudible reply. Crown Prince Friedrich presented her to the Grenadiers who had lined up. His son Wilhelm was at their head.

The future Kaiser announced to them that the future Kaiserin would henceforth be "the mother of the company." Later in his career he made more eloquent speeches.

Arabian Nights, 1914

It was nonetheless a truly auspicious day. But the day when Wilhelm would lead Germany into the modern world was still far off.

Chapter 2

Tuesday, July 7

Zade waited for Ali in a small open-air café in the Hermannstrasse while he said his prayers in the mosque. It had been built in 1866 and had its own cemetery but no minaret. She had said hers in the early morning in her small room in the Ouda embassy. After Ali finished the mullah joined them for coffee.

The mullah, a bearded old man from Cyprus, was greatly upset by the decision the Kaiser had made on Sunday to give the Austrians a blank cheque to do whatever they wanted to punish the Serbs for assassinating his friend Franz Ferdinand, with whom he had gone hunting in Konopischt in mid June, only two weeks earlier.

"Mark my words — he will rue the day," the old man warned. "Nothing good can come out of this."

"What else should he have done?" Ali said. "They're allies, aren't they?"

"He should have said 'The guilty must be punished — let us consult together how to do that without setting fire to the world.' The Russians won't let anything happen to the Serbs. All the Slavs will stick together, you'll see. No, no, no, this is reckless nonsense. The man never thinks anything through. He is impossible!"

Zade usually found out anything she needed to know without asking questions. Men adored talking to her. But this time she wanted to probe.

"Can't somebody talk to him before it's too late?" The mullah looked straight at her, his eyes wide open.

"Why don't you try?" There was a twinkle in his eye.

There was no point telling him that this was exactly why she had come all the way to Berlin from Ouda. He politely took his leave. Ali and Zade ordered more coffee. Ali said he was developing a number of ideas but he was not quite ready yet to talk about them.

Nearby sat two workers, to judge by the caps on their heads, drinking beer. This was the first time that Ali witnessed the hypnotic effect Zade's beauty had on the inhabitants of the Abendland, this evening land, where the sun sets. The two men could not take their eyes off her. They were used to seeing oriental women in the neighbourhood, mainly the wives and daughters of Persian rug merchants. But they had never before been in the presence of a truly stunning beauty from the Morgenland, the morning land. At last, one of the two screwed up enough courage to get up, walk over to their table, take off his cap, make a slight respectful bow to Ali, and say directly to her:

"What do you think the weather will be like tomorrow?"

"The sun will shine," she said in her delightfully accented German.

"That's what I believe, too. Thank you."

He turned round, went back to his table and sat down in triumph.

In the Droschke on the way back to the Luisenstrasse, Ali told Zade that before going upstairs to the embassy he would like to introduce her to his friend on the second floor, Alois Penner, of the Double Eagle news agency in Vienna. But at the entrance of Number 16 they were waylaid by the Hausmeisterin, the concierge, who had a special fondness for Ali.

"Ah, I see you have a beautiful lady visitor from far away," Frau Vogelsang said, with a meaningful wink. "And I can see you have very good taste."

She shook hands with Zade.

"You came at a very exciting time," the concierge said to her cheerfully. "My three sons are in the reserve and can hardly wait for the shooting to start. Hans wants to shoot Russians and Fritz wants to shoot Frenchmen. Klaus wants to shoot both. But my husband says the Kaiser is too much of a coward to break the noose around our necks. All talk and no action, he says."

Alois Penner's tone, when they finally managed to reach the second floor, was somewhat different.

He bent low over Zade's hand and inhaled her perfume. "Küss die Hand, madame," he said. "A ray of sunshine from the Morgenland. What a delight. Just what is needed on this gloomy Tuesday."

Penner was in his late fifties and his desk was a jungle of newspapers and magazines. He had grey Franz-Joseph-whiskers sprouting on his cheeks and the world-weary melancholia so characteristic of his once glorious multinational empire. Its armies had not won a single war in two hundred years, including the one nearly fifty years ago that the Sau-Preussen, the piggish Prussians, had provoked in order to wrestle from them the ancient imperial hegemony over the entire German-speaking world. And now here he was, reporting to Vienna from their unbearably brash and vulgar nouveau-riche capital.

THE FIRST ALOIS PENNER MONOLOGUE

1699:	Ottomans lose Croatia to Austria
1878:	Serbia achieves independence from Ottomans
1908:	Ottomans are forced to yield Bosnia and Herzegovina to Austria-Hungary; Albania revolts, raising the question whether Ottomans can retain loyalty of any non-Turkish subjects
1912–13:	Ottomans lose almost all their remaining Balkan territories

Why did God ever create the Serbs? Those odious peasants have openly declared their intention create a Greater Serbia. At whose expense? At *our* expense. Without a moment of shame, and egged on by the loathsome Russians, their prime minister Nicola Pasic says this is the only purpose of their existence, to steal our Croatians, Bosnians and Slovenes and turn them into Serbs. This is in line with the latest fashion of pan-Slavism, which decrees that all Slavs belong together whether they like it or not. If this happens, it will be the end of Austria-Hungary as a Great Power. The poisonous passions of nationalism will destroy it. Kaiser Franz Joseph and everybody in Vienna and Budapest know this. He is eighty-four and has seen his empire decline for sixty-five years, ever since he came on the throne in 1849, and he wishes to oversee what he — and everybody else — suspects will be the last phase of the Dual Monarchy with dignity and decency. In the meantime he knows that in order to do this we have no choice but to punish those responsible for the crime committed in Sarajevo. In the whole of human history no one has ever given up power voluntarily. Let us not rush things. If we allow the Serbs to get away with this we will lose the Czechs and the Poles and all the others long before the time for their departure is ripe. Nothing in human affairs is inevitable, and — who knows? — the Wheels of History may reverse themselves. The question is how do we take military action without causing a world-wide fire? Behind Serbia stands the Tsar, who may very well welcome a war in the vain hope that this will divert his unpleasant revolutionaries from trying again what they failed to achieve in 1905 — less than a decade ago — topple him. And the Tsar is allied to the excitable French, who are desperately waiting for a chance to take revenge on the Germans for defeating them in 1870 and seizing Alsace and Lorraine. That war was, of course, revenge for the crushing defeat, dismemberment and financial ruin Napoleon had inflicted on the Prussians at the Battle of Jena in 1806.

Clearly, this requires diplomacy of the highest order. If only it was simply a matter of our persuading the Serb government to arrest their murderous terrorists and put them in jail! But, regrettably, this is impossible. It does not take into account what every journalist knows, namely that behind the terrorists stands official Belgrad, that the secret organization the Black Hand is in fact — let us for once call things by their name — an arm of the government. Alas, Vienna has to pretend that they know nothing about this, even though they may have seen the Black Hand's solemn constitution, as have I. Article Two reads, "This organization prefers terrorist action to psychological [*geistige*] propaganda." Each member has to be prepared to pledge his life [*seine Person zu verpfänden*]. Their emblems are cross-bones, a dagger, a bomb and a bottle of poison. Naturally, last week the newspapers in Belgrad celebrated the murderers as heroes and martyrs.

So, as you can see, Vienna and Budapest face a gigantic problem. The stakes could not be higher. If military action is required, what kind? When and where? Things can get out of hand very easily.

For Vienna, the case for immediate action is overwhelming. They have been waiting for an opportunity to crush Serbia for many years, since long before Archduke Franz Ferdinand's murder. This gives them a perfect opportunity. Will not the whole civilized world support a war to smoke out the assassins? In particular, will not Kaiser Wilhelm be proud to join hands with his allies in such a morally impeccable punitive action? Especially since his well-known sense of humour does not include jokes about assassinating heirs to the throne. Will he not be happy to take considerable risks to fight terrorists? Even the men running the French republic, good, solid bourgeois all of them, men whose great-grandfathers had cut off the head of Louis XVI but whose fathers in 1871 did not hesitate to crush the Commune, will they not also applaud enthusiastically a drastic action against murderous terrorists? And will not even the Tsar overlook his blood ties with his disreputable fellow Slavs in the interest of upholding the principle of God-anointed monarchy?

Before he turned his attention to Franz Ferdinand, Apis, the popular name for the leader of the Black Hand, had already done an exemplary job in 1903 of masterminding the assassination of King Alexander Obrenovich of Serbia and his unsavoury Queen Draga. He had them both thrown out of the window of the Royal Palace in Belgrad. But he was sloppy in planning the murder of King Ferdinand of Bulgaria, and also bungled five attempts to kill the governors of Croatia and Bosnia. Sometimes his incompetent assistants dutifully committed suicide before they were caught.

Of course, the Black Hand was absolutely right to kill Archduke Franz Ferdinand. Although the Archduke had no use for the "national aspirations" of the minorities within our Dual Monarchy, he did believe in internal reform. He shared Bismarck's view that the Serbian plum trees and pigs were not worth the bones of a single Austrian soldier — Bismarck's translated this into "a single Pomeranian grenadier" — but Franz Ferdinand's main antipathy was directed at the Hungarian aristocracy, which he thought threatened Austrian predominance. He wanted to split up the Empire into three parts, the Austrian, the Hungarian and the Slav parts, but he had no precise idea how to bring about this laudable solution. Some thought he was working towards a federation of ten or twelve equal states modelled on the United States of America. None of this was of interest to the Serb terrorists. For them he was a believer in internal reform standing in the way of a Greater Serbia, and that was reason enough to kill him.

Last Sunday, on July 5, a special emissary arrived with a personal letter from Franz Joseph, to be presented to the Kaiser the next day by the Austrian Ambassador, Count Szögyény. The Dual Monarchy of Austria-Hungary could withstand the pan-Slav flood,

Franz Joseph wrote, only if Serbia's role as a power factor in the Balkans was ended. What would Germany's position be if such a course were followed?

The Kaiser had an affable lunch with the Count. Reversing a previous policy of urging restraint on Vienna in all matters concerning Serbia, this time he threw all caution to the wind and declared that, even in the event of serious European complications, Austria-Hungary could count on Germany's full support. Why not strike against Belgrad right now? Russia was not ready for war and would certainly think very carefully before resorting to arms.

In short, Wilhelm gave Vienna a blank cheque. In the afternoon, his Chancellor Theobald Bethmann Hollweg arrived and approved of the Kaiser's reply. It had been his position all along that Germany needed a strong Austria-Hungary as a counterweight to despotic, aggressive Russia whose military and industrial strength was rapidly growing. The assumption was Vienna would act with lightning speed and present the world with a *fait accompli*.

Did they not know that we Austrians are no longer capable of doing anything with lightning speed? That this is a German *spécialité*?

The Debut

Tonight, o mighty King, I must tell you about the dramatic first day in the reign of Kaiser Wilhelm, June 15, 1888, more than seven years after his wedding, the day on which the world learned how this truly modern monarch intended to lead his nation to a glorious future. He was twenty-nine years old and still very much the disciple of Bismarck, and he may very well have thought it was a compliment when Bismarck said of him, "The Kaiser is like a balloon. If you don't hold the string tight, you never know where he'll be off to." Wilhelm approved wholeheartedly of Bismarck's view that Vicky was a grave danger to the nation. She had inherited her alien — that is, English-liberal — views, he thought, not only from her mother but also from her father, Queen Victoria's Prince Consort Albert of Saxe-Coburg, who had looked with favour on the revolutionary aspirations of 1848. Wilhelm knew very well that his other grandfather, Wilhelm I, had fled to London in 1848 when the revolutionaries stoned the windows of his Berlin palace. Bismarck owed his rise to power to his firm resolve to stamp out all revolutionary aspirations in Prussia once and for all.

Like her parents, Vicky believed in government responsible to parliament, not to the monarch — an absurd concept, Bismarck and Wilhelm agreed, which was just about the last thing Germany would need. If a conflict were to arise in Vicky's mind between English liberalism and Prussian monarchical autocracy, both were certain she would be on the wrong side. This, to put it in a nutshell, made her a potential traitor, if not an actual one.

Your Majesty will not be able to relish the full flavour of the eventful opening scene of the Wilhelmian drama unless I first tell you this: You may thank Allah a thousand times every morning, noon and night that you were (no doubt) a beautiful baby when you were born, with all your limbs intact. As everybody knows, your mother was a model of modest Ouda womanhood and not the ambitious, domineering daughter of the most powerful woman in the world.

As I have told you before, Wilhelm was born with a crippled arm. His left arm was useless. Some said that both mother and father were at first delighted with their son and merely sorry for his little misfortune. Others claim to remember that from the very beginning Vicky felt profoundly guilty for having produced a deformed baby and that there were times when she could hardly bear to look at him. She knew that the injury to his arm was the result of an accident during birth and was in no way her fault. No one, not even Wilhelm, ever said it was. But there was nothing she could do to shake off an overwhelming sense of responsibility.

I would have thought that to overcome this sense she would give the child more than the usual maternal love and affection. But for some very profound reason which I do not understand the opposite seems to have been the case. If only she had been able to overcome this sense and given him the occasional praise, instead of her constant, frowning disapproval! All his life he had to fight to overcome an overwhelming, no doubt mother-induced sense of inferiority. She had eight children in thirteen years. As far as I know, she was a good mother to all of them. Only with Wilhelm did she have serious problems from the very beginning.

One of the reasons may have been political. By giving birth to a deformed child, she must have felt she had let England down. For an English woman to produce the future German Kaiser, the baby should have been perfection itself. Instead of that — a withered arm!

In her view everything English was superior to everything Prussian. This attitude had not exactly endeared her to her in-laws when she arrived in Berlin as a young bride. As a result, the wife and sister of her father-in-law, Kaiser Wilhelm I, snubbed her. When her own father, the Prince Consort Albert, died, she was not allowed to go to London to the funeral on the grounds that she was two months pregnant.

While the old Kaiser had his occasional bath in a tub, she had English bathrooms installed in her Schloss. The Prussians like to eat their asparagus white, but she had to have her asparagus green, as they do in England. Wilhelm's arm should be treated by bathing in the English Channel, not in the Baltic Sea, which would do no good.

Vicky felt superior to her husband, even if she did truly love him. She had dominated him from the moment she married him, at the age of eighteen. Even infidels believe wives should not dominate their husbands. But she did, without seeing anything wrong in it, not just because she was English and he was only Prussian and, to boot, a member of what she thought was the paltry dynasty of Hohenzollerns, but because she realized she was more intelligent than he.

Naturally Wilhelm rebelled against both of them as soon as he was old enough. He adopted as his guidelines everything they opposed, above all admiration for Bismarck. Once he was an adult, though, this was no longer a matter of juvenile rebellion but an expression of genuine devotion and conviction. In return, Bismarck went to great lengths to build up Wilhelm's self-confidence, going as far as to tell him that one day he would have to be his own chancellor. On the old Prince's seventy-first birthday in 1886 Wilhelm sent him a bust of himself and a letter in which he declared himself to be "one of his most ardent followers and firmest friends."

Now let me tell you my story.

The moment that Wilhelm's father, Kaiser Friedrich, who had commanded the Second and Third Armies with distinction in the wars against Austria and France, died in the Neue Palais in Potsdam, Wilhelm became Kaiser. Friedrich left behind diaries that were expected to contain critical material about Bismarck. If they were published, it would harm Bismarck as well as Wilhelm. The new Kaiser correctly assumed that the diaries stated that some of the credit Bismarck claimed for founding the Reich really belonged to Friedrich. Who can blame Wilhelm, therefore, when, in his first official act, he attempted to gain possession of them? He did not know that during Friedrich's last illness Vicky had already smuggled them out of the country. By now they were in Windsor. In his view these documents belonged to the German state and to remove them was an act of treason. Most patriotic Germans would agree with him.

Minutes after the flag was lowered to half-mast, Vicky, dazed with grief, went to the park to cut a few white roses to put on her husband's body. A soldier politely begged her to return to the palace. No one, he said, was allowed to leave the palace without written authorization. Soldiers, with rifles in their hands, had been placed in all strategic positions. Wilhelm, garbed in the full dress uniform of the Hussars, sabre at the ready, frantically searched his mother's room. At the same time, the late Emperor's aide-de-camp, at Wilhelm's orders, ransacked Friedrich's writing desk.

All that was found was a faded telegram from his grandmother in Windsor sent on the day of his birth, asking "Is it a fine boy?"

Chapter 3

Wednesday, July 8

Soon after his arrival in Berlin Ali Hassan discovered that there was a strong erotic element in the German penchant for the Orient. This, he thought, must have something to do with the universal appeal of A Thousand and One Nights, especially of the harem life that was so appetizingly described in these stories. You did not have to be more than normally bored with your wife to envy men like Harun-al-Rashid, who could call upon any belly dancer of his choice any time of the day or night and ask her to perform for him in ways any German reader could only dream about.

He was therefore not surprised to observe yesterday morning, in the small café in the Hermannstrasse in Neukölln, Zade's effect on the two beer-drinking workmen. It confirmed what he already suspected and hoped — she would have a galvanizing effect on every normal German male who saw her. It made him decide that all that was required for her to succeed in her mission was to construct a situation in which she would catch the Orient-loving Kaiser's eye and the rest would follow inexorably. Having set the style for the Wilhelminian age, Wilhelm was bound to respond to her in the way his normal male subjects did, only more so. When, a year or two ago, somebody remarked in his presence that His Majesty had a little cold, he thundered that His Majesty only had big colds.

Sending Zade's flattering stories to him while the Kaiser was cruising in the northern seas might help — this Ali called the Arabian Nights Strategy — but it was not safe for him to rely on only one strategy. He had to think up several others.

Two days after Zade's arrival in Berlin, while Vienna was preparing an ultimatum to be sent to Belgrad, Ali devised his second strategy, the Swiss Strategy. He did not say anything about it to Zade as yet, but it was very much on his mind when he had a conversation that morning in his embassy with the two Turkish officers in civilian clothes who occasionally came to see him, the gaunt Captain Ismail Hazim and the stubby Captain Fual Kamil. They were both natives of Salonika, the Macedonian port in the western frontier region of the Ottoman Empire, the bustling un-Turkish port that had been the birthplace of the Young Turkish rebellion. (The Young Turks had been one of many secret societies there, many of them modelled on the Italian carbonari. Some were intellectuals who had gone to the West, produced newspapers to be smuggled back to Turkey and then, after the revolution in 1908, returned.)

The two officers relished their occasional conversations with Ali because they knew Ouda's Ambassador had the same mission in life as they did. Like Ouda, the drowsy, languid Ottoman Empire had to modernize or perish.

The Ottoman Empire was not an empire like any other. It was a relic of its great past, essentially a myth, its central authority almost non-existent. In effect, local sheiks ruled, and the sultan's authority was largely make-believe. In certain areas there was no government at all — brigands roamed at will. Only five percent of the taxes were collected by the government, the remaining ninety-five percent — well, no one knew where that went. England, France and Russia were watching the gradual disintegration of the Ottoman Empire with barely disguised greed. They hope to benefit from what they expected would be its eventual dismemberment.

Many foreign governments, including Germany, enjoyed extra-territorial rights. The Ottoman Public Debt Administration was composed almost entirely of representatives of European and American bondholders. Foreigners did not have to pay taxes at all. They were subject to the civil and criminal laws of their home countries, not to Ottoman law. They even had their own postal system. No policeman could enter their premises without consular permission.

The two Turkish visitors wore flamboyant mustachios reminding the opera-loving Berliners they encountered of characters in Mozart's Abduction from the Seraglio. Their friends were usually delighted to discover, after listening to their quaintly florid German for a few minutes, that they had an endearing and an almost naive admiration for everything German. Ali had met them several times at receptions given by Baron Edgar von Toplitz, the chairman of one of the banks financing the Berlin-Baghdad railway, in his sumptuous Villa Suleika, near the Tiergarten.

1875:	Ottoman Empire defaulted on public debt
1881:	Administration of public debt was placed in European hands
1882:	German military advisers sent to Constantinople to help reorganize the army; British advisers did the same for Ottoman navy
1908:	Young Turk Revolution, under leadership of C.U.P. (Committee for Unity and Progress) and inspired by Turkish nationalism; the Young Turks were committed to reversing the seemingly relentless disintegration of Ottoman Empire; abdication of Sultan Abdul Hamid in favour of his younger brother Mehmed Reshad
1909–14	C.U.P. liberalism eclipsed by nationalism; pan-Turkism and pan-Islamism became political movements; revolts and massacres; before the events in Sarajevo in 1914, government divided about which great power — Britain, France, Russia or Germany — should be invited to assist in life-saving reforms; Turkish- and Arabic-speaking populations roughly equal at ten million each; Constantinople, a city of one million, had one hundred and ten cars

Source: David Fromkin, A Peace to End All Peace, André Deutsch 1989, pp. 46–48.

Ali introduced Zade, a distinguished visitor from Ouda. She took a seat on an armchair near the window. The two Turks were not used to seeing westernized Arab women and at first did not quite know how to behave. But they soon got used to her, especially since she was so singularly beautiful.

"Your Excellency," the gaunt Captain Hazim began, "Constantinople is assuming there will be a major war."

Ali thought this was a prudent assumption but he saw no reason to say so. "The Kaiser," he said, in the slightly mocking tone common in sophisticated military and diplomatic circles when speaking of the German Emperor, "is about to embark on his usual summer cruise in the North Sea, on his beloved imperial yacht the Hohenzollern, on which he has so far spent a total of one fifth of his time since he came to power."

"So we understand," the stubby Captain Kamil observed.

"Admiral Alfred von Tirpitz," Ali continued in the same manner, "is climbing mountains in Tarasp in Switzerland. No doubt he needed a change of scene from the high seas. The Chief of the General Staff, Helmuth von Moltke, is taking the waters in Karlsbad. Immediately after the events at Sarajevo, the Chancellor Theodor von Bethmann Hollweg withdrew to his estate in Hohenfinow, northeast of Berlin, and comes to the capital only on urgent matters of state. Gottlieb von Jagow, the Secretary of State in the Foreign Office, is on his honeymoon in Lucerne. Does that sound like war, gentlemen?"

"Germans have telegraphs and telephones," Hazim reminded the Ambassador. "Many years ago Bismarck told the Kaiser that any damned foolish thing in the Balkans could one day start a world war."

"Did he really?" Ali pretended that this was new to him. "I am very pleased to hear that. His Majesty always had the greatest respect for the Iron Chancellor's judgement." He changed his tone. "My friends, I know what is on your mind. Up to now you have worked towards a close relationship with Germany in economic and administrative matters. You have understood that the other Great Powers thought it was in their interest to see the Ottoman Empire poor and weak in order to benefit from its ultimate dissolution. You know that the Bulgarians, the Greeks and the Italians, too, have designs on you. They all have their knives whetted — whereas the Germans want you to be strong. And if you were to recover some of the territories you lost, the Germans know they have nothing to fear. They have never annexed a single village belonging to you. And should there ever be a war between Germany and France, England and Russia — let us pray to Allah that it will never come to that! — the Germans understand that your empire could be of immense strategic advantage to them. They also know, of course, that they could help you reconquer Egypt, Algeria and the Caucasus. So you are absolutely right to look to Germany for help. I have even heard talk of the Germans possibly supporting a holy war in the name of Islam — because such a war could really make a lot of trouble for the British, the Russians and the French. I am sure there is nothing I can say about these matters that you have not thought of yourselves. So you have to make a decision. No doubt some of your people think you can stay neutral if there is a war, like Switzerland, and make a lot of money doing business with both sides."

"Yes, that would be very, very tempting," Captain Kamil nodded.

They talked about this possibility wistfully for another few minutes, and came to the inevitable conclusion that, alas, they were not strong enough to remain neutral in case of war among the Great Powers.

Then they left.

As soon as they had gone Ali tried out his Swiss Strategy on Zade.

"I think it is safe to say," he said, "that the Ottoman government will agree with our two friends and side with the Germans."

"Right."

"Don't you think, just as the Austrians are having trouble with their minorities, the Turks will have trouble with theirs?"

"I certainly do," Zade replied. "Not only that. The British will do everything they can to persuade the Arabs to stab them in the back."

"And they will succeed."

It was no surprise to Ali to note once again that Zade had an excellent political imagination. This she had already demonstrated when she converted the mostly anti-Kaiser material he had sent to her from Berlin into pro-Kaiser stories.

"That is where you come in," he said. "As soon as the Kaiser comes back, you will go to him as my emissary and tell him that Ouda is an Arab Switzerland, a neutral country in the desert that can be of immense value to him as a base for intelligence and for anti-British propaganda. What do you think?"

Zade rose and silently kissed him on the forehead.

❈ The Ottoman Locomotive ❈

A little more than year after the Kaiser made his debut by asserting the rights of the German state against his English mother, he decided to proclaim his interest in the Near East in a symbolic act. He paid a state visit to Constantinople to call on Sultan Abdul Hamid II, Caliph of Islam and so Shadow of God to three hundred million True Believers. Dona and Herbert von Bismarck, the Chancellor's son and the foreign minister, came along. The Sultan was also known by some as the Red Sultan because of the amount of blood he had shed, and by others as the Ogre of Yildiz Kiosk, his fortified palace on the hill above the city. His mother had been a consumptive Circassian slave girl and his father a plump, lazy ruler remembered only for having introduced the four-poster bed to Turkey.

For thirty years Abdul Hamid had been the despotic leader of that huge state, writing poetry while facing conspiracies at home and abroad, fighting wars and suppressing revolutions, shooting down suspected assassins with a pearl-handled revolver.

I am sure Your Majesty remembers the Sultan well — a shrunken little man, with a great beaked nose and a wispy beard died red as the custom demanded. You may even have met his Belgian mistress and some of the women in his seraglio. You probably did not know, however, that his favourite books were about an English detective by the name of Sherlock Holmes and his favorite composer Jacques Offenbach.

I have no idea whether Wilhelm ever found out

how terrified the poor Sultan was of electricity, diseases and crowds. After all, the modern world had not yet had a chance to establish itself in the Ottoman Empire. That is why Wilhelm, quite rightly, considered his visit so important. But somebody must have told him that he was likely to be watched. The Sultan employed more than twenty thousand secret agents to spy upon his own guards, none of whom he trusted. Who knows how many were required to spy upon his guests.

I am sure, though, Wilhelm understood very well that the only way in which the Sultan could at least pretend to try to keep his country together was by military force. Young rebels were constantly plotting against him, as were some of our fellow Arabs, Armenians, Greeks, Kurds and Jews. I am sure Wilhelm was well briefed on them all, including the Kurds who, as you know, were not supported by any foreign power. But the Armenians were backed by Russia. Since Wilhelm was well acquainted with Jewish bankers — Bismarck had one — he may have heard of the Jewish banker Mizray Qrasow. He had offered to pay all the debts of the Ottoman state in return for permission to Jews to visit Palestine any time they pleased. I don't know why the Turks refused the offer. Since the time of the Prophet, relations between Muslims and Jews have usually been better than relations between Muslims and Christians.

The imperial party arrived in the Bosporus in their yacht, the Hohenzollern, on October 31, 1889, and received a heart-warming welcome from the population. By then, the first few miles of the Anatolian Railway — the stretch from Haida Pascha to

Eskisehir — was already being built, financed mainly by the Deutsche Bank, an undertaking naturally strongly opposed by England, France and Russia. I have no doubt that the Kaiser's visit delighted the German financial and business community, even if Bismarck had frowned on it because he thought it was an unnecessary provocation of Russia. He could have stopped it, of course, but since the Kaiser had set his heart on the journey he let him go, and even allowed his son to go along.

Bismarck was right — the Russians did consider the visit an affront, and said so most vociferously, unlike the French who pretended to be amused by what they considered "an absurd Cook's tour." The English were at first pleased because the Russians were displeased. However, as Your Majesty no doubt recalls, they soon changed their minds and concluded a defensive agreement with the Russians to join forces to expel the Germans from those territories between the Black Sea and the Persian Gulf which they considered vital to them. This was the first time the English and the Russians were on the same side since the time of Napoleon.

But by then it was too late. German locomotives had began to supplant Ottoman camels.

Chapter 4

Tuesday, July 14

There was a tacit agreement between Ali and Zade that they would not discuss what, if anything, Zade would actually say to the Kaiser at the critical moment, to dissuade him from causing a world war. The assumption was that the act of lovemaking per se — somehow — could not help but lead to that result. It would be a waste of time for Ali to question that assumption. Instead, intense thought was given to the avenues that would lead to the encounter.

This was an overwhelmingly difficult undertaking. So far two strategies had been worked out, the Arabian Nights Strategy, sending Zade's stories to the Hohenzollern cruising off the coast of Norway, and the Swiss Strategy, which Zade was to put before His Majesty as soon as he came home. The first one was essentially a device to attract the Kaiser's attention to the author's presence in Berlin and to entice him to summon her. The second one was more demanding.

Zade had arrived in Berlin on Monday, July 6, 1914. Ali told her about the Swiss Strategy on Wednesday, July 8, the day he met with the two C.U.P. officer. That Wednesday afternoon he had telephoned Manfred von Kosenburg, his one reliable contact in the Hausmarschall's office at the Neue Palais in Potsdam. (Manfred was the younger brother of the prominent neurologist and author Professor Hermann von Kosenburg whom we will meet later). Kosenburg gave him assurances that he would do his best to arrange an audience with his emissary as soon as His Majesty returned from the cruise. Ali had no access to anybody closer to the court than Kosenburg.

While Europe continued to enjoy an unusually lovely summer, Ali conceived the third, the Mustache Strategy, a direct result of the meeting he had on July 14 with the journalist Alphonse Picard in the office of the Mériot agency on the floor below the Ouda embassy in the Luisenstrasse.

Hardly taller than a dwarf, attractively ugly, Picard reminded some of his older friends in Montmartre of the painter Henri de Toulouse Lautrec, who had died in 1901 and whom many remembered vividly. Picard was the painter's journalistic equivalent. His office was dominated by a large black-and-white poster of the Kaiser. Only the mustache was red.

Picard observed the French national holiday by not writing a single line. So he had plenty of time for Ali Hassan and his enchanting visitor from Ouda.

THE FIRST ALPHONSE PICARD MONOLOGUE

My perverse readers never got tired of reading about the Kaiser until last March when they became transfixed by The Case of Madame Caillaux, which all Frenchmen find even more exciting. I know Your Excellency is well informed on the subject. But you, *madame,* must allow me to explain. I am referring to the sensational and highly significant trial of Henriette Caillaux, the wife of the French Minister of Finance and head of the Radical Party, who shot to death the editor of *Le Figaro,* Gaston Calmette, who was Caillaux's political opponent. Calmette had done something unprecedented in French journalism. He had published Caillaux's love letters to his first wife, written when she, a married woman, was his mistress.

When one day this scandal will be over, one hopes in the not too distant future, the French public will think about the Kaiser again, and possibly with better reason than before. Up to now my countrymen thought of him merely as a buffoon sporting Europe's most aggressive mustache. I have been telling them for years to take him seriously, but they would not listen. A man in his position, I told them, who can be intelligent for no more than five minutes at a time, is dangerous. His Ambassador in Paris told our minister Jean Louis Barthou the other day that he hoped our two countries would soon live together peacefully. Barthou said, "Nothing would please us more. Give us back Alsace and Lorraine and we will be the best friends in the world."

So I wrote a piece following up this splendid idea. Nobody would publish it. I suggested we should give the Kaiser a few of our colonies in Africa in exchange. They cost us far too much of money, anyway, and give us no joy. For us, having lost Alsace and Lorraine is a bleeding, festering wound. For the Kaiser, they mean very little. He loves colonies. Alsace and Lorraine were important to Bismarck, but he thought Germany should stay out of the colonial games. Bismarck was yesterday's man. Wilhelm thinks of himself as a truly modern monarch and therefore believes colonies will secure him a place in the sun. Well, let us give him a place in the sun in return for Alsace and Lorraine and we will have peace for ever.

I really think this is an idea that, in its grand sweep, would appeal to him. He likes grand sweeps. For five minutes at a time. Once we have secured the friendship of this truly enlightened monarch, his mustache will become the most beautiful mustache in Europe!

But suppose the Kaiser wants to have a war with Russia? Well, let him go and have his war with Russia. We will keep out of it. It is true that Russia is our ally, but every ally, on all sides, has always understood that, when the chips are down, his own interests come first. If the Russians were so sure of us, why in the last presidential election did they bribe our newspapers to back Raimond Poincaré? They thought he would not let them down while his opponent Georges Clemenceau might.

And, two weeks ago, was there any real need for the Kaiser to give *his* ally the famous *carte blanche*? Of course there was no need for such folly. He could have dreamed up a thousand excuses. He could have said the terms of the alliance did not cover acts of murderous terrorism directed at present and future monarchs. But for five minutes he was in one of his bravado moods, drunk with *Nibelungentreue,* a veritable Siegfried slaying the Serb terrorist dragon, fighting to the death a war in defence of the sacred right of emperors, kings and heirs of the throne not to be assassinated. In 1894, terrorists even assassinated the President of the French Republic! Can you imagine?

Giving Vienna a *carte blanche* was really the most stupid thing for the Kaiser to have done. He handed the Austrians the entire initiative, leaving himself stark naked, wearing only his mustache, not even a fig leaf. You watch — he will tell the world he is being encircled. Of course he will be encircled! He has given away all the means to break out of the circle. When the five minutes were over he probably did not give the matter another thought. If he did, he probably thought he had gone through a whole string of crises, two Morocco crises, two Balkan Wars, without the Russians making a single move. Why should this one be different? And besides, did he not now have a navy? It would take care of things.

Only in a country that prefers Grimm's Fairy Tales to a sensible constitution would a Kaiser behave that way. In Germany, two or three dozen people have all the power. They never ask for advice. They only talk to each other. The country is full of bright, civilized people who are completely shut out of things.

It is disgusting.

◆

While Picard was talking he noticed that Zade was staring at the poster, her eyes fixed on the Kaiser's red mustache.

"*Madame,* you like the mustache?"

"Yes," she confessed. "I do."

"Every honest woman does," Picard nodded gravely. "Even in France. I have talked to dozens of women about it. I know what women feel about his mustache, German women, Italian women, even English women. It's the waxed corners that are thrust upwards that arouse them. I'm composing a major piece about this, for a satirical woman's magazine. And of course I have cross-examined Herr Haby, the court barber, who trims it and moulds it, using his own beard lotion, which is enjoying excellent sales. It's called *Achievement* — in English, to capture the English market, very clever — and of course anything English is chic in both France and Germany. Herr Haby accompanies His Majesty on all state visits."

An idea seized Ali.

"Has he allowed you to watch him while he works on His Majesty?"

"I have not asked him."

"Well, what do you think?"

"I have no idea."

"You are brilliant." Zade beamed at Ali while Picard wondered what was on their minds. She left it to Ali to ask the next question.

"Don't you think you need to find out *from a woman* what it feels like to trim the All Highest's mustache? I'm sure that's still missing from the article you're writing. True?"

Alphonse Picard's eyes twinkled.

"Yes, that is true. You mean you, *madame,* would enjoy watching Herr Haby at work?"

"I think it would be an adventure to remember."

He promised to telephone Herr Haby immediately.

The Court Preacher

Tonight, o glorious King, I have a revealing story to tell you. It shows how a modern prince, who is inevitably exposed to many conflicting influences, must choose his own way and stick to it.

In November 1887, there was an official announcement that Wilhelm's father, Crown Prince Friedrich, had cancer of the throat. It suddenly became clear that the new era that Wilhelm and his friends were awaiting so impatiently was no longer in the distant future. After the venerable Kaiser Wilhelm I's death, Kaiser Friedrich III reigned only for ninety-nine days before he died and Wilhelm succeeded him.

Around the time the announcement of his father's fatal illness was made Wilhelm chaired a meeting in Count Alfred von Waldersee's house on behalf of the Berlin City Mission, which was headed by Court Preacher Adolf Stoecker. Waldersee was the right-wing Deputy Chief of the General Staff and Wilhelm's friend. The Mission did good works for the poor in the slums of Berlin.

Adolf Stoecker had formed the Christian Social Party and was a member of the Reichstag and the Prussian Landtag. As a politician he advocated social reforms under the auspices of the church and the monarchy. Stoecker was an outspoken anti-Semite, which, I must explain to Your Majesty, means he was against the Jews. By chairing a meeting to give him a platform, Prince Wilhelm seemed to associate himself with Stoecker's views. As a student he had not been known to have had any anti-Semitic feelings. He had even been friendly with a Jewish fellow student. But after he left university and got married, he heard Stoecker preach and was deeply impressed. The man had something of Martin Luther about him, he said. Dona wholeheartedly agreed. It was thanks to them that he was appointed court preacher.

Stoecker's objection to Jews was that they were dangerous aliens who should not have been allowed to emerge from their ghettoes and participate in German life. What was happening today, he preached, was a battle of race against race. The Jews were "an alien drop in our blood," he said. They were "leeches leading a parasitic existence in Germany," not "part of the German nation but a nation unto themselves, linked to other Jews in the world to form one mass of exploiters." In one speech the pastor said, "We offer the Jews a fight until we have achieved complete victory, and we will not rest until they have been thrown down from their pedestal on which they have placed themselves here in Berlin into the dust where they belong ... We want to be a Hohenzollern city and are proud of this from the bottom of our hearts, but we wish to prevent Berlin from becoming a Jewish city."

Stoecker was not the only outspoken anti-Semite in Berlin. In 1881, a mass petition was submitted to the government, signed by a quarter of a million citizens, against permitting Jews to gain the upper hand, calling for the prohibition of Jewish immigration and the exclusion of Jews from all government offices. The petition also asked for their removal from all positions as primary school teachers, and a reduction of their number at the universities. The prominent historian Heinrich von Treitschke bemoaned the dangerous preponderance of Jews in German public life, and wrote that "even in the best-educated circles we hear as if with one voice The Jews are our misfortune."

Bismarck found Wilhelm's siding with Stoecker openly a matter of grave concern. Of course, like Wilhelm's friends, he, too, was a right-wing conservative, but he was far too sophisticated and experienced a politician to accept an open association of the future Kaiser with a sectarian rabble-rouser even if he was the Court Preacher, a member of the Reichstag and the Landtag. And even if the Berlin City Mission helped the poor. In any case, by now Bismarck was acutely worried about Wilhelm, found him vain, far too eager to be popular among the masses, immature, shallow, superficial and far too susceptible to flattery.

No doubt he thought this was a good moment to take him to task. Since he was skilled at using the press for his own purposes he inspired an article attacking Wilhelm's participation in the meeting in Count Waldersee's house. There followed an exchange of letters between Bismarck and Wilhelm, which led to a marked cooling-off between them. For Bismarck, a Prussian monarch must stand, like Frederick the Great, above the parties. "The Christian notion," he wrote, "was decidedly unsuitable as a weapon in the Crown's hands in the battle against social and other democrats." In his polite, carefully composed reply, Wilhelm indicated between the lines that he deeply resented Bismarck's reprimand, but assured him that he would instruct the Court

Preacher to withdraw as official director of the City Mission. Those who sympathized with Wilhelm told him, with an eye to the future, that Bismarck was not irreplaceable, and that even men of lesser talent could do the job, since after all, according to the constitution devised by Bismarck himself, it was the monarch's responsibility to direct policy.

As I have mentioned to Your Majesty several times, Prince Wilhelm's parents adhered to the liberal, humanistic ideals that had preceded Bismarck's creation of a military state. They went as far as to call Stoecker's anti-Semitism "a shameful blot on our time" and made it public that they were ashamed of these trends and, by implication, of their son following them.

So, in early 1880, as a protest against Pastor Stoecker's preachings, Wilhelm's father, the future Kaiser Friedrich III, attended a service at the Berlin synagogue — that is a Jewish mosque — in full dress uniform as a Prussian Field Marshal.

Your Majesty is no doubt wondering whether Wilhelm is anti-Semitic today. The answer is yes, he is. There is no doubt about it. He has been consistently anti-Semitic since the age of twenty, but this attitude is tempered by the exceptions he makes in favour of a few wealthy and gifted Jews, preferably if they have international connections which are useful to him. I am referring to distinguished men such as Albert Ballin, Walther Rathenau, Max Warburg, Franz Mendelssohn, and Simon and Carl Fürstenberg. In his relations with these men he ignores that they are Jewish, or simply forgets it, as in the case of Albert Ballin, the chief of the Hamburg-

Amerika Linie who is an ardent supporter of German colonization in Africa. Moreover, since Ballin believes the Ottoman Empire can no longer justify its existence as an independent state, he also favours German colonization in the Near East. His ships, known for their luxury and elegance, are always at His Majesty's disposal.

Of course, access to the Kaiser is flattering to men like Ballin and the other prominent Jews I mentioned. They are, in a sense, royal favourites and are sometimes called Kaiser-Juden or Kaiser-Jews. Those who disapprove of this exception abuse Wilhelm for being a Juden-Kaiser who is debasing the crown.

At the time under discussion, the time immediately before he became Kaiser, he announced that when he came on the throne the Jewish influence over the press would be stopped. The Minister of the Interior objected, on the grounds that this would contravene the Constitution. I am not sure whether this is true, but Wilhelm was supposed to have answered, "Very well. Then the Constitution would have be got rid of." Of course this may have been one of his many jokes.

May I jump ahead to the year 1901 when Wilhelm personally met Houston Stewart Chamberlain, the author of Evangelist of Race, a book that had great influence at the time. Its purpose was to demonstrate to his readers the superiority of the Aryan race over all non-Aryan races such as Semites, a race to which we Oudanians happen to belong as well as the Jews, and to advocate the need to avoid contamination, both cultural and physical, by the Jewish race. The

Aryan race, was, in the sense in which Chamberlain used the term, the blond race of Teutonic northern Europeans. He had borrowed the word from the study of languages. All Indo-Germanic languages are "Aryan".

When this long and weighty book appeared in 1910, it made a deep impression in Germany. Though much of it was not new and had already been anticipated in the music and writing of Chamberlain's father-in-law, Richard Wagner — in 1908 he had married Wagner's daughter Eva — its main message had never before been conveyed in this persuasive manner in the context of philosophy and world history. The book also had the attraction of not having been written by an academic. Chamberlain was eloquent in his attack on the idol-worship of Roman Catholics and single-minded on the need to eradicate Jews from German cultural life because their materialism was evil and a characteristic of their race. The book was, generally speaking, not found to be shocking at all in the Kaiser's entourage, nor among people who read books in Germany generally, nor in other parts of Europe, nor, so someone told me, in the United States of America, where talk about the superiority of one race over another was common practice.

Following Chamberlain's lead, Wilhelm cried out in indignation and disbelief whenever it was suggested that England may one day side with Russia against Germany, how it was possible that the "Germanic English" could ever side with Slavs against their racial Stammesgenossen, or tribal comrades?

The Kaiser's anti-Semitism is conditioned by his moods. When he is furious with the English, he often talks about Juda-England, equating the hated Jews with the hated English and suggesting that the English and the Jews were jointly ganging up on him. On the other hand, there are occasions when he says that anti-Semitism should have its limits. The radical Pan-German League, for example, which is supported by his eldest son, Crown Prince Wilhelm, went too far, he thought, when it demanded, in the anti-Semitic brochure Wenn ich der Kaiser wär — If I Were Kaiser — the removal of the Jews' right to vote. And in 1907, in a conversation with Sir Edward Grey in London, he said that there were too many Jews in Germany. "They want stamping out," he said, surely not meaning this literally. But he added that if he did not keep his people in check there would be "Jew-baiting" in Germany.

In our world of Islam, too, there has been — and is today, as Your Majesty knows, — a similarly wide range of antagonistic attitudes towards Jews. Therefore, many of us were surprised to learn, after we left school, that when Muslim forces invaded Spain in 711 A.D. the Jews were on our side against the Christians. Also, that during the middle ages — for example at the Caliph's court in Cordoba — Jews flourished and made important contributions. And some of us have forgotten, or never knew, that in the fifteenth and sixteen centuries, when Jews were expelled from Catholic Spain, they found homes and hospitality in our Arab lands in North Africa.

In the light of all this, I must confess to Your Majesty that I do not fully grasp why the "Jewish Question" has become such a big subject in Germany.

Arabian Nights, 1914

I decided I needed some help to understand it. This is what I found:

While other countries such as Spain, Portugal, Holland, England and France formed nations and acquired overseas colonial empires overseas, Germany was left behind. The reason is that throughout the Middle Ages and, in fact until quite recently, Germany was not a country but consisted of hundreds of different principalities and city-states in a Reich that was more important as an idea than as a political structure. Jews did not participate in that world. They lived in a kind of exile in ghettos in the cities and in small communities in the country, very much like many Jews live in our Muslim world, for example in the mellah of Fez in Morocco. Often such ghettoes were said to be founded originally for their protection. In any case, the Jews considered confinement in them, wherever they were, to be a tragedy. In the German ghettoes they made a poor living in low-level trades, with hardly any contact with Christians, who avoided contact with them and from time to time persecuted them. Jews living under these conditions naturally shared a sense of community with Jews living under similar conditions elsewhere. Unlike Christians, they pray for liberation in this world, not in the next, because for them no Prophet or Jesus Christ had as yet appeared. While waiting for their Messiah they studied the Hebrew Scriptures, which contain the chronicles of their lives as the "Chosen People" two thousand years ago, in the immediate proximity of Ouda, before most of them were dispersed to Europe and North Africa. The concentration on liberation in this world rather than the next encouraged them to think about all the things that were wrong with the human condition as they saw it and how it could be improved.

The Middle Ages waned slowly, from the sixteenth century to the late eighteenth century. New ideas, culminating in the revolution in France, opened the door to the modern world, the same doors that should soon open Ouda's. Germans and Jews went through these doors in a similar condition. Both were citizens of the world, not of any one nation. The German nation did not exist as yet. Both had a passion for the written word. So the "Chosen People" chose Germans as their partners as, full of joyful excitement, they together welcomed the nineteenth century as the century of progress for everyone. A period of unprecedented creativity followed. Jews — who spoke German without any trace of a non-German accent, never amounted to much more than between one and two percent of the entire population, but the importance of their contributions in those fields of activities to which they had access far exceeded their relative numbers. This resulted in some confusion. People wondered whether Jews were Jews because of what they believed or because of what they were. I don't know how this question was answered. All I know is that Germans did not at first seem to have any serious difficulties accepting Jews as equal partners in their parallel journeys into the modern world.

Once the nineteenth century had passed its middle, there was, however, for the more thoughtful Jews a parting of the ways. Under the guidance of Bismarck's Prussia, foundations were laid for the formation of a strong, autocratic, militarist state pursuing objectives very different from the humanistic ideals both Germans and Jews had cherished earlier in the century. Many Jews had no problem at all adapting themselves to Bismarck's world and prospered in it. The rest remained faithful to the progressive, democratic and cosmopolitan ideas — the ideas of Wilhelm's parents against whom he rebelled — of the early part of the century.

Once this was pointed out to me, I saw more clearly what I imagine were the roots of Wilhelm's anti-Semitism.

Chapter 5

Friday, July 17

The Governess Strategy is next.

On Thursday, July 16, at a reception in the Bulgarian embassy, the talk was about the departure the previous day of French president Raimond Poincaré and his prime minister, René Viviani, for a state visit to Saint Petersburg. People wondered when the arguments between Vienna and Budapest would end and when a note would finally be sent to Belgrad, and whether the French and the Russians would have a chance to discuss it.

> The ultimatum to Belgrad was deliberately not sent until July 23, after the departure of the French leaders from Saint Petersburg, in order to prevent them and the Russians from coordinating their plans.

While these matters were being debated in one corner of the room, Zade, in another, discovered from the daughter of the Swedish Ambassador that the wife of Fritz von Tiedemann, one of the secretaries of Chancellor Theobald von Bethmann Hollweg, was looking for a Turkish governess for their children. Only for a few weeks. The Tiedemanns lived in Hohenfinow, near the Chancellor's estate, but would soon be moving to Constantinople where he was to take charge of a bank. It was mentioned en passant that His Majesty liked visiting Hohenfinow, northeast of Berlin, just west of the Oder River, and much preferred conferring there with his Chancellor than in Potsdam. He was expected to be driven there by car after returning home from the cruise, after conferring with the Chief of the General Staff. There was also good hunting at Hohenfinow.

Zade decided to apply. The job interview took place the next afternoon, on the veranda of the Tiedemanns' comfortable house, overlooking a nicely kept garden.

"You say you are from Ouda, madame, and your language is Arabic?" Frau von Tiedemann asked. She was blond, well-groomed and polite. "But you speak Turkish?"

"I do indeed."

Frau von Tiedemann explained that she thought it would be good for the children to learn a little Turkish before moving to Constantinople, even though they would of course attend a German school there.

That made a lot of sense, Zade said.

The oldest Tiedemann boy was fifteen and a half. His mother wondered for a moment how he would respond to Zade's beauty. In the aristocracy, and among the wealthy all over Europe, attractive governesses were often employed with implied, and sometimes specific, instructions to introduce adolescent sons to the mysteries of sex, to prevent them from seeking such introductions from unsavoury women elsewhere. Having had this thought Frau von Tiedemann quickly dismissed it as absurdly far-fetched. No such thing could ever happen in her family.

"Do you have any letters of reference?" she asked.

"I'm afraid not."

For a moment Zade thought her Arabian Nights stories might serve as evidence of her good character. But no, surely it was a little risky to expose herself at this stage to questions about their genesis.

"I will not claim that I have ever been a governess before," she said. "But I am in Berlin on a visit for a few weeks, and, to tell you the truth, I am getting a little bored. I like children. Ali Hassan, Ouda's Ambassador to Germany, can vouch for my character."

The telephone on the little side table rang.

"Please excuse me," Frau von Tiedemann said. "Oh really?" she said "General Conrad von Hötzendorf went on holidays, at this time?"

> <u>Vienna:</u>
> Count Leopold von Berchtold, Foreign Minister
> General Conrad von Hötzendorf, Chief of Staff
>
> <u>Budapest:</u>
> Count Istvan Tisza, Prime Minister. He first opposed military action against Serbia on the grounds that he abhorred war and had no interest in "diminishing Serbia" nor in incorporating parts of Serbia, on the grounds, that Hungary already enough Slavs. But then after long arguments he yielded.

"I can't believe it! The Austrians have really gone crazy! The Chancellor is at his wits' end. He had gambled everything on quick action. Of course he agreed when His Majesty consulted him before he gave the Austrians carte blanche. They were determined to crush the Serbs right away — they had wanted to do it for years. If His Majesty had left the Austrians in the lurch, they might have gone over to the Entente, who were waiting for them with open arms. If that had happened we wouldn't have a single ally left in the entire world! The Chancellor thought another Balkan War could bring Austria a great diplomatic triumph and a realignment of the southeastern states. And if Russia insisted on intervening and France refused to go along with it, there was the possibility of the Entente breaking up. That had been a long-term objective of the Chancellor's for years. It was all a leap in the dark. But it was not a frivolous gamble. And if this went wrong and there was a general war, the whole nation would no doubt follow His Majesty, driven, the Chancellor says, by necessity and peril. You are quite right. Many young people are looking forward to a quick war leading to victory as a kind of liberation. I understand exactly how they feel. Thanks for telling me."

Frau von Tiedemann had some difficulty concentrating again on the matter at hand.

"Oh yes, you said your Ambassador could vouch for you. I believe I have heard he is highly respected in the diplomatic community. So that is good. And you are a Muslim?"

"Of course."

"Is there any food you don't eat?"

"I don't eat pork. And I don't drink alcohol. But, as you notice, I don't wear the usual veil."

"All this is very promising."

The telephone rang again.

"No, my dear. Fritz is with the Chancellor. What? No, I wouldn't do that. Fritz is always very annoyed when people say that Bethmann Hollweg is not cut out to be a chancellor ... Yes, but that was private. It is quite true Fritz said the Chancellor was a man of the old school, a brooding thinker steeped in the classics, in Kant and Hegel, in Bach, Mozart and Beethoven, not really surprising in a member of a great banker's family from Frankfurt. Pardon? But how can anybody deny that he is an effective statesman and politician? After all, by now he's been in office for five years! And Heaven knows, His Majesty is not the easiest man to get along with ... Yes, of course, he has the rank of a major in the army. His Majesty insists that all his civilian ministers are also officers and wear uniform when they address the Reichstag. Bismarck did. ... But everybody knows Theo's relations with the General Staff are often strained. There's nothing new about that. What? Yes, I've also heard that. Theo says that Bismarck was a great man but nobody trusted him, and everybody in Europe trusts him — Theo — especially the English. He has become a pillar of European peace, Theo says ... The last thing he would worry about is if people say he has no sense of humour. That may be so. He certainly thinks this is not a time for making jokes. What do you mean? That nobody could be both popular and successful? And that a true statesman should not seek popularity from his adversaries? Now, what you repeat that? I didn't quite understand it. What was it? An American journalist wrote that if Bethmann Hollweg had to sit down at a negotiating table with the current leaders of the Entente, he would be lucky if in the end he retained Berlin? No, no, no. this is absurd. Those American journalists will write anything for effect. You must excuse me now. I have a visitor."

Once again, Frau von Tiedemann returned to Zade.

"Oh yes, you say you don't drink alcohol. Now tell me this. Do you think the children of 'infidels' — isn't that what you call us Christians? — will have any difficulties in Turkey? I realize that we grown-ups will have little contact with ordinary people, and the children will of course go to a German school, but still, I mean, they can't help meeting native children occasionally. I don't suppose they should ever go on the street by themselves, without an adult going along with them?"

"Oh, I wouldn't say that. I have never heard of any trouble of the sort you are worried about. But of course I am an Arab, not a Turk, and I have never lived in Turkey. In Arabia the Turks are the masters and are usually very unpopular, to say the least, and therefore behave very differently from the way they behave at home. Turks come to Ouda only on a visit."

Once again, the telephone rang.

"Oh, I'm not at all sure the Chancellor will be pleased to hear that.

> On July 13 Dr. Friedrich von Wiesner, a Legal Counsellor of the Austrian Foreign Ministry, who had been sent to Belgrad to investigate any possible connection between the Serbian government and the terrorists, wired that there was "nothing to indicate, or even to give rise to the suspicion, that the Serbian government knew about the plot, its preparation or the procurement of arms. On the contrary, there are indications that this is impossible."

"Vienna has been waiting for years for an excuse to crush those Serbian terrorists once and for all. This was such a good opportunity! After all, we've always believed in a strong Austria-Hungary, haven't we? This makes it very difficult, doesn't it? You say the report came out on July 13? But that was last Monday! Today is Friday. How come we haven't heard of it? Doesn't that make it impossible now for Vienna to act? What do you mean, 'where there's a will there's a way'? Who would support them? Dr. Wiesner's is just one opinion, they say? Let's talk about this later."

"We were discussing the natives." Frau Tiedemann made a valiant effort to concentrate, "You see, we have never been outside Germany, except for our annual summer holidays in Switzerland. And we don't know anybody, outside the diplomatic community, who is not Christian. So this is all a little new for us."

A pleasant-looking man with horn-rimmed glasses, wearing a light summer suit but a stiff collar, appeared in the garden, looking up to the veranda. Clearly this was Fritz von Tiedemann. The last thing he expected to see was his wife talking to a stunning beauty.

Galvanized, he hesitated.

"Do come up, Fritz. I want you to meet, I hope, our new governess."

Fritz ran up the few steps and shook hands with Zade.

It suddenly occurred to Frau von Tiedemann that there was far more need to worry about her husband than about her son.

After a few words about Ouda and Ouda's relations with the Ottoman Empire, Frau von Tiedemann asked her husband whether the Chancellor had heard of the Wiesner report. He had.

"I left him in a deeply pessimistic mood. Everything is going wrong, he says. If the Austrians had acted fast, and the Russians had mobilized — against the Austrians? against us? — this might have split the Entente. The French might have felt under no obligation to help their Russian allies. Nor, of course, would the English. What did it matter to them how the Serbs behave? Splitting the French from the Russians would have been a magnificent diplomatic coup, almost unbelievable, a coup that would have earned Bismarck's highest praise. But now — with the French on the high seas en route to Saint Petersburg to make firm decisions together …"

"But surely," Frau von Tiedemann said, "now, after Dr. Wiesner's report, the Austrians' hands are tied."

"That's not the way they look at it, my dear. The Chancellor has had reports that the Russians are actively considering mobilization. And everybody knows what that could mean. He thinks the pan-Slavic dream has turned their heads and they've become extremely dangerous and might very well do something stupid."

She sighed.

"When I left the Chancellor he was talking to one of the leaders of the Social Democrats."

"That's very brave of him," his wife said. "The generals won't thank him for that. Nor will His Majesty who once told the world that matters will not improve until the troops drag the Social Democratic leaders out of the Reichstag and gun them down." She turned to Zade who up to now had carefully refrained from showing any interest in the political talk she overheard. "You may not know, madame, that His Majesty regards Social Democrats as enemies of the fatherland. That's what he's said on more than one occasion. He wants to take revenge for the revolution they made in 1848. So you see it is very courageous of our chancellor to talk to them. The generals want to shoot every red the day war break out, a day which, of course we all hope, will never come. Of course, they can't wait for it — they've got all their plans ready and are rearing to go. Theo thinks by talking to the socialist leadership, by taking them into his confidence, he can persuade them to support a war, should it come, if they think it's a just war forced on Germany. Especially a war against tsarist despotism. He's well informed about their mass meetings, in which their leaders bitterly attack imperialism, militarism and all those war-mongering, rabble-rousing, super-patriotic professors. After all, the Sozis are a very large party and deserve serious consideration. Of course, they're in close touch with their friends in France who have staged similar mass meetings but who've recently lost their battle against the three-years-military service bill. But they're still determined to block a war if they can. I don't know whether their prime minister talks to them."

Zade's expression revealed neither interest nor disinterest.

"But we must not bore our visitor," Fritz von Tiedemann said. "So you are going to join us for a few weeks?", he asked hopefully.

"We have not quite reached that point yet."

"Before you make up your mind whether to employ me," Zade said as she rose, "I think I should mention that I'm afraid I can't join you right away."

"Oh, why not?"

It had always been Zade's practice to keep the number of lies that had to be told to the irreducible minimum. How could she say she wanted to wait for the Kaiser to return to the mainland?

"I promised my Ambassador to finish some work for him first."

❆ Mayerling ❆

Your noble Majesty, your heart will bleed for Wilhelm when you hear the terrible story I am about to tell you. On the 29th of January in 1889, the day after his first birthday as Kaiser of Germany and King of Prussia, he was shattered by the news from Vienna. Archduke Rudolf, the Austrian heir to the throne and therefore his Austrian counterpart, had been found dead, together with his mistress, the Baroness Marie Vetsera, in the bedroom of his hunting lodge, in the wooded hills south-east of Vienna, at Mayerling. It seemed that Rudolf had first shot her and then himself.

Wilhelm had detested Rudolf intensely and Rudolf had detested him. Now, Your Majesty may well ask, if they detested each other so intensely, why was this such a devastating blow? The answer is that the two heirs to the thrones had been almost exact contemporaries, had married at about the same time and were, in a certain sense, twins. There was no point asking why Rudolf had done it — it was obvious. The immensity of the obstacles in his future path had crushed him. Rudolf was the victim of his prescribed, predestined role, just as if, instead of murdering himself, he had been murdered. (His mother Empress Elizabeth was to be stabbed to death ten years later and Rudolf's successor, Franz Ferdinand, was, as Your Majesty knows, assassinated in Sarajevo.) Rudolf had failed because he had lacked the drive and the intellectual power to develop a grand design of his own. At fifteen he had already prophesied the doom of his father's dynasty. He thought Austria's alliance with Bismarck's Germany a calamitous, a hugely dangerous mistake. He despised Russia as a reactionary power, and liked and admired France. And then there was something else. He felt powerless against the overwhelming weight of his father's clerical, feudal bureaucracy and his, to him, misguided policies.

The death was a warning to Wilhelm, a reminder of the extreme precariousness of his position. Wilhelm, having just become Kaiser, was resolved to prove that, unlike his twin, he had the character, the courage, the devotion to duty, the strength and single-mindedness to succeed in his mission while Rudolf had so conspicuously, so tragically failed in his. Besides, to Wilhelm — he had to admit it — this suicide was typically Austrian: sloppy, weak, decadent, irresponsible, self-indulgent and cowardly.

But he certainly did Rudolf an injustice if he thought that he lacked devotion to duty. Rudolf never lost awareness of his responsibilities. One motive for his suicide may well have been that he felt he had compromised himself in so many ways and was so steeped in deceit in his relations with his father that he saw no honourable way out.

The sordid circumstances of this double-suicide only became known gradually. Twice before, Rudolf had tried to persuade other girls to die with him. In the weeks preceding his death Rudolf was clearly unwell: he had drunk compulsively, made love wildly, taken drugs and his handwriting had gone to pieces. His wife sought a private interview with Kaiser Franz Joseph and begged him to send his son on a long voyage to recover his health. But the old emperor said all he needed was time to be with her.

That was not good advice. The marriage was a disaster. Stephanie was a thoroughly boring and colourless girl. She was the daughter of King Leopold II of Belgium, who had extracted a vast fortune from the Congo. She was eighteen when they got married, five years younger than Rudolf. As the daughter of the Archduchess Marie Henriette she was — so I was told — her husband's aunt. She was also, on her father's side, a descendent of the House of Coburg and therefore related to Wilhelm. Still, since this was not a close relationship, Vicky had wanted Rudolf to marry one of her daughters. But Rudolf had no interest in marrying a Prussian princess, even if she was a granddaughter of Queen Victoria. Instead, he went to Brussels, "in the company of pretty and sassy Jewess," I read in one book, resigned to obey his father and marry Princess Stephanie. His mother, Empress Elizabeth, thought the girl was thoroughly unsuitable and protested vehemently.

Rudolf was an intellectual, not interested in military affairs, rebellious, ironic, free-thinking and liberal, anti-Prussian to the core, a champion of a peaceful, united, multinational Europe and a friend of Jews and republicans. Paradoxically, his bearing was that of an imperial officer. At first, the two princes seemed to get on quite well, each trying to conceal his low opinion of the other. Once or twice a season they invited each other to hunting parties, just as protocol demanded. In fact, Wilhelm enjoyed his frequent trips to Austria. More about that later. Two years after his wedding, on a visit to Berlin, Rudolf remarked that Wilhelm, for all his youth, was a dyedin-the-wool Junker who spoke of the Reichstag as "that pigsty" and of the members of the opposition as "those dogs who deserve to be whipped." On other occasions in the years to come, Rudolf told friends that he had grave fears for the future of Europe once Wilhelm came on the throne. I have no doubt that Wilhelm said similar things about Rudolf.

I said a moment ago that Wilhelm had enjoyed his hunting expeditions to Austria. The reason is what somebody called Eros in Austria. Eros is the infidels' god of love. Before and after he got married, Wilhelm enjoyed the company of Austrian women who found it flattering — and no doubt useful in their careers — to have shared the bed of a crown prince. Sometimes there would even be two women at a time. Such diversions were expected from a prince, of course, and no Viennese operetta would be complete without them. It would have been a source of considerable worry had it been otherwise. Sometimes the ladies also visited him in the north. Wilhelm was not particularly careful in keeping these pleasures secret, although I found no evidence that Dona ever found out about them. He wrote letters to one or two of them, which could, and were, used later to blackmail him. One of his companions stole his cufflinks, with the letter W engraved on them, which perhaps helped her raise her rates. I don't know whether it was Rudolf who put him in touch with Frau Wolf, one of Vienna's most popular madams, to whom he wrote letters without disguising his handwriting. He was not known for his generosity in rewarding his companions, no doubt on the assumption that the distinctinction of having been with him was reward enough. I do know that Rudolf occasionally lent him money.

Once he was Kaiser all this stopped.

At least, as far as I know.

Chapter 6

Sunday, July 19

After breakfast in the embassy Zade proudly reported to Ali that the groundwork she had done to implement the Governess Strategy was likely to pay off magnificently. He was sorry to have to tell her that he did not think the Kaiser was likely to travel to Hohenfinow soon after his return.

"Why not?" Zade asked. "He will need his Chancellor more than ever."

Before Ali could answer, an imposing, amiable man appeared in the doorway, cheerfully waving a newspaper. Zade had seen him several times on the stairs and correctly guessed it was Jonathan Lind, the head and only member of the English Talbot News Agency, which had its office on the floor below. Ali had mentioned him to her several times, but they had not met.

"Jonathan, meet my friend from Ouda."

He bowed to her.

"Why else do you think I have come to visit you on this beautiful Sunday morning?" he said to Ali. "But you must forgive me. I am always shy in the presence of a beautiful woman. I am, in fact," he added, obviously meaning the opposite, "tongue-tied."

"Not for long, I hope," Ali said.

"It is very curious," Jonathan said to Zade. "I have been dying to meet you. And now I don't know what to say. And I hate the preliminary small talk."

"Preliminary to what?" Zade wondered.

"Who can tell the future?"

Lind had been a classics teacher at Eton and still sported a school blazer and an old school tie. He was a bachelor. Ten years ago, when he weighed twenty pounds less, he became bored with

Eton, even though he had enjoyed teaching and loved coaching the First Eleven Cricket Team. He was devoted to the game and always read the cricket scores in The Times before reading anything else. He decided he could do that in Berlin just as well as at home. The life of a foreign correspondent in one of the world's most interesting cities struck him as alluring. Since he had excellent connections in Whitehall and on Fleet Street he had no trouble constructing the right job for himself. He was close to Sir Edward Goschen, the British Ambassador in Berlin, and was one of the best informed journalists in town. Since his father was a German banker who, for business reasons, had never become a British subject, Jonathan too had German citizenship. This would give him immunity from internment as an enemy alien in case there was a war with England. This he considered most likely.

"What is in that newspaper?" Ali asked.

"Evidence that we are about to enter Phase Two of the unfolding crisis. In Phase Two we will discover that the conflict cannot remain localized. The conflict, in short, is spiralling, or — if I may coin a new word, to show you that I know the French word escalier — escalating. Who can tell the future? I just asked melodramatically. The answer is, I can. And I know it's all your fault, Ali Hassan. If you Turks had not behaved like such swine, you could have held on all to all those piffling little countries in the Balkans, and none of this would have happened."

July 6:	Wilhelm leaves for Norwegian cruise	
July 7:	Austro-Hungarian Ministerial Council meets	
July 8:	Ultimatum to Serbia prepared; Hungarian prime minister Tisza argues against military action	
July 15:	General Conrad von Hötzendorf, Austrian Chief of Staff, goes on holidays; Poincaré and Viviani leave for Saint Petersburg	
July 19:	Austro-Hungarian Ministerial Council approves memorandum to be handed over on July 23; Tisza yields on condition that no annexation of Serbian territory is contemplated	
July 20:	Poincaré and Viviani arrive in Saint Petersburg	

"We are not Turks!" Ali cried. "We are Oudanians! We are Arabs!"

THE FIRST JONATHAN LIND MONOLOGUE

Oh never mind. It's all the same to me. Asia Minor starts at Calais. Now let me answer your question. This newspaper is the *North German Gazette*. It is known as "semi-official." Which means it is the horse's mouth. I happen to know that in this case the horse who wrote a brief notice of great significance for publication in this journal is the foreign minister Gottlieb von Jagow himself. He is a little man in stature and in spirit who has at last returned to Berlin to recover from his no doubt exhausting honeymoon. Nothing happens here without the Kaiser's imperial inspiration. No doubt His Majesty told his Chancellor and his Chancellor told his Foreign Minister that the time had come to suggest to the Russians and to the French cautiously, in tortuous diplomatic language, but of course with crystal clarity, for Heaven's sake to keep their fingers out of the Austrian-Serbian conflict. If they did not comply with this subtle but crystal-clear request, there would be unpleasant consequences. As you know, the Russians and the French are about to feast together in Saint Petersburg. That is a very convenient occasion for them to figure out what consequences the Kaiser had in mind. Herr Gottlieb von Jagow should proclaim to the world that when composing their ultimatum the Austrians are acting entirely on their own, without the Germans looking over their shoulder in any way, and that therefore the Germans have not the slightest idea of the content of the forthcoming note. At the same time he should assure the world that under no circumstances would he, the Kaiser, ever leave his Austrian allies in the lurch.

All the statesmen assembled in Saint Petersburg, of course, know a lot about the two calling the shots in Vienna — the Chief of Staff, Baron Conrad von Hötzendorf, and the Foreign Minister, Count Leopold von Berchtold. They know that Conrad is determined to crush Serbia with or without a pretext. They also know that he has a razor-sharp intelligence and a quite un-Austrian toughness. And they know — not that this matters — that he speaks all the eight major languages of the Double Monarchy fluently, that he has travelled, disguised as a peasant, in Russia, Rumania, Serbia, Bulgaria and Turkey, that he is just about the opposite of the Count, who has none of Conrad's toughness, being thoroughly Viennese, rich, elegant, timid, charming and, in the little time left over from enjoying the company of pretty Viennese shop girls, hardworking and conscientious. They know that, even though he happens to be a Hungarian in spite of his German name, he does not speak a word of Hungarian. And they must have heard what a character said to him the other day: "I'm going to tell His Majesty to shelve you. You clearly can't cope. He should dismiss you immediately." The Count replied, "Oh my dear friend, by all means do so. Please tell him. I've been saying it to him for a long time. But he just won't believe me."

I wonder whether, while toasting each other in Saint Petersburg, they will ask themselves whether the Austrians will really be so foolish as to imagine that they can dismember Serbia without the Russians coming in to stop them. Wouldn't they know that the Russians simply could not allow that? Do they really think they can simply occupy Belgrad for six months, string up a few dozen terrorists and play the Austrian National Anthem on the main square every day at noon? Wouldn't the Austrians know that it is not within their means to move in on Serbia without unleashing a major European war?

Now you're going to ask me, what should they do? Obviously they have to do something. All I can say about that is that there are hundreds of people in Vienna, Budapest — and in Berlin — who could dream up thousands of ingenious and effective ways to punish the Serbs while still preserving the austere authority of the Double Monarchy — and the peace for the world. But the kind of un-British governments they have makes it impossible for these sensible voices to be heard.

Now — I can see it in your faces — the next subject you want me to talk about is Kaiser Wilhelm. What is going on in his mind, you ask, as he is cruising in Norwegian waters, supervising his guests' gymnastics on deck of the *Hohenzollern* and receiving and sending telegrams? Does he think the conflict can remain localized? Does he not know he is on a sticky wicket? Oh, I am sorry, I forgot. In Ouda you don't play cricket. A sticky wicket happens when the cricket field is partly dry and partly wet, creating a treacherous bounce, which makes the batter's life difficult. In other words, a sticky wicket describes any situation which is full of hazardous uncertainty. Well, I happen to know what is going in his mind. He is thinking of his former teacher and idol, Prince Otto von Bismarck. He is saying to himself that if Bismarck could play the diplomatic game for twenty years, from the time he created the Reich until his time was up, keeping ten balls in the air simultaneously, so can I.

Please let me digress for a moment and tell you a little story.

In the summer of 1879, two years before he got married and nine years before he came on the throne, Wilhelm attended army manoeuvres in Alsace which, as you know, after Prussia had beaten France, had become German. There, in Strasbourg, he met a *fille de joie*. He was twenty, she was thirty-five. Her professional name was Miss Love. Her real name was Emilie Klopp. They had a number of encounters. One of the many things she taught him was to tie her arms — obviously she helped, because he could only use one arm — and then — forgive me, *madame,* for being so crude — and then to enter her. He enjoyed that very much. I very much doubt whether two years later, after he was married, his wife, Dona, permitted him to do the same, but I cannot say so for sure.

Some time after he was married he invited Miss Love to Potsdam and put her up in a place near the *Marmorpalast,* in the Russian quarter around the corner from the church of Alexander Nevski. There he could enjoy her company whenever he liked.

All this worked perfectly smoothly except for one little thing. He gave her a signed photograph of himself and wrote her at least six letters containing hints of their practices which in her answers she described as *pikant,* meaning spicy. In return for these services he gave her a present of one hundred marks, but only once, promising to pay her more later.

Among Miss Love's many other customers was Bill von Bismarck, the younger son of the Iron Chancellor. What was more natural for her than to wait a few years until Wilhelm had acceded to the throne, then to approach Bill and to suggest to him gently that unless she received a significant sum of money she would give the six letters the Kaiser had written to her to the press? Her overall expenses, including the expense for moving to Potsdam, she said, and for the apartment furniture, amounted to at least twenty thousand marks.

Bill von Bismarck knew about at least three other affairs of Wilhelm's of this kind, which, to avoid scandal, had been smoothly settled with generous payments out of secret funds. But compared to twenty thousand marks the sums were trifling. Bill did not know how to proceed. So he consulted his brother Herbert, who did not have the answer either. They decided to consult their father.

There was no need for alarm, Bismarck said. Both Friedrich Wilhelm IV and Wilhelm I, our Wilhelm's revered grandfather, had faced similar situations when they were young. There was always money available to settle these things, and no reason to worry about a scandal. Public opinion would never condemn a prince for seeking entertainments of this nature from a professional. It would be different if Wilhelm had seduced a lady who was respectable. This, by the way, was a point on which Bismarck's two sons differed from their father. Times had changed, they thought. Today the public would no longer approve of their future monarch consorting with prostitutes. The press was more mean and more puritanical than it had been earlier in the century. That may be so, Bismarck said. In any case, the one thing to avoid was to try to pay off Miss Love behind the Kaiser's back. She could always go to His Majesty and demand more. No, there could be no resolution of this affair without involving His Majesty himself. He asked Herbert to speak to the All Highest directly.

When Herbert von Bismarck did so the Kaiser said he did not remember any Miss Love. But then, after pretending to reflect deeply, he confessed that he did vaguely remember one encounter, in Strasbourg, after the manoeuvres. The rest of the relationship, including her move to Potsdam, Miss Love had invented, he said, for obvious reasons. He did not wish to discuss the matter any further.

I am sure you will agree that this story illustrates two points. First, Bismarck understood perfectly how the world works and knew how to fix things that were fixable. Secondly, more than thirty years ago, the Kaiser was able to escape the consequences of his actions with the greatest of ease, on this and no doubt many other occasions. The question is, now that the Kaiser is his own Bismarck, can he escape the consequences of his *carte blanche?*

The Friend

If Rudolf was Wilhelm's worst friend, Count Philipp von Eulenburg-Hertefeld was his best. He was the only true friend he ever had.

Even though you, my noble lord, have been spared the succession of crises that have shaken the long reign of Wilhelm II with ever increasing intensity, no one knows better than you do how important it is to have at least one male friend with whom you can talk freely and whom you can trust without reservations. A loving queen, however intelligent and well informed, cannot take his place, because her interests and yours are intertwined. Furthermore, friendships can usually be dissolved with fewer unpleasant consequences than marriages. For these reasons it is most important for kings to have true friends. In Wilhelm's case, Dona's main role in his life was to be his bedmate — Bismarck thought the prince had a powerful sex drive — and to be the mother of his children, rather than that of confidante and adviser in matters of high policy.

Prince Wilhelm was twenty-seven when, at a hunting party, he first got to know Philipp, who was twelve years older. They had met once before, in Munich. The Eulenburgs were a leading Junker family, belonging to the oldest nobility, the Uradel. They had served the Hohenzollern family for half a millennium. Wilhelm was immediately drawn to him, instinctively recognizing in him qualities he felt he himself lacked, surrounded as he, Wilhelm, was by courtiers, military men and bureaucrats. In many ways he felt unfulfilled. Only his military duties captivated him. All his other duties stood in the way of his many interests. He was not particularly self-analytical but he could not have failed to have noticed the enormous effort he had to make to act as a decisive, cold-blooded, hard-headed Prussian soldier with an exemplary family life while he knew he was vulnerable, changeable and burdened by a devoted wife whom he called the ideal German woman, although she bored him to tears.

Philipp's interests were artistic. He disliked hunting, he did not shoot and hated the idea of killing. He was the centre of the Liebenberger Freundeskreis, or Circle of Friends. Liebenberg was his castle and country seat, not far from Berlin, north of Brandenburg. He had served in the Garde du Corps in the Franco-Prussian War when he was twenty-three and was decorated with an Iron Cross for his work under the German governor of Strasbourg. But he soon decided that he had no use for the military, nor was he interested in politics until he met Prince Wilhelm, sixteen years later.

In contrast to other members of his class he was highly cultivated. He was a Schöngeist, an enthusiast for beauty, with a special feeling for medieval chivalry and northern folklore. His temperament was arch-conservative, romantic and mystical. He was a great admirer of Richard Wagner and corresponded with his wife, Cosima, even after she was widowed. He thought all Germans could identity with Wagner's national art and he regretted that Bismarck, preoccupied as he was with political, economic and military considerations, had never paid attention to the cultural unification of Germany. That is why he hoped that Wilhelm would assume cultural leadership once he was in power and would move a few steps away from what he thought was the excessive materialism of the new Reich. It was largely thanks to Philipp that Wilhelm supported the Bayreuth Festival, in northern Bavaria, although, very tactfully, Philipp thought the Bavarian government would consider it an affront if Wilhelm did more than support it and actually became a patron. Bavarians do not, as a rule, like Prussians.

Philipp was not particularly ambitious and spent every moment of his spare time at the piano, composing ballads and songs. He also wrote plays that became quite well known. Sometimes, in the early years of their friendship, in the evenings, after a day's hunting on his estate, he accompanied himself on the piano, singing his own ballads for his guests, while Wilhelm turned the pages.

Philipp had an unusually close relationship with his highly artistic mother, an amateur painter of some distinction, to whom he wrote every day, and a distant one with his austere, reserved, hard-working, practical, very Prussian father who could barely hide his disappointment in his son's dilettantish pursuits. The choice of an artistic career, which Philipp later said he had really wanted, would have meant a complete break. Quite apart from the financial implications, this would have triggered the kind of confrontation he had tried to avoid all his life. So he accepted his father's choice of a profession for him, that of a civil servant, while trying to live in his spare time in the artistic world of his mother. He had a (to him) dull wife with whom he had fathered eight children, and perhaps, so it was rumoured, the occasional extra-marital affair.

Philipp was always on stage. No one ever heard him say an angry word. He and his friends used a special vocabulary to express their feelings for each other, which, in its mannered sentimentality, was reminiscent of romantic letter-writing in the early nineteenth century. He was excellent company, an amusing conversationalist, a born raconteur, full of witty anecdotes, kind-hearted, smooth and even-tempered His interests were European, and, although he approved of some of the political views of both Richard Wagner and Adolf Stoecker, both strong anti-Semites, he did not seem to have been more anti-Semitic than the average German. He became a friend of the head of the Austrian branch of the Rothschild banking family and was an admirer of Dr. Theodor Herzl, the founder of Zionism. In short, his world was light years away from the barbaric sergeants who were drilling the goose-stepping sons of his peers on the parade grounds of Potsdam.

Philipp considered himself an orthodox Lutheran and was a firm believer in life after death. Like many others of his generation he was a spiritualist and it was he who introduced the Kaiser to it.

I only have a vague idea of what goes on during the spiritualists' so-called séances. I am told they try to contact the dead through a person who is a medium. It's certainly something we Muslims know nothing about. I heard rumours that Queen Victoria also occasionally participated in spiritualist sessions.

After finishing his legal studies Philipp joined the civil service and became a judge at lower courts in several small towns in Prussia. But the formalism of the law filled him with disgust and he found it difficult to sentence poor people for minor offences. The Eulenburg and Bismarck families had enjoyed a close relationship for generations, and he was a friend of Herbert, which no doubt helped him to be transferred to a position in the Trade and Commerce section of the German Foreign Office. Soon he became one of the few people free to call at the Bismarck residence for tea or dinner without an invitation. When Philipp tried to leave the foreign service after his father's death and devote himself entirely to the arts, it was Bismarck, together with Wilhelm, who persuaded him to stay. Bismarck at first thought Philipp's friendship with Wilhelm could be useful to him since he could use him as a source of information and perhaps as a means to influence him.

Philipp was concerned that the industrial masses were largely alienated from the monarchy. By introducing progressive social security measures very much ahead of their time, Bismarck had hoped to gain their support. But this policy had failed, the Social Democratic Party was stronger than ever, and he saw no alternative to enacting repressive measures to curb it. Philipp agreed with Bismarck that no compromise with socialism was possible, but he opposed the degree of repression Bismarck contemplated. He also disapproved of Bismarck's anti-Catholic Kulturkampf, which had triggered the formation of the Centre Party. Like the Social Democrats, it was hostile to the government. On a personal level, he objected to Bismarck poisoning Wilhelm's relationship to his mother. The mother-son relationship was sacred to him.

But most disagreements were connected with the rapid industrialization that was taking place. Philipp thought Bismarck's introduction of universal manhood suffrage had produced the opposite effect from that intended. Philipp never thought that the working class should participate in the political process, specifically in electing the Reichstag. He believed workers lacked the necessary political education and could easily be manipulated to subvert the position of the Prussian nobility, and of the property-owning classes generally. Of course, he never doubted that the privileges of his own class were in the interest of the German people as a whole.

But by far the most important area of disagreement between him and Bismarck in the years before Wilhelm became Kaiser had to do with the powers of the monarch. He was convinced that only a strong monarchy could preserve traditional society. A strong monarchy meant that the monarch, and not the chancellor, had to govern. This had not been an issue until Wilhelm became Kaiser. Wilhelm's venerable grandfather, Wilhelm I, had allowed the legendary creator of the Reich to make policy and have the last word. In Philipp's view, in that sense Bismarck's extraordinary achievements had actually, as it turned out, undermined the power of the monarch. Philipp considered it his main task to ensure that his friend, rather than the chancellor, become the decisive voice in government, whether the chancellor was Bismarck or Bismarck's successor. He also thought it was his job to help Wilhelm resist any temptation to democratize. While their friendship largely flourished as a result of Wilhelm's initiative, it also furthered Philipp's own interests and those of his family and friends.

Once Wilhelm was Kaiser, it soon became evident that Bismarck was unwilling to relinquish any of his powers. It seemed to be only a matter of time before Wilhelm would attempt to curtail them. The Iron Chancellor was bound to dig in his iron heels. What would Wilhelm do if Bismarck used all his enormous, almost mythical prestige to challenge him publicly? And what role, if any, would Philipp play in such a duel?

I must beg Your Majesty to await the outcome of this drama with the admirable patience that is so much in keeping with the high office with which Allah has entrusted you.

Chapter 7

Monday July 10

The weather was still perfect when Zade and Ali visited Manfred von Kosenburg in his office at the very back of the Neue Palais in Potsdam, beautifully situated just west of the Palace of Sanssouci, both built by Frederick the Great.

Kosenburg had called Ali Hassan to suggest a discussion of the Swiss Strategy. He was a stout, friendly, middle-echelon functionary on the staff of Oberst-Marschall August zu Eulenburg, a relative of Philipp's and the general manager of the imperial establishment, who did his job so smoothly that he was often criticized for making it too easy for Wilhelm to lead his hectic and confusing life.

According to the Court Precedence Regulations of January 19, 1878, the rankings of the Imperial Household were as follows:

> 1. Der Oberst-Marschall, or Principal Marshall
> 2. Der Oberst-Truchsess, or Lord High Stewart
> 3. Der Oberst-Schenk, or Principal Cupbearer
> 4. Der Oberst Jägermeister, or Principal Hunt Master
>
> Source: John C.G. Röhl, The Kaiser and His Court, Cambridge University Press 1987, p. 87.

As soon as Manfred saw Zade he was blinded by her beauty. He had to make idle conversation until he could compose himself.

"His Excellency may have told you," he said to her, "that we are His Majesty's housekeepers. But we are really far more. We are, in a sense, his guardians. That's why we are so upset by what the Crown Prince did."

Zade and Ali were puzzled.

"So you haven't heard," he went on. "Once again the young man has come out publicly on the side of the war mongers. He can't wait for the war with Russia to start. These bellicose statements drive Bethmann Hollweg to a state of white fury. If there's going to be a war, the Chancellor thinks, it must be a defensive war, not one provoked by irresponsible sabre-rattling. The Crown Prince is a real enfant terrible, you know — although he's really no longer an enfant. He must be well over thirty by now. His father had to send him a telegram from his yacht to please stop this sort of thing immediately. Also, not to make any more inflammatory speeches. After all, this is a very sensitive moment. Everybody is aware that the French are arriving in Saint Petersburg today. Who knows what sort of mischief they're going to plan now, after the poor Tsar had to stand at attention while the band played the Marseillaise and the heir of the French Revolution, the republican president Poincaré, had to inspect the Imperial Guards. The Tsar may well prefer a war to another French Revolution staged in Russia — I mean a repetition of the 1905 revolution — only a little better organized this time. Even if his railways are not in very good shape and it may take him a few weeks to mobilize. In the end he may well have both, a war and a revolution. But that is not what you've come here to discuss with me."

He took another look at Zade. Will His Majesty be able to say no to anything this stunning lady suggests? Those gorgeous eyes. And such lovely, smooth skin, the colour of desert sand in twilight. And such natural grace. He certainly will need us to guard him against these lethal charms. How much more dangerous than our harmless, prosaic German beauties.

"Ah yes, now I remember." With some effort he pulled himself together. He addressed Zade directly. "You want to tell His Majesty that Ouda is an Arab Switzerland, a neutral oasis in the desert that can be of immense value to Germany as a base for intelligence and anti-British propaganda. If there is a war.

And if the Turks are on our side."

Zade was prepared.

"I understand the situation is by no means resolved," she responded. "But you are right — it is most likely they'll be on your side. So let us talk about that. You must face the truth — we Arabs can't wait for the Ottoman Empire to breathe its last. We hate the Turkish governors for their brutality and despotism. It is a safe bet that the British will try to make use of us Arabs to make life miserable for the Turks. If the German Ambassador in Ouda has the right sounding posts, he can find out what the British are up to and thwart them at every point. And in Ouda there are plenty of sounding posts."

"I can see that," Manfred nodded. But he did not seem altogether convinced.

"Let me give you an example," Ali said. "I understand the Kaiser is interested in archaeology."

"Oh yes!" Manfred became excited. "It is really amazing. Archaeology is a real passion of his, an escape from all his troubles. I can't think of anything that fills him with more enthusiasm. He has an extraordinary, commanding knowledge of it. He is particularly interested in the way ancient art reveals concepts of kingship and the idea of the sacred. The professionals are often astounded. His Majesty could not be more serious about it. And he talks about it at great length — some people think at too great length. You have heard about his palace the Achilleion? No? Well, that is his place in Corfu, on a wooded hill, overlooking the sea towards Albania. It used to belong to the Empress of Austria, Sissi, you know, the one who was assassinated. He purchased it out of his own funds in 1906, and it became his favourite place of refuge. Unlike the northern cruises it is not reserved for men only. The Empress enjoys it as well, and so does their daughter Victoria. He himself took charge nearby of the excavations of the head of a Medusa, dating from prehellenistic times. Then, two years ago, they started new excavations on the Greek mainland. He got himself a shovel and participated in the digs himself, for six or eight hours a day! Someone told me he said to one of the archaeologists there, 'At last I've found something I can concentrate on!' — Now, what was Your Excellency asking?"

"I was going to give you an example of the sort of situation that may arise in which a neutral Ouda might be useful to His Majesty in wartime. My example involves an archeological excavation that might appeal to him."

"Oh yes?"

"Our King Shahriyar shares the Kaiser's interest. Mesopotamia is very close to Ouda. Three years ago the British Museum in London undertook a major project, excavating Crachemish, the old Hittite city beside the Euphrates, not far from Aleppo. At first it was no more than a mound. King Shahriyar sent Zade and me to the site as observers, and to offer whatever help we could. That is where I met a bright Oxford student who was working on this project. I don't think he worked very hard on it, though he knew a great deal about the Hittites. What really captivated him was Arabia, everything about Arabia. He had even learned Arabic and spoke it well. Even some dialects. His name was Lawrence, but his friends called him Ned. It occurred to me that, should the British and the Turks ever find themselves at war, here was a young man who could gather Arab fighters in the desert for the British and lead an Arab rebellion against the Turkish oppressor. If you people had the right contacts, you could prevent that."

Manfred von Kosenburg thought this was a very good argument.

"Do you remember the boy Dahoum?" Ali asked Zade.

"Very well," she said. "A beautiful Bedouin boy, bright-eyed, slim. Fair hair, very rare among us. About fourteen or fifteen. Lawrence employed him as an assistant, taught him to read and write, and also photography. And later took him to Oxford with him. It was clear to everybody, and Lawrence made no attempt to conceal it, that he loved the boy."

Manfred shook his head and frowned.

"In Germany we don't talk about that sort of thing," he said. "My brother is a well-known neurologist and has written a good deal about it, but I would never mention it to His Majesty. Does the Koran allow it?"

"No, certainly not, it's strictly forbidden, a very great sin. I only mention it because Lawrence made no secret of it and I am not aware that he suffered any unpleasant consequences." Zade suddenly changed the subject. "Oh, by the way," she said, "I am surprised the Kaiser has not come home from his cruise, to take charge."

"We expect him any day now. However, he is in complete control wherever he is. The yacht is fully equipped will all the latest means of communication. I wouldn't be surprised if His Majesty was even in direct contact with his cousin the Tsar, who I am sure would rather be on his yacht than having to listen to the Marseillaise."

He paused, trying to remember the purpose of the visit.

"Oh yes," he resumed, "I will certainly do my best to arrange a time for you to be received by His Majesty, so that you can make your presentation."

"That would be very good of you," Zade said. "I fully realize, of course, that this matter may not be at the top of his agenda, at a time like this."

"On the contrary." Manfred rose to accompany his visitors to the door. "The greater pressure, the more time His Majesty has for exotic diversions. Especially a touch of oriental romance. This concept you suggest — a sounding post in the desert to subvert the British — is just the sort of thing that appeals to his imagination."

An Act of True Courage

O mighty King, let me tell you what the wise and courageous Kaiser Wilhelm did less than two years after ascending the throne. He had never heard of the tale of the young Sultan Al-Rashid and his old Grand Vizier Khalifah, and yet he acted exactly the same way. You remember that the young Sultan took over the venerable old Grand Vizier from his father and grandfather. Khalifah had been showered with honours for serving his country masterfully for three decades. He had become more famous than any other grand vizier anybody could remember, even though his father and mother could not abide him. When young Al-Rashid was growing up, Khalifah was one of his teachers. Khalifah even told him on one occasion, "One day you must be your own chancellor." So, once Al-Rashid ascended the throne, he took the venerable old Khalifah at his word. He summoned him, thanked him for the services he had rendered to his father and grandfather, gave him a pot of gold and a palace to live in with his wife and his harem, and dismissed him. Soon after the old Grand Vizier died, Al-Rashid built a mosque and named it after him.

I have mentioned Prince Bismarck to Your Majesty many times before. I told you that he had unified Germany in 1871. To achieve this he saw no alternative but to waging three aggressive wars. After that he became a man of peace and the foremost statesman in Europe. He wrote the most beautiful German prose since Goethe and Heine — two poets Your Majesty may not have heard of. He spoke magnificently and was a man of enormous flexibility. He even disarmed Queen Victoria with his charm. He was a great realist, the opposite of a romantic. One gets a whiff of his sober approach and of his power of expression when, in 1888, he remarked, on the subject of Germany's flirtation with acquiring colonies in Africa, "My map of Africa lies in Europe: here lies Russia and here lies France and we are in the middle. That is my map of Africa".

He surrounded Germany with a wall of secret treaties and brilliantly succeeded in his most important objective, to keep France and Russia apart.

What I have not told Your Majesty is that he ruled Germany with an iron hand, manipulating politicians and journalists in a manner no one had done before in Germany since the Dark Ages. His opponents, including, of course, the Kaiser's mother and father, took the view that he acted with "the utmost cynicism." Some said he corrupted Germany. He certainly used whatever method seemed to work, including the highly effective payment of generous bribes, including bribes to the press. One of his objectives was to use his "anti-Socialist laws" to prevent the large Social Democratic Party from exercising any influence at all. So he tried to outwit and outmanoeuvre it whenever he could. To keep it off balance, he introduced health and unemployment insurance legislation, which no other country had adopted as yet, and which Ouda, under Your Majesty's inspired leadership, may be able to introduce in the near future. In the early 1860s, at the beginning of his reign as chief minister of Prussia, he even proposed an all-German parliament elected by universal suffrage, a proposal so radical that at the time even the socialist leader August Bebel thought Germans were not yet ready for it.

As I mentioned before, when Wilhelm ascended the throne, in order to become widely popular, he wanted to be the Kaiser of the Poor. What, I ask Your Majesty, could have been more honourable? And who stood in the way? Bismarck! Public opinion overwhelmingly considered Bismarck Yesterday's Man. In the Reichstag election of 1887 four and a half million out of a total of seven million votes had gone to groups hostile to Bismarck. However, Germans still worshipped him as the creator of the Reich.

For the young man to dismiss his former model and teacher, this granite monument, this — I am sorry, Your Majesty, words fail me — this personification of The Great Man, this incarnation of Eternal Germany, required the courage of a David confronting Goliath. So did young Wilhelm's subsequent cancellation of the secret Reinsurance Treaty with Russia of 1887, Bismarck's proudest achievement, on the grounds that it was incompatible with Germany's treaty obligations with Austria-Hungary. The Reinsurance Treaty guaranteed neutrality on the part of both Germany and Russia if either should find itself at war with a third great power.

For some time, the two men thought they could work together, but by March 1890 the time had come for a showdown. I will spare Your Majesty the details on how the final break came about. It may be enough to say that on March 5, 1890, Wilhelm told the assembly in Brandenburg that he would smash anybody who stood in his way to pieces. A few days later, Wilhelm was the patron of an international conference for the protection of workers. It was a failure. Bismarck had done his best to sabotage it. And so on. At first, both Wilhelm and Philipp thought he might agree to giving up some of his powers voluntarily, right away, but this came to nothing. Perhaps later, he said, but not now. I don't think in the end Philipp played an active role in the actual decision-making, though Bismarck thought he did. I cannot swear that the following is true, but this is what I have heard: The climax came when Wilhelm got wind of negotiations between Bismarck and the Catholic head of the Centre party, in Bismarck's house, with the object of compelling Wilhelm to stand aside when a new constitution was proposed that would relieve enemies of the Reich — socialists and others — of their right to vote. Of course, this plot, if indeed it took place, was designed to thwart what they considered Wilhelm's ludicrous and highly dangerous attempt to win popularity by becoming Kaiser of the Poor. Bismarck's Jewish banker was said to have participated in these discussions. This allegedly elicited the observation from Wilhelm that Jesuits and Jews have always gone together. In the morning of March 15, Wilhelm ordered a coach and drove to the lodgings of Bismarck's son, Herbert, where Bismarck was staying. There are different versions of what happened. The one I like best is this one — Bismarck had not finished dressing and kept the Monarch waiting. When he at last made his appearance, both men were tense. They clashed. Wilhelm said unpleasant things about Bismarck's Jewish banker and the Jews generally. Bismarck replied that Jews were a useful element in German society and carried out important tasks, especially at foreign courts. At one moment, Bismarck covered a letter lying on the desk with his hand. The Kaiser grabbed it. The letter was from Tsar Alexander III and referred to Wilhelm as an "ill-mannered boy of bad faith."

Who can blame Wilhelm for immediately demanding Bismarck's departure?

In due course, he issued a statement that said it was with the deepest emotion and a troubled heart that he had accepted Bismarck's resignation. He bestowed on him the rank of Field Marshall, granted him a large sum of money and a new title, Duke of Lauenburg, which Bismarck refused. He also sent him a life-sized portrait of himself. Bismarck moved his belongings, including three thousand bottles of wine and three hundred boxes of cigars, to his estate Friedrichsruh near Hamburg.

From that day on, every time Bismarck used a coin, he turned it upside down in order, as he said, not to have to "look at that face."

That is one of the few minor details in which this story differs from that of Sultan Al-Rashid and his Grand Vizier Khalifah.

Chapter 8

Thursday, July 23

While the world was waiting for the text of the Austrian ultimatum to be submitted to Belgrad later in the day, Ali and Zade went for a stroll in the Tiergarten hoping to dream up more strategies to entrap the Kaiser.

Ali had received a confidential telegram in the morning containing the main points.

> The Belgrad government was to cease and desist immediately from all subversive activities on the territory of the Austro-Hungarian monarchy, as well as from all anti-Austrian propaganda in Serbia itself. Judicial proceedings were to be instituted against any person in Serbia who had been accessory to the Sarajevo crime, with delegates of the government of the Double Monarchy taking part in the investigation. The Serbian government was to cooperate in putting an end to the illegal traffic of arms. The reply was expected by six p.m. on Saturday, July 25, at the latest.

"Ali Hassan!" cried the familiar voice of Jan van Steensel, the former deputy to the Dutch Ambassador in Constantinople. "Getting married at last?"

"No, no, no," Ali laughed. "My friend and I have more important things to do."

He was delighted to see Jan, who was a good friend and had unusually reliable sources of information. Moreover, he was a first-class strategic thinker. Recently dismissed from his position for reasons perhaps not unconnected to a few alleged indiscretions directly attributable to his enjoyment of distilled spirits on public occasions, a habit particularly heavily frowned on in a Muslim country, he was peacefully sitting on a bench near the Goethe Memorial reading Le Monde. Jan was married to the wealthy and tolerant daughter of a German banker and intended to spend the rest of his days comfortably in Berlin, doing nothing other than drink and talk. He must have had at least five glasses of schnapps for lunch at his favorite restaurant, Borchardt in the Kaiserhof on the Wilhelmplatz. This was evident only in his slurred speech, but by no means in the quality of his mind, which was exceptionally fertile, especially when drinking.

Ali introduced Zade. They sat down.

"What a delightful surprise," Jan said. "I want some busybody to report to my wife that I was seen in the Tiergarten sitting on a bench in the closest proximity of a stunning beauty."

"This can easily be arranged," Ali replied.

"Now let me ask you this, Ali Hassan," Jan van Steensel went on. "What could be more important than marriage? I find mine entirely satisfactory. Mind you, I had to do a good deal of experimenting first." Lurid stories of the Dutchman's experimentations had reached even Ouda. The Germans in Constantinople called him the Flying Dutchman. "I can't think of anything more important. But obviously you can. Tell me what."

Ali took a deep breath.

"Zade intends to seduce the All Highest."

Jan looked at her, his eyes wide open.

"Do you know something, madame? Many have tried and failed. But none so far, as far as I know, from Ouda. And none as beautiful as you. I really think you will be able to pull it off. May I ask whether you have ever shared the bed of a reigning monarch?"

"Oh yes, monsieur," Zade replied truthfully. "Many, many times."

"Good. I assume you want to do it once again, just for sport?"

"Oh no," Zade replied indignantly.

"Surely not for profit?"

"Why else? Of course. But not financial profit. Political profit."

It took Jan van Steensel a few seconds to work this out.

"Not only to you?"

"To the whole world."

Jan looked at Ali.

"I am dumbfounded by this lady's idealism, enterprise and imagination. I think I can guess what she has in mind. Have you made arrangements to meet him? He will be rather, hm, busy when he comes back."

"We have a few ideas," Ali said. "But perhaps, Jan, you can help us."

"I most certainly can. But only on one condition. Nobody ever tells him the truth. He hears what he wants to hear. He can only take criticism if at the same time you flatter him. That's what you've got to do, tell him the truth while flattering him. I am sure you know how to do that. After you have told him what you want to say, you must convey to him what I am about to tell you. Will you listen to me?"

"With the greatest interest."

He took out a small silver flask and swallowed a few mouthfuls of the content.

"You must tell him there is a real possibility — unless he acts quickly — that, in the war that's bound to come, the Turks will go with the British. He can prevent that if he pays attention to what you will tell him. There is a lot of pro-British sentiment in Turkey, especially after last year's Anglo-Turkish agreement in which the British even withdrew their objections to the building of the Berlin-Baghdad railway — under certain entirely manageable conditions."

> On May 17, 1913, The Times of London referred to the Anglo-Turkish agreement as "further demonstration of that spirit of cooperation among the Great Powers which has done so much of late to preserve the peace of Europe. It should convince Germany that Great Britain does not oppose the essential elements of the Baghdad railway scheme provided her own special interests are protected. Above all, it will relieve the financial disabilities of Turkey and will enable her to press forward the great task of binding with bonds of steel the great Asiatic territories in which her future chiefly lies."
>
> Source: Edward Meal Earle, Turkey, The Great Powers and The Baghdad Railway, New York Russell & Russell 1966, p. 257.
>
> In consideration of Britain withdrawing her opposition to Germany's construction of the Baghdad railway, Germany accepted a subordinate place in southern Mesopotamia and recognized British interests in the Persian Gulf.
>
> Source: Ibid., p. 265.
>
> In 1913 the United States produced 140 times more oil than Persia.
>
> Source: David Fromkin, A Peace to End All Peace, André Deutsch 1989, p. 29.

Neither Zade nor Ali said anything.

"The Germans may have reorganized the army," Jan continued, "after the Turks' crushing defeat two years ago in the Balkans, but the British were just as effective in doing the same for the Turkish navy, and Rear Admiral Arthur Limpus with his British Naval Mission is at least as influential as Liman von Sanders, the head of the German military mission. Willy does not seem to understand what Turkey can do for Germany. Just look at the map — Turkey can attack Russia from the south. And Turkey can cut off England from India. That's not what his ambassadors in Constantinople and in London tell him, either because they don't see the obvious, or because, if Turkey joins the British, they think it would serve the British right to be saddled with the lazy, incompetent, corrupt, unreliable, moribund Turks. I know for sure that Hans von Wangenheim thinks an alliance with Turkey would be more trouble that it's worth. As you know, he's the German Ambassador in Constantinople. And just a few weeks ago, the German Chief of Staff, General Helmuth von Moltke, himself said it would be most inappropriate for Germany to assume the Turks would be on their side in case of war. In fact, the Germans had sent their military mission to Turkey reserving the right to recall it in case of war, which certainly suggests that from the beginning they thought the Turks might very well side with the British, or at least try to remain neutral."

The pair continued to listen intently.

"As to Willy, everything with him is personal. He used to be quite friendly with Enver Pasha, the dashing Young Turk who is now war minister. He's in fact the virtual ruler of Turkey. Enver used to be military attaché in Berlin for two years, speaks fluent German and even sports a mustache like the Kaiser's. In Berlin, he was known as a heavily perfumed lady-killer — that's more than anybody ever said about me. But Willy's friendship rather cooled. He disapproves of the way Enver has dealt with the Ottoman dynasty. And he was upset last year when he heard that during an attempted coup the then minister of war was shot dead in Enver's presence. Even if Enver didn't do it himself. Willy probably thought Enver should have seen to it that this sort of thing was done somewhere else. Or maybe he believed it's a foregone conclusion that in the end the Turks will come along because of all those business and banking ties to Germany, the Baghdad railway and all that. For all I know, he may even think of Turkey as his personal colony that, in the end, will do what he tells them. Also, he may have heard that not too long ago the American Ambassador in Constantinople, Henry Morgenthau, told everybody that he was deeply disturbed when he noticed that the Germans had successfully 'prussianized' the Turkish army. He had just witnessed a parade of goose-stepping Turkish soldiers.

Whatever the reasons, Willy has done nothing. He is waiting for the Turks to make the first move. Which may never happen. The Committee is hopelessly divided. They're desperate. They know they must be allied to one of the Great Powers or they are lost. I hear one member has sounded out the French. Another the Russians. Yes, imagine, even the Russians, the Turks' old enemies."

Jan van Steensel took out his silver flask for refreshment.

"Madame," he asked, turning to Zade, "are you wondering why I care so much about this — I, a patriotic Dutchman, the citizen of a neutral country?"

"Yes, monsieur, that is exactly what I am wondering."

"The answer is, I think the Germans are going to win this war but only if the Turks are on their side. The British Empire is big enough. It will survive, whatever happens. It's time the Germans got a chance. And I am saying this not only because my wife says so. I'm saying this because they don't seem to realize they will lose the war if the Turks go with the British. There is one man in the British government who will do anything to prevent the Turks from lining up with Germany. Have you heard of their minister of the navy, the Lord of the Admiralty they call him, a young man called Winston Churchill?"

Ali had, Zade had not.

"Unlike almost everybody else, especially in his own Liberal party, he does not think the Ottomans' disintegration is inevitable. On the contrary. He admires the Young Turks. Like Willy, who's nearly twice his age, he's met Enver but, unlike Willy, he still likes him. He is convinced Britain, more than any other power, can and should help the Turks. And for a very good reason. Britain happens to be the greatest Muslim power in the world."

> In 1910: Sixty-two million Muslims lived in India, ten million Muslims in Egypt.
>
> Source: Martin Gilbert, Churchill, Boston: Houghton Mifflin, vol. 3, p. 189.

Jan leaned forward.

"Now listen to this. The British are building two powerful dreadnoughts for the Turks. It's a terrific expense for them, since their treasury empty. They've raised the money by public subscription, throughout Turkey. Those battleships are a serious challenge to German influence and are now ready to sail to Turkey. But if there's danger of war and there's a possibility the Turks will go the wrong way, I bet Churchill and the entire Cabinet will make sure they stay in Britain."

"But," Zade said, "presumably the Turks have paid for them in advance?"

"Of course. This is extremely painful for Churchill, since he's so pro-Turkish. But he understands in times like these the national interest must come first. No doubt the British government will pay the money back. I am sure in Constantinople they're talking about nothing else. So this is the time they will certainly listen to Willy. You must whisper to him to hurry up and make them an offer."

Once again, he reached for his flask and this time emptied it.

"Now," Jan said, "did you say you want me to arrange a meeting?"

"You would earn the gratitude of all of mankind," Zade replied.

"I'll tell you what I will do. Can you keep a secret? Wilhelm occasionally has séances. Just for the fun of it, he says. Table-knocking, and all that. He doesn't really believe in it, he says. But, on the other hand, he always says with a wink, one never knows. He claims he never lets the spirits dictate to him what to do. But unless he wants them to guide him, why bother? There's no such thing as pure, disinterested curiosity. My wife is a great friend of Frau von Halbgebauer. She's a most talented medium. None better. Very good family, too. And very discreet. If you ever need a medium, just let me know. I wouldn't be at all surprised if Willy will call her the moment he returns to Potsdam. All that's required is that she invite you, madame, to their séance. He won't be able to concentrate on the table-knocking once he sees you. I spoke to her yesterday. It costs me nothing to call her again."

"Oh? What did you talk about yesterday?" Ali asked.

"I told her that it would be a good idea to have Frederick the Great speak to Willy directly, through her. She did not know that Frederick also needed the Turks when times were rough. And he's bound to listen to the Hohenzollern king he reveres even more than his grandfather."

"So you gave her a history lesson?" Zade asked.

"I certainly did. In 1762, the last year of the Seventh Year war, Frederick suffered disaster after disaster. He was in a terrible state. All his friends, including the English, had deserted him. But then the tide turned. His enemy, the Tsarina Elisabeth, died and his friend Peter became Tsar and, as a reward for doing his best to modernize Russia, earned the title Peter the Great. In June, Frederick made sure that Prussian officers drank the health of his new ally Mustapha III. I did not tell Frau von Halbgebauer that all Frederick got out of the Turkish alliance was a brace of camels that Mustapha sent to Postdam. But with Peter on the throne he didn't need the Turks any more."

Zade mulled this over.

"What you're saying, monsieur, is that, unlike Frederick, Willy needs the Turks."

"More than he realizes. Everything depends on them."

"I will whisper this to him," Zade promised.

"Good. You will hear from Frau von Halbgebauer."

The Pilgrim

Please stop me, my honoured and beloved King, if you have heard this story before. You will remember my telling you about the Kaiser's and the Kaiserin Dona's first visit to Constantinople soon after he ascended the throne. My subject today is their second visit, nine years later, in October 1898. You are well aware of the magnificent progress made during these nine years in the building of the railway from Berlin to Baghdad, which symbolized what the Germans called Der Drang nach Osten, the drive towards the East, in which large segments of German industry participate with great enthusiasm. As I will show you tonight, there is no better salesman for German industry than Kaiser Wilhelm himself. Although he knew that his host, Sultan Abdul Hamid II, was responsible for the persecution of his Armenian minority, and he also knew that recently the Sultan's troops had brutally attacked the German scholar Waldemar Belck in Eastern Anatolia while he was studying cuneiform characters in ancient inscriptions, Wilhelm always put first things first.

Once again he and the Kaiserin enjoyed the Sultan Abdul Hamid II's sumptuous hospitality. The Kaiser was presented with a sabre studded with diamonds and the Kaiserin with a necklace estimated to be worth thirty thousand lires [Turkish pounds] and a number of precious silk carpets. The Kaiser presented the Sultan with something he, but perhaps not the Sultan, considered even more valuable — one of Frederick the Great's walking sticks.

Somewhat indiscreetly I was told that the Kaiserin and her ladies, who, like all German women worship on the altar of cleanliness, complained of the dirt and the flies and spent anxious moments chasing insects with their hat pins. One afternoon the Kaiserin was taken inside a harem where, so it was reported, she was repelled by the sight of a crowd of very fat women in ill-fitting Paris clothes, eating chocolates and looking bored.

The only European potentate who had never annexed any territory from Sultan Abdul Hamid II or his predecessors was his guest, the Kaiser, who, together with the Kaiserin, was on his way to the Holy Land on a pilgrimage and who was to spend altogether four weeks in the Ottoman empire. The Sultan assigned two Syrian soldiers to them to protect them. Far more significantly, he presented to the Kaiser the Dormition Church in Jerusalem where the body of Mary was said to have rested before the Christians say she rose to Heaven. This holy place was designed to become the property of German Catholics. Wilhelm hoped that it would compensate them, at least in part, for the bad treatment they had received from Bismarck during the Kulturkampf not very long ago. Considering what the Sultan had lost already, he could easily spare a church that meant nothing to him.

I must unfortunately admit, dear master, that one purpose of the Kaiser's pilgrimage was the wish to give his Christian missionaries the chance to convert us Muslims. When I hold him up to you as a model of a modern monarch, I do not wish to claim that I can defend every action of his. All I wish to do is to explain him, with all his faults. I might add that if I had the chance to convert him to our faith I would do so at a moment's notice, using whatever methods were at my disposal. Who knows? Perhaps one day I will be given the chance.

The fact remains that the new railway promises to link German cities with Christian holy places in Syria and Palestine. Therefore, it was not only German businessmen who were meant to benefit, I repeat, but also German missionaries. By the time Their Majesties arrived in Jerusalem, the Lutheran Jerusalem-Verein, an organization of which the Kaiserin Dona was the patron, was already flourishing. It ran a large orphanage and was dedicated to the propagation of Deutschtum, meaning German civilization, which included the teaching of the German language. The Deutsche Orient Mission supported Lutheran missionaries. German Catholics were no less zealous to save our souls.

One high point of the pilgrimage to Jerusalem was the ceremonial inauguration of the Protestant Church of the Redeemer on Muristan Square, which German Lutherans shared with English Anglicans. The bell tower, 137 feet high, had been — so I was told — designed by the Kaiser himself.

Two days before this inauguration, on October 29, in suffocating heat, mounted on a black charger, the All Highest led his brilliantly arrayed court, including the Kaiserin, a number of Protestant clergymen and the court painter Hermann Knackfuss, through the gates of the Old City in Jerusalem. He was dressed in gleaming white, with a gold eagle on top of his helmet. A fifty-foot section had been broken out of the roof of one of the battlements next to the Jaffa Gate, so that His Majesty did not have to descend from his horse.

I am not in a position to dispute that His Majesty was genuinely moved by the knowledge that this was the city of Jesus Christ. That is what he said later. But he was certainly not moved by anything he saw. He thought the Christian buildings were not in harmony with the spirit of the holy sites. It seemed to him that there had been a race for the highest towers and the biggest churches, which was only to be expected since the clergies of the different churches spent all their time carrying on intrigues against each other. This fostered hatred, not love, he said. Also, it made a very bad impression on us Muslims. The way religion was understood in Jerusalem, he observed, it would never lead to the conversion of a single Muslim. If he had come here without any religion, he would certainly have become a Muslim, not a Christian. Not only that, but the Church of the Saint Sepulchre compared very badly with the Mosque of Omar in its simple and awe-inspiring grandeur.

Throughout the pilgrimage, I am happy and, frankly, a little surprised to report, that Wilhelm found the Muslim world much more appealing to him than the Christian world. In Damascus he appeared dressed as a Bedouin sheik and was duly greeted by the ecstatic crowd with their customary cries of lululu, lululu, lululu. He placed a wreath on the tomb of Salah ad-Din, (the Germans call him Saladin), who became popular in Germany, I am told, because of a famous eighteenth-century play about tolerance, equating him in his wisdom with a wise Christian and a wise Jew. After all, the Kaiser could not know that hardly any one in our world remembers Salah ad-Din and the few who do realize he was an unscrupulous, brutal politician who, far from being tolerant, hated all infidels. We must forgive the Kaiser this little lapse. After all, his intentions could not have been more praiseworthy, especially when he gave an address, at Salah ad-Din's tomb. After first speaking movingly about the affection Haroun al-Rashid had had for Charlemagne, he made this declaration: "Let me assure His Majesty the Sultan and the three hundred million Muslims who, in whatever corner of the globe they live, revere in him their Caliph, that the German Emperor will ever be their friend and protector." It is unlikely that this generous speech gave much pleasure to the three Great Powers, England, France and Russia, to whom most of these three hundred million Muslims owe allegiance.

But the story I want to tell you is about another event altogether. During this pilgrimage, Wilhelm met Dr. Theodor Herzl, the founder and leader of Zionism. Let me say something about Zionism. You will remember what I told you about anti-Semitism. I have not spoken about the ways in which the Jews respond to it. There are mainly two ways. Either they try to integrate themselves into the culture of the country in which they live, without necessarily abandoning their religion and traditions, or if they find this undesirable or impossible, they become Zionists, meaning adherents of a movement that has as its purpose the formation of a state of their own.

In the Russian Empire, they are not allowed to integrate themselves. They can be accepted in Russian society only if they become Christians. Anti-Semitism is official policy and Jews have no civil rights. The state permits, and often even encourages, persecution and periodic massacres. Therefore, Zionism was primarily designed to liberate Russian Jews, but there is anti-Semitism everywhere in Christian Europe. Therefore, Zionism soon became an important movement in Jewish communities everywhere. At first, Zionists did not dare to dream of Palestine. Instead, they thought England or France might let them form a colony in one of their territories. But then the focus shifted to Palestine. Everything depended on the Sultan, the ruler of Palestine. Would he permit this? It was understood that the Jews themselves would supply the necessary finances.

Dr. Herzl was an imposing, regal-looking newspaperman who also wrote plays and novels. Not yet forty years old and sporting a black beard, he had no interest whatsoever in the Jewish religion. He was strongly drawn to the Kaiser and considered him the model of a modern prince, exceptionally gifted and imaginative and, as a result of his physical defect, very human. Moreover, he thought of him as a kindred spirit. Both men, he thought, had a gift for making their mission in life dramatic. And both had a wish to please. The Kaiser's anti-Semitism was of course assumed, and any manifestation of it therefore not a bit surprising.

So Dr. Herzl approached the Sultan. But he did not get very far. Only one of his emissaries was granted an audience. He presented his case. It was categorically rejected. Palestine was holy to the Muslims, the Sultan explained, and he would never surrender it voluntarily. He would not listen to any plans to let the Jews come in even if they carefully respected Muslim interests, which they assured the world they intended to do it. "Let the Jews save their billions," the Sultan said. "When my empire is carved up, they might get Palestine for nothing. But only our corpse will be divided. I will not consent to vivisection."

Dr. Herzl's next move was to approach the Kaiser and propose to him the formation of a Jewish chartered company under his protectorate, to settle Jews in Palestine. He hoped that the Kaiser, who was known to have a flair for imaginative new ideas and was the Sultan's friend, would welcome any scheme that would encourage Jews from the East to settle somewhere other than in Germany. He might also favour any scheme that might reduce the number — and therefore perhaps the influence — of Jews in Germany. Also, it was well known that the Sultan needed to placate the Kaiser. Perhaps, in this political context, the Sultan, if approached by the Kaiser and not by a Jew, would see matters in a different light.

A few preliminary conversations took place between Dr. Herzl's people and German officials, including the Chancellor, Bernhard von Bülow, who from the beginning thought Zionism unrealistic and misguided. But he did not say so. Kaiser Wilhelm agreed to receive Dr. Herzl twice, first at a preliminary interview in the German embassy in

Constantinople and a few days later, during his pilgrimage to the Holy Land, at a formal audience in Jerusalem.

At the preliminary interview in Constantinople, the Kaiser received Dr. Herzl in the presence of Chancellor von Bülow, and listened to him politely.

"There are elements among your compatriots in Germany" — a term the Kaiser used to describe Jews throughout — "for whom it would be a good thing to settle in Palestine. I am thinking of your compatriots in Hessen, where they practise usury among the local population." The implication, of course, was that he would welcome their departure from Hessen. Chancellor von Bülow added that the Jews had shown their gratitude to the House of Hohenzollern by joining the left opposition in droves, adding that neither the wealthy Jews nor Jewish newspapers supported Dr. Herzl.

But the Kaiser was by no means rude to Dr. Herzl. He assured him he would be happy to put the matter to the Sultan at a state dinner that evening — the date was October 18, 1898 — which, according to German press reports, was staged with all the magic of A Thousand and One Nights and ended with fireworks and a boat ride on the illuminated Bosporus. In the meantime, in preparation for the formal audience planned in a few days' time in Jerusalem, would Dr. Herzl please prepare a speech and submit it in writing to the Chancellor, for editing and approval.

At the lavish banquet, Kaiser put the matter to the Sultan as promised, emphasizing that the Zionists were no threat to him. The Sultan was adamant. He would not hear of the scheme. He was quite satisfied with his Jewish subjects, he said, but he did not wish to have any more.

The formal audience with Herzl took place in Jerusalem ten days later, in gruelling heat, in the imperial compound, which consisted of twenty-six tents supplied by Thomas Cook, Inc., on the rocky slope north of the Old City. Dr. Herzl had duly submitted his speech to the Chancellor in advance. Bülow deleted all references to the national Jewish revival, the Zionist congresses and, above all, to the idea of a German protectorate. Dr. Herzl, dressed in his formal best, delivered what was left of his speech as best he could, though he was not well and suffered greatly in the heat. The Kaiser wore a veiled helmet and was fidgeting with his riding crop as he listened. In his reply he said he was well acquainted with Dr. Herzl's movement, which did contain the core of a sound idea. The matter, he said, required further study. After the official exchange was over they had a brief chat. They agreed the most urgent need for Palestine was for water.

"That," Herzl assured him, "we can bring to the country. It will cost billions, but it will yield billions."

"Oh well," said the Kaiser, whipping his boots with his riding crop, "you people have got lots of money. More money than all of us put together."

On this somewhat inconclusive note, the audience ended.

◆

Your Majesty, I cannot conclude this story without quoting from a letter that has recently come my way. The subject is Zionism. The Kaiser wrote it before the Sultan had turned down his suggestion of a Jewish chartered company under his protection, an idea in which he soon lost interest. The letter was addressed to Grand Duke Friedrich of Baden, whose wife Luise was his father's sister.

"I am convinced," he wrote, "that the settlement of the Holy Land by the wealthy and hard-working nation of Israel would soon bring to it unexpected prosperity." He went on to say that this could be a blessing that might soon produce a significant economic revival of Asia Minor. That, in turn, would restore the financial fortunes of Turkey, and so the sick man of Europe would be sick no more. "The energy, creativity and efficiency of the tribe of Sem would be diverted to worthier goals than the sucking dry" — the German word he used was aussaugen — "of the Christians, and many an oppositional Semite now supporting the Social Democrats would go off to the East where there is rewarding work to be done ... Now, I realize that nine tenths of all Germans would recoil in horror if they were to discover that I sympathized with Zionism or would even, as I intend to if asked, place them under my protection ... Our dear God knows even better than we do that the Jews killed Our Saviour, and He has punished them accordingly. But neither the anti-Semites nor others, myself included, have been asked or empowered by Him to bully these people after our own fashion in majorem Dei Gloria, which as you know means "to the greater glory of God.'

Finally, he wrote to his uncle that one should always remember the Christian exhortation to love one's enemies: "From an earthly, realistic, political standpoint, it should not be forgotten that, considering the immense and extremely dangerous power that international Jewish capital represented, it could be a huge advantage to us Germans if the world of the Hebrews looked up to us in gratitude."

Chapter 9

Friday, July 24

Alphonse Picard left a message upstairs at the Ouda Embassy to the effect that he had spoken to Herr Haby, the imperial barber, and wished to report the result in persona. Would His Excellency and the beautiful lady please honour him by allowing him to visit them as soon as possible?

They suggested six thirty.

"I have spoken to His Majesty's barber, Herr Haby," Picard announced as soon as he arrived. "He said with great regret that it would be unthinkable for a woman to be present during his ministrations. Any woman."

"Did he explain why?" Ali Hassan asked.

"I did not ask him why. Because I know the answer. I should have thought of it before asking him. The waxing and moulding of the imperial mustache is a male ritual. Women have no place in it."

Zade smiled.

"Madame, I am sure you feel quite at home in Germany. In Ouda, too, I am sure only a few women are permitted to enter male territory. The anointing of His Majesty's mustache is not the only priestly activity from which women are excluded. Bismarck's Reich is a man's world, which the Kaiser inherited. It has three natural enemies — Social Democrats, Jews and women. They are excluded from all important decision-making. With a few exceptions."

"Jews?" Zade frowned. "I know a lot of Europeans have trouble with Jews."

"So it seems. However, many do very well in the Kaiser's Germany. So do many women. As long as the women don't involve themselves in matters men think important. Well, we must now think of another way for you to come close to His Majesty." Alphonse Picard seemed to fall into a trance. It did not take very long. He emerged with an exciting new idea.

"What about doing a Dance of the Seven Veils for him? Like Salomé?"

Ali Hassan and Zade looked at each other.

They thought it imprudent to show too much enthusiasm.

"I think," Zade said, after some hesitation, "that may be a very good idea."

"But wouldn't that be very hard to arrange?" Ali Hassan asked.

"Not at all," Alphonse Picard beamed. "You may safely leave that to me!"

No one had noticed that Alois Penner had silently entered the room.

·

THE SECOND ALOIS PENNER MONOLOGUE

Do my ears deceive me? Taking off seven veils for the All Highest? You want to arouse His Imperial Majesty, *madame*? Why in Heaven's name would you want to do that? But that is none of my business. I have never understood women. In any case, if you want to meet him face to face why did you not ask me how to go about it, once he returns to the mainland? I may come up with an idea or two.

But first, I must give you the latest news. At home in Vienna, everybody says the Emperor Franz Joseph assumes that the Serbs have no choice but to accept the ultimatum. He firmly believes all those belligerent people around him will be forced to postpone their plans to crush Serbia. This he thinks is just as well because all he wants is to end his days in peace.

The Tsar, too — so I hear — will do everything he can to put the brakes on his generals. He loathes war. He thinks that as soon as a war starts, the Finns will rebel against him, and so will the Poles, and Heaven knows who else. However, my guess is the poor man will not be able to control events. Franz Joseph may be right. The Serbs may be willing to accept the ultimatum, although it was deliberately phrased to be unacceptable to any self-respecting government. But the Russians will pressure them to reject it, even at the risk of unleashing a European war. In Vienna they did not worry for a second about Herr Dr. Wiesner and his investigation clearing Belgrad of collusion. After all, Sarajevo was only one of many provocations, they said. So they prepared their diplomatic note in the strictest secrecy, taking great care not to frighten their German allies.

From a note from Gottlieb von Jagow, the German Foreign Minister, to the Kaiser, dated July 23, 1914:

"Your Majesty's Ambassador in London is in receipt of instructions, for the benefit of his conferences, to the effect that we do not know what the Austrian demands are, but that we regarded them as part of Austria-Hungary's internal affairs, which it would not become us to influence."

The Kaiser wrote this note in the margin:

"Right! Grey [Sir Edward Grey, the foreign Secretary] must be told this plainly and seriously! So that he will see that I am not fooling ... Serbia is nothing but a band of robbers that must be punished for its crimes! I will meddle in nothing the Emperor is alone competent to judge!

Source: Imanuel Geiss. July 1914, Selected Documents, New York, Scribner 1967, p. 171.

Now, the question arises, was that *carte blanche* Wilhelm gave Franz Joseph on July 5th really such a mistake? I thought at first it was. But now I'm not so sure. He believed the Austrian case against Serbia was just, and so did all the European powers. The moment he decides the Austrians are reckless he can always interpret his undertaking to have meant sympathetic mediation rather than military support. And as to the danger of Russian intervention, he was informed that Russia did not yet have the arms, after their crushing defeats by the Japanese nine years ago, to wage a major war. Again, that is what much of Europe assumed. In any case, his military intelligence reported that an attack by Russia was not to be expected until 1916. And he knew the Tsar's heart would rather be on the side of those who punish regicide than of those who use the occasion to fight a war for the greater glory of the Slavic race. Besides, the Russians had not intervened in the recent Balkan wars. Why should they do so now? And he knew another thing. The Austrians did not really need German military support to crush the Serbs if they moved fast. But if they did nothing and, in effect, allowed the Serbs to break away, and possibly setting an example for others to follow, a dismembered Double Monarchy, followed inevitably by Russian expansion in the Balkans, would decidedly tip the balance of power in the Russians' favour and be a catastrophic setback for Germany. Furthermore, if the Russians did intervene and the French attacked Germany to help their Russian allies, Germany would be in a defensive position. Under those circumstances the English would most probably stay out.

From everything I see in the left-wing press, fear and indignation is reaching fever pitch.

In Der Vorwärts:

Because the blood of Franz Ferdinand and his wife has been spilled by the shots of a crazy fanatic, the blood of thousands of workers and peasants is to be spilled. A mad crime is to be capped by a crime even madder. For this ultimatum, in its tone and in its demands, is so shameless that any Serbian government that should humble itself and bow down before it must

> reckon with the possibility of being kicked out by the people mercilessly.
>
> In the Leipziger Volkszeitung:
>
> In Austria the chauvinistic circles are even more completely bankrupt than elsewhere. Their nationalistic howls are meant to cover their economic ruin, and the loot and murder of war is to fill their pockets.
>
> Source: Emil Ludwig, Juli 14, Hamburg, Rutten & Loening 1961, p. 175.

Enough of that. I am sure you can compose any number of editorials along those lines yourself, even if in Ouda you probably don't have much of a left-wing press. From what I hear from my friends around the corner — in the Wilhelmsstrasse — all eyes are now on London. The Chancellor and many others in his camp are hoping desperately that the Foreign Minister, Sir Edward Grey, will do all he can to keep the conflict localized, just as he did two years ago, successfully But that is not what Admiral Tirpitz is hoping. He thinks Germany is now ready for a showdown.

> From a 1911 report to the Kaiser:
>
> The historical verdict on our naval policy will depend on whether it will achieve its purpose of gaining a good defensive position vis-à-vis England ... Only two choices are open to Your Majesty today, that of an agreement [with Britain] of a voluntary limitation of armaments on the basis of a two to three ratio, or a continuation of the arms race.
>
> Source: V.R. Berghahn, Germany and the Approach of War in 1914, Houndsmills, Basilstroke, Macmillan 1993, p. 118.

By the way, Admiral Tirpitz was so effective in making up figures to persuade the Reichstag to approve his naval estimates that a joke was doing the rounds in Berlin. When taking a *Droschke* home after work, he would give the driver the wrong house-number because he could not bring himself to give the right figure.

Oh, I nearly forgot — did you not say, Madame, that you wanted to meet the Kaiser? And that you would like me to make a suggestion how to bring this about? Well now, let me think. Ah yes. A few years ago the American banker and collector Pierpont Morgan bought the only extant letter by Martin Luther, for 120,000 marks. Somebody suggested to him that it might be a good for American-German relations — and sound business — to give it to the Kaiser as a present. Morgan saw the point. He did what was suggested and in due course His Majesty sent it to the Luther Archives in Wittenberg. But then he had a problem. What to give to Mr. Morgan in return? He decided a bust of himself was by far the best idea. The suggestion was discreetly passed on to Morgan, who was a man of some taste. He gently declined and suggested a decoration instead. His Majesty obliged.

Now, this is what I suggest. What is the name of the King of Ouda? Oh yes, King Shahriyar. We all know that he is a man of fabulous wealth. The City of Berlin is dominated by Social Democrats, who are, of course, always anxious to subvert the Kaiser. The city is chronically short of money. I understand it recently sold to King Shahriyar the statue of the Kaiser's revered grandfather, Kaiser Wilhelm I, in the Tiergarten, for 500,000 marks, to be put up in the royal park in Ouda. The deal was negotiated through agents who obviously did not know what they were doing. You just heard about it, didn't you, *madame?* So you seek an audience with His Majesty. You pretend to be a close friend of King Shahriyar. He had conveyed to you that he had only recently heard about the purchase and now asked you to inform His Majesty that he would much prefer a statue of himself.

Wilhelm will be putty in your hands.

❈ The Almost-Alliance ❈

My gracious king, put yourself into the Kaiser's shoes at the turn of the century, when there was an acute danger of Germany becoming involved in a war between Austria-Hungary and Russia over the Balkans. Who had the means and the international stature to prevent such a war? England, of course — who else? All that was required was that Germany declare itself prepared to protect the British Empire against Russia. The Kaiser saw clearly that active cooperation between the greatest land power in Europe, Germany, and the greatest sea power in the world, England, could jointly determine the outcome of any conflict of this kind without it erupting into a major war. "I am the balance of power in Europe," he declared. The Balkans had been a tinderbox ever since pan-Slavic aspirations, actively promoted by imperialist Russia, threatened an area that the Austro-Hungarians considered their sphere of influence — ever since, one by one, the former Turkish possessions in the Balkans successfully rebelled against the despotic sultans.

If only others had had the Kaiser's insight! England needed Germany. The Boer War was not going well. Russia was threatening British India by advancing in Asia, and the French were threatening British Egypt from the south, from Central Africa. Futuristic novels appeared in London describing a Russian-French invasion of England. Westminster was sounding out Berlin, dropping vague hints suggesting that it might be useful to have some serious talks. The Chancellor was the light-weight, slick, slippery, charmeur Bernhard von Bülow who was, compared to the Iron Chancellor, made of rubber. But the man who, back stage, held all the strings in his hands was a sinister, secretive, mischievous, hugely influential grey eminence in the German Foreign Office, Friedrich von Holstein, who at every critical point deliberately thwarted the intentions of the All Highest. Public opinion was in an anti-British mood. Both men, Bülow and Holstein, were determined to follow public opinion and prevent the Kaiser from going his own way and coming to some kind of an arrangement with London, even though Wilhelm knew that the future king, the Prince of Wales, his Uncle Edward, had a very low opinion of him. In 1900, Queen Victoria, the Kaiser's grandmother, was eighty-one years old.

Edward thought Wilhelm incarnated distasteful Prussia. He called him "Willy the bully" and thought he was weak and cowardly and he took little trouble to guard his tongue when speaking of Wilhelm. Some time before 1900 he went as far as to say that his "illustrious nephew" should learn that he lived at the end of the nineteenth century and not in the Middle Ages. And a few days before his death in 1910 he wrote to an old friend that "I have not long to live. And then my nephew will make war."

Wilhelm already knew at the time he became Kaiser in 1888 what his uncle thought of him. Who could blame him therefore, very soon after ascending the throne, when he was about to undertake his first state visit to Vienna and discovered that his uncle would be staying at the Grand Hotel too, for insisting that his uncle leave the city while he was there? I certainly don't. Who knows what Edward would have done to distract attention? So, he obediently left town but duly returned the moment the Kaiser's state visit was over. I don't know whether it was on that occasion that he was seen emerging from one of Vienna's most expensive brothels, in broad daylight, at noon.

Your Glorious Majesty, I have forgotten the Ouda fairy tale in which the Jinn concludes that "To a Beduin, one grandmother is worth more than a dozen mothers." No doubt Your Majesty remembers the story clearly. Whatever it was about, Queen Victoria was in his estimation worth more than a thousand mothers of the kind he had. And the Queen hardly disguised that of her many grandchildren he was her favourite.

But she occasionally scolded him. She did so in 1896, after the Jameson raid in South Africa, when anti-British feeling was at its height in Germany. On that occasion the Kaiser sent a telegram to Paul Kruger, the President of Transvaal, saying that Germany was prepared to restore peace and to defend the independence of the land from without — that is, from his grandmother's subjects. But even then, when scolding him, she was careful not to hurt his dignity.

Queen Victoria may have been the only person on earth for whom he felt genuine respect. Once she died, he may have told himself, he would only have inferiors in the world — with the exception, I suppose, of the seemingly immortal Emperor Franz Joseph. He always treated Tsar "Nicky" as a little boy. So he didn't count.

At the beginning of 1901, just before the lengthy celebrations to mark the two hundredth anniversary of the Prussian Crown, the Kaiser heard that Queen Victoria was dying. He immediately decided to cut the celebrations short and to proceed to London. He sent a message to Uncle Edward begging him not to receive him as an emperor, that he came as a grandson. During the rough crossing everybody was seasick. Not he. He reported that he "let himself be buffeted by the sea-air for six hours and never felt better."

Edward was in a benign, forgiving mood. He came to Victoria Station to meet Wilhelm wearing a Prussian uniform. When he arrived someone opened the carriage door and said "Thank you, Kaiser, for coming." Edward overheard this and said "That is what everybody is saying. Nobody will ever forget your coming here." Clearly, this was not a moment to bear grudges. When the Kaiser had been in London not so very much earlier to celebrate the Queen's Diamond Jubilee, someone in the crowd shouted to him, "If you want to send a telegram to Kruger, the post office is just around the corner!" The Kruger telegram was now forgotten.

Wilhelm made his way to his grandmother's sickbed in Osborne, on the Isle of Wright. Many of her children and grandchildren were there. He surprised everybody with his firmness and tenderness. She occasionally recognized those about her, but at first she thought he was his father, Friedrich. Her difficulty in breathing was the only sign of pain. On January 22 she began to fade. When he was asked later whether it was true that she died in his arms he said, "Yes — she was so little — and so light." He insisted that the coffin be placed on a Union Jack, which he later took to Berlin as a souvenir. The uncle left for London, to become King of England and Emperor of India. The Kaiser was left in charge at Osborne, the only time, it was observed, that a German sovereign had ever ruled over any part of England. The funeral did not take place until two weeks later. He decided to remain in England. In Berlin, it was feared that the British, at a time when their morale was low, would take advantage of their kind and gullible Kaiser. Every day they received bad news from South Africa where the Boers were waging unconventional guerilla warfare by blowing up trains and ambushing British troops and garrisons. General von Plessen, the head of the Kaiser's suite, referring to the Boer War, observed that the Kaiser gave the British self-assurance. "But," he added, "they will certainly soon recover their historic insolence."

Dona objected to his staying away from her for so long, afraid that he might be seduced by an English beauty. As far as I know, this did not happen.

As was feared by Chancellor von Bülow and the grey eminence in the German Foreign Office, Holstein, the British made good use of those two weeks. The Foreign Secretary, Joseph Chamberlain, discreetly asked the Kaiser what he thought of a British-German alliance. It was all over with splendid isolation for England, he intimated. England had to choose between the Entente (with France and Russia) and the Triple Alliance (with Germany, Austria-Hungary and Italy). The cabinet was divided, he said, but he, Chamberlain, was among those who preferred the Triple Alliance. To sweeten the idea he offered British diplomatic support to Kaiser's well-known designs on West Morocco. This would have the charm of balking French ambitions in that area. The French were so upset by their setbacks in another area, Egypt, that in recent years the late Queen had been advised not to make her annual visit to the Riviera.

There was no concrete offer, but the invitation, however tentative, was clear enough, even if the British balked at the idea of a formal alliance. At a special dinner given for him at Marlborough House before his departure, the Kaiser stated his belief that sooner or later England and Germany would get to know each better and between them keep the peace of the world. "We ought to form an Anglo-German alliance," he said. "Not a mouse could stir in Europe without our permission." He sounded like his grandfather, the Prince Consort.

On the day of his departure the crowds gave him a tumultuous ovation. He was in such a pro-British mood that he even awarded Lord Robert, the man who defeated President Kruger, the highest German decoration — the Order of the Black Eagle.

The British overtures were followed by months of diplomatic exchanges. On one occasion Edward, now king and emperor, wrote him a letter expressing the hope that the two countries might work together to maintain the welfare of the world. The Kaiser agreed. After all, he wrote back, the people in the two countries belonged to the same great Teutonic race 'to which Heaven has entrusted the culture of the world'.

Chapter 10

Sunday, July 26

THE SECOND ALPHONSE PICARD MONOLOGUE

My editor in Paris is delighted with me. And quite rightly so. Who else would have rhapsodized the Kaiser's barber Herr Haby and his beard lotion called *Achievement*? Yesterday I wrote three stories, almost as good as my story about Herr Haby. One, a piece about the collision between the mounted police and the protesters in the Schadowstrasse, and about the few hundred workers marching from the Friedrichstrasse up Unter den Linden singing anti-war songs. My second story reported several conversations I had with my secret informants in the Foreign Ministry leaving no doubt in anybody's mind that German diplomats, not only the generals, had been pushing Vienna hard to make their ultimatum as tough as possible. My third story was an interview with the pacifist Alfred Fried, one of the co-founders of the Peace Society, who often writes in their monthly journal *Völker-Friede*. He is working day and night organizing meetings and briefing speakers. He and his colleagues are in close touch with their friends in Paris. He said he was quite encouraged by the reception they got and said the most dangerous thing to do at the moment was to give up hope. The most foolish people, he said, were the professors. He heaped scorn on those who would welcome a war to demonstrate the superiority of German *Kultur* over French *civilisation*, which was vulgar and shallow and no better than the Zulus' babbling.

So naturally my publishers are delighted with me. Today I am going to indulge in a fantasy. What goes on in the minds of President Poincaré and Premier Viviani on board the *France* on their way home, I will ask, after their convivial banquets with all those grand dukes and grand duchesses in Saint Petersburg, and all those toasts about living through historic days together like brothers? Even if they cancel their state visits to Denmark and Norway, they cannot reach back home before Wednesday. But I have been told by my contacts that secret military preparations are proceeding in their absence, and that French troops have been called back from Morocco.

Poincaré is a lawyer from Lorraine. That says all. He went to school in the years immediately after the French defeat in 1870. Lorraine had just become German. There was only one reason for existence, the children were told, namely to shake off the German yoke, so that Lorraine could be returned to its rightful owner. Nothing else mattered. My friend Clemenceau despises Poincaré because he refused to take a stand in the Dreyfus affair, which Clemenceau most certainly did, with great courage, together with Émile Zola. As to Viviani, he is a socialist, but, above all, he is a French patriot. So what will I say about Poincaré and Viviani? I will say that both men are more skilled at the political game than their clumsy German counterparts and that most probably they cannot wait to reach home to conduct a war they will welcome with great eagerness, provided that Germany attacks them first. Even so, they will have more trouble stirring up enthusiasm among the masses than the Germans because the French are a nation of proud citizens and the Germans are a nation of subjects who will do what they are told.

I am also planning a piece about revenge. Why did Prussia provoke a war with France in 1870? To take revenge for the humiliations she suffered at the hands of Napoleon when he crushed the army of Frederick the Great at Jena. And for all I know, Frederick took revenge for all the burnings and lootings Louis Quatorze's armies committed during their invasions in Germany in the previous century. And so it goes.

Tomorrow I am going to ask my superiors what plans they have for me when I return to Paris rather than being interned here as an enemy alien.

◆

The occasion for Ali and Zade meeting Prince Otto was a dinner given by Richard von Hollmann, one of the directors of the Deutsche Bank, in his mansion opposite the Charlottenburger Schloss. An elegant man wearing a monocle, Hollmann was one of the chief negotiators with the Turks in all matters touching on the Berlin-Baghdad Railway. Ali had had dealings with him on several occasions. Apart from the Prince, the guests were Admiral Moritz von Finckelstein, who was a tall, thin man close to Admiral Tirpitz, the voluble American banker Lloyd Field, who was a close business friend of the host, and the Turkish surgeon Dr. Fuad Idrisi, a pale man wearing a goatee whose wife was Frau von Hollmann's sister. One of Dr. Idrisi's patients was Enver Pasha. Neither Ali nor Zade had any reason to participate in the conversation until dessert was served.

It did not matter that Ali and Zade did not clearly understand the full name of their host. Was it Prince Otto, Prince Erich or Prince Alfred? Was his family name Saxe-Gotha or Saxe-Weimar? But they did understand that he was second cousin three times removed of the Kaiser's grandfather, the Prince Consort Albert. The Prince never corrected them when they called him 'Prince Otto," but he clearly preferred it when they called him "Your Serene Highness," or *Durchlaucht.*

The subject of conversation was, of course, the Serbs' acceptance (with only one qualification) of the deliberately unacceptable Austrian ultimatum, five minutes before the deadline expired. The world would have been immensely relieved had the Austrians not immediately broken off diplomatic relations. The one qualification was contained in Paragraph Six.

> It goes without saying that the Royal Government [of Serbia] consider it their duty to open an enquiry against all such persons as are, or eventually may be, implicated in the plot of 28 June, and who happen to be within the territory of the Kingdom. As regards the participation in this enquiry of Austro-Hungarian agents or authorities appointed for this purpose by the Imperial and Royal Government, the Royal Government cannot accept such an arrangement, as it would be a violation of the Constitution and of the law of criminal procedure; nevertheless in concrete cases communication of the results of the investigation in question might be given to Austro-Hungarian agents.
>
> Source: Geiss, p. 203.

"I am delighted," Dr. Idrisi said while the soup was being served, "that we don't have a monopoly on confusion. I understand the Kaiser thinks the Austrians have just achieved a tremendous moral victory and that the Serbs' acceptance was a triumph of Austrian diplomacy. There was no longer the slightest reason for war, he told everybody. And still, the Austrians immediately broke off diplomatic relations and now have issued an order for partial mobilization. Clearly they were determined to invade Serbia whatever the reply said. What kind of an alliance is that? I'm asking this question because our people in Constantinople are debating at this very moment whether we should become Germany's newest ally. Couldn't the Kaiser have stopped the Austrians? What about the Chancellor?"

"I am glad you asked, Dr. Idrisi," Admiral von Finckelstein said with some heat. "It's Chancellor von Bethmann Hollweg who is responsible for all this. He is the most incompetent, insensitive man in Berlin. A mess like this is what happens when high-minded idealists go into politics. They don't know how the world really works. Everybody knows the Austrians can't do anything in a hurry, and this man built his entire strategy on the Austrians crushing Serbia fast, before the Russians had time to wake up. Anyone could have told him this was sheer madness. Well, four weeks have passed and the Russians are by now so much awake that they — at least some of them — told their Serb friends to put in that Paragraph Six, hoping that the Austrians would use it as an excuse to march in. In Saint Petersburg, of course, there's also total confusion but the war party seems to be taking over. Before that, the Serbs were quite prepared to swallow their pride and accept the Austrian note in its entirety and bide their time until a better moment comes along for them to strike."

"How do you know all this?" Hollmann asked, adjusting his monocle. "It can't be Admiral Tirpitz who told you. He is still climbing mountains in Tarasp."

"I have my sources," the Admiral said with a smile. "In any case, Admiral Tirpitz is coming back tomorrow. The Chancellor didn't want him in Berlin, but he's coming anyway. Now that the Kaiser has ordered the return of the fleet into home waters, he's got to be here, whatever the Chancellor says. He has to make sure the ships move to the Baltic to face the Russians, and not to the North Sea to frighten the British."

"Aren't you being a bit unfair, Admiral?" Prince Otto asked, stroking his double chin. "I was told the Austrians waited so long because they didn't want to hand the Serbs their ultimatum until the French had left Saint Petersburg. Their original plan was to present it on July 16."

"Any excuse for dithering," Admiral von Finckelstein growled. "By now nobody remembers what caused all this in the first place — Sarajevo. Murder. Terrorism."

"That's very true," Prince Otto said. "But isn't Wilhelm absolutely right, for once? Didn't the Serb reply satisfy Austrian honour? Is that Paragraph Six really worth setting the world on fire? Who has ever heard of a Serbian constitution? I am sure most Serbs have never heard of one."

There was general laughter.

"Your Serene Highness is absolutely right," Herr von Hollmann said. "It's on the basis of Austrian honour having now been satisfied that a process of mediation must begin. And we Germans have to participate in it."

"My Ambassador, Mouktar Pascha," Dr. Idrisi said, "told me this morning he is convinced there will be no war."

July 26:	Russia asked Germany to exert moderating influence on Austria-Hungary; Grey proposes a four-power conference in London of ambassadors not directly involved in the conflict: England, France, Germany and Italy
July 27:	Bethmann Hollweg rejects the London conference on the grounds that it could not haul Austria before a European court of justice; Vienna decides to declare war not later than July 29 to block any attempt by outside powers to intervene
July 28:	Grey tries to persuade Austria-Hungary and Russia to enter into direct negotiations

Up to now the voluble Lloyd Field had said nothing. Now the time had arrived for him to speak.

"Pessimists make terrible bankers," he said. "I have often been criticized for erring on the other side, for being overly optimistic. Fortunately I have usually been able to recover from the very sizable number of disastrous loans my chronic optimism led me to authorize over the years. But on this occasion, I confess I am very pessimistic."

"Oh?" Hollmann said, frowning. "Tell us why."

"What has happened in Russia where you say the war party is taking over will happen here. The Kaiser couldn't say no to the Austrian generals who want their war even if the excuse for it has gone. The military here, too, want their war. They think it's inevitable sooner or later and that their chances are better now than later. The Kaiser won't be able to stop them. Even if he could. The system wouldn't let him."

"The system?" Dr. Idrisi asked. "They have the best technology, the best universities, the best medicine."

"Maybe, but I am talking about their society. They have a very crude caste system here. All European countries have, but France and England are democracies. The only people who count in Germany are people on top, and they are the generals — and, forgive me, Admiral, the admirals and their friends in industry. The people are helpless. They have absolutely no voice."

"I don't want war," Admiral von Finckelstein objected heatedly. "All Admiral Tirpitz and I have ever said was — *si vis pacem para bellum.*"

"I beg your pardon?" Lloyd Field asked.

"If you want peace, prepare for war."

"And, out of nothing, in a few years, build a navy at a rate two thirds that of the British."

"If you want to be a great power," Admiral von Finckelstein retorted, "you have to have a great navy. We learned that from you Americans."

"Do you know something, Admiral? I think you did it to show that the British are in decline and that you want to take over from them."

1850:	50% of world's industrial production was British-owned
1870:	32%
1910:	15%
Source: Fromkin, p. 30.	

"My dear friend," the Admiral shook his head, "you have a very lively imagination."

"I have never been accused of that," Lloyd Field replied cheerfully. "But you don't really need it to be able to predict that this is going to go out of control and that Sir Edward Grey will get nowhere with his noble efforts. Unless..."

"Unless?" Richard von Hollmann raised his eyebrows.

"Unless President Wilson takes over the mediation. The British are allied to the French. The French are allied to the Russians. The United States belong to neither alliance. I spoke to my Ambassador about it this morning. James Gerard said the same idea had occurred to him. "But he thought it was too soon to raise it with Washington."

"Stop!" Prince Otto cried. "I have an even better idea! Let Teddy Roosevelt mediate. He's a private citizen. Who better than the winner of the Nobel Peace Prize?"

> In 1906, President Theodore Roosevelt received the Nobel Peace Prize for drawing up the peace treaty between Russia and Japan the year before.

"What a fascinating idea!" Dr. Idrisi said.

"I know the Kaiser likes him enormously," Hollmann said.

"A sentiment very much reciprocated," the Prince observed. "He and my nephew Kaiser Wilhelm had a great time together at Edward VII's funeral. I was there, so I know. With my own ears I heard my nephew call Colonel Roosevelt 'my friend'. And at the reception that the new king, George V, gave for all the assembled sovereigns Wilhelm pointed out to the Colonel which royalty was worth his attention. When Roosevelt was talking to the King of Bulgaria, the Kaiser shooed him away, even though he used to be Prince Saxe-Coburg-Gotha and is related to us, and directed him to the King of Spain and said 'Now *he* is a man worth talking to.' And later when Roosevelt visited us in Berlin, the Kaiser met him at the station, something absolutely unheard of! A commoner who no longer held office! At dinner, Wilhelm asked him how he was regarded in the United States. Roosevelt answered, 'Well, Your Majesty, I don't know whether you will understand the political terminology, but in America we think that if you lived on our side of the water you would carry your ward and turn up at the convention with your delegates behind you — and I cannot say as much for most of your fellow sovereigns.' The Kaiser invited him to attend the field manoeuvres of the German Army. No civilian had ever been so honoured. Did you ever see the photograph of the two men chatting on horseback together?"

None of the guests had seen it.

"Wilhelm had copies made and presented to his guests. On the back he had written, 'When we shake hands we shake the world.'"

It was perfectly permissible and by no means *lèse majesté,* on occasions like these, to laugh a little at His Majesty's lovable posturing. So they did.

"Won't the British, the French and the Russians think the two are a little too friendly? " Ali asked. It was the first time he spoke.

"Oh no," Prince Otto replied. "Teddy Roosevelt has a tremendous reputation all over the world." He looked at Zade. "An idea just occurs to me."

Prince Otto had been eyeing Zade throughout the evening, barely managing to conceal his amourous intentions, but had not found an opening to address her directly.

"I want to see my nephew as soon as possible after he returns," he said, his double chin trembling with anticipation. "I'm told he is coming back to Potsdam tomorrow. There is not a minute to lose. I happen to know he is very fond of dazzling beauties from the *Morgenland. Madame,* would you do me the honour of coming with me?"

✺ How to Attack America ✺

Your Majesty will remember the warm flow of affection between the British public and Wilhelm at the time of Queen Victoria's funeral and the discussions about the possibility of an Anglo-German alliance. Even relations between him and his uncle, now King and Emperor Edward VII, mellowed, as did the feelings between Wilhelm and his mother in her Schloss in Kronberg, north of Frankfurt. Vicky never recovered from a riding accident and then developed cancer. He visited her frequently and together they followed the ups and downs of British fortunes during the war in South Africa. The German press, in contrast to the Kaiser, was violently pro-Boer. He made a determined effort to make his mother feel that they were at last becoming reconciled. In August 1901, Vicky died, seven months after her mother. Edward came to Kronberg for the first part of the funeral. It was a deeply emotional event for him and for Wilhelm. They accompanied the coffin to Potsdam, for the second part. There, she was laid to rest in the mausoleum next to her husband.

A funeral is no occasion to discuss politics. Instead, Edward passed on to his nephew a confidential memorandum his Foreign Secretary had written for him, probably suggesting to him to be careful when talking to the Kaiser. The King was highly embarrassed later when he was respectfully reproached for this indiscretion. The Kaiser passed it on to his ministers, who must have been delighted because they, too, were far from enthusiastic about an Anglo-German alliance and, no doubt had worried that their boss would, as usual, talk too much. In short, neither sovereign found much support for his attempts to strengthen relations. What was strengthened instead, on the German side, was a move in the opposite direction — Germany's resolve to build a navy to challenge Britain's.

Some time earlier, Wilhelm had read a book by the American naval strategist Alfred T. Malan, The Influence of Sea Power on History. He found it so important that he had it translated into German. The book made a deep impression on Alfred Tirpitz, the young commander of a division of cruisers in the Far East, who had caught the Kaiser's attention. Soon he was appointed Secretary of State of the Reichsmarineamt. Malan's book became a bible for the Kaiser and for many others who believed that without a strong navy Germany could never become a world power and conduct Weltpolitik, or world politics. The temptation of an alliance with England would soon fade into the background. A big navy was more attractive.

Your Majesty, you raised an eyebrow just now when I mentioned an American having written a book on naval warfare. It is true that we in Ouda know little about the United States of America. All we know is that Americans have cowboys and buildings they call skyscrapers and a lot of money, and that they threw out the British King. We certainly have never heard of any American writing books! Also, we don't seem to realize that, in the last fifty years, both the United States and Germany have grown much faster than England and France, and that their industries are now far more productive and efficient. In fact, they are more modern.

The Americans are also late-comers to the game of Weltpolitik. Until a few years ago they deliberately avoided it and concentrated on developing their huge country. But, thanks to their rapid growth and enormous wealth and energy, they, like the Germans, have recently developed a strong appetite for flexing their muscles and playing a role overseas. They had read Malan's book. When there were insurrections against Spain in Cuba and in the Philippines, the American government, with the enthusiastic backing of their popular press, backed the rebels and, in the Spanish-American War that ensued, crushed Spain. Many prominent Americans, however, were against the U.S.A. playing what they called the "imperialist" game. One of these was another American who wrote books by the name of Mark Twain, and a rich businessman called Andrew Carnegie. That was in 1898, the same year the Kaiser made his pilgrimage to Jerusalem. It was the first time the Americans had defeated an old European colonial power. The Kaiser and his people sat up. They had read the same book. Could it be that one day, on the high seas, they would clash? The Kaiser's sympathies, of course, had been with Spain — a monarchy! — and not with the insurgents. Nothing was further from his mind. The Americans assume that to be modern you had to be for the rebels and against the monarchies. No doubt Your Majesty thinks that is absurd. So does the Kaiser.

It so happened that in 1901 a man became president of the United States who was in many ways very much like the Kaiser. His name — Theodore Roosevelt. His predecessor, President McKinley, had been assassinated by a terrorist in the Temple of Music in a city called Buffalo. Roosevelt was three months older than Wilhelm and had spent part of his youth in Germany. Both were flamboyant personalities and great conversationalists, and both wanted to be popular. And both talked tough. The only way to curb the anarchic spirit of the proletariat, Roosevelt declared, was to shoot ten or a dozen of their leaders. During a tramway strike in Berlin, when troops were called out, Wilhelm declared he hoped that five hundred strikers would be "snuffed out" before the troops returned to barracks.

Wilhelm immediately recognized a kindred spirit. They began a lengthy correspondence. Soon, he went to great lengths to be friendly to Americans who visited Germany. If they came to Potsdam, he showed them around the Neue Palais. He found them amusing and was pleased when they appreciated him. He even allowed a Mister Armour from Chicago to clap him on the shoulder and he hardly flinched when a Mister Vanderbilt called him a "good fellow." But he found the American habit of wanting to buy everything they saw a little irritating.

In view of all this, I was very upset when I heard that Wilhelm was being accused of, on the one hand, smiling at the Americans and, on the other, planning to attack them. This criticism is grossly unfair. All that was happening was that a few young naval officers, as part of their normal strategic exercises, devised theoretical plans on how to inflict a quick military defeat on the U.S.A. in order to force them give Germany a free hand in the Atlantic and the Pacific. Exercises of this kind are normal in military establishments anywhere and do not imply any intention to put them into practice. All they mean is that it is wise to be prepared for any contingency. I have no doubt that in this and similar cases the Kaiser promoted the work. Why not?

These exercised began long before Theodore Roosevelt became president. In the winter from 1897 to 1898, the young lieutenant Eberhard von Mantey wrote a paper on the premise that neither a naval war with the U.S.A. nor a naval blockade could succeed, only direct attacks on big cities on the East Coast. As ports of entry he listed in particular Norfolk, Hampton Roads and Newport News, all in the state of Virginia, and advised against a direct attack on New York, which he considered too well fortified. By the way, he had a low opinion of the discipline of the American military.

This study might have been forgotten had it not coincided with the Spanish-American War. The Kaiser was grumbling that once again, with the disintegration of the Spanish position in the Pacific, Germany had missed an opportunity to pick up some of the pieces. It seems that at that time many people in Berlin were certain that sooner or later clashing interests, both in the Pacific and the Atlantic Oceans, were bound to lead to naval conflicts between Germany and the United States. Some said the world might not be big enough for both of them.

In March 1899, the Kaiser himself assumed the supreme command of the navy. Mantey was asked to undertake a second study. This time he reversed himself on several counts. He contemplated a defeat of the American navy, followed by the conquest of two forts in the bay of Manhattan. The crossing would take twenty-five days. Seventy-five thousand tons of coal were required, which between forty and sixty freighters could easily handle. As the guns of German cruisers bombard New York and two or three infantry battalions pour on U.S. soil, three million inhabitants would panic. The American President would soon sue for peace.

Other studies followed. One question examined was how to take Boston. A strategic thinker proposed a double attack from Cape Cod and from Rockport, two towns on either side of Boston. At the end of August 1901, Kapitänleutnant Hubert von Rebeur-Paschwitz, a naval officer attached to the German embassy in Washington, went to Cape Cod to survey the terrain. He found it unsuitable and thought the troops should land in a place called Manomet Hill on the west side of the bay of Cape Cod. From there artillery fire could effectively protect the invading troops. Provincetown, a town in the state of Rhode Island, was also mentioned as a possible point of entry. He thought a direct attack on the rich Atlantic cities in the North would undoubtedly force the Americans to yield, but a bombardment of Washington would not make much of an impression on the American public. The Kaiser himself thought his navy should first establish itself in Cuba and proceed from there.

Your Majesty will remember my saying that the Germans were not the only ones who drew up plans of this kind. The Americans no doubt did precisely the same.

But I think President Theodore Roosevelt definitely went way too far when he declared with his usual bravado that, after Spain, the next enemy America would have to fight was Germany.

Chapter 11

Monday, July 27

The genesis of the Bronevski Strategy was as follows.

By a pure fluke, a copy of the report by Count Friedrich von Pourtalès, the German Ambassador in Saint Petersburg, to Gottlieb von Jagow, Germany's Foreign Minister, was among two dozen diplomatic dispatches received in the Ouda Embassy on the morning of July 27. This misadventure demonstrated beyond a shadow of a doubt that, probably because of the summer heat, there was something gravely wrong with the way diplomatic communications were being transmitted in Berlin.

The report concerned a conversation Austrian Ambassador Count Friedrich Szàpàry von Szàpàr had with Sergei Dimitrievich Sazonov, Russia's Foreign Minister, in the afternoon of the previous day. The Austrian reassured the Russian that Austria-Hungary was not contemplating any plans of conquest and was simply anxious to have the peace kept along its borders. This assurance visibly eased the Foreign Minister's mind. As to Clause Six of the Austrian ultimatum, which Serbia had rejected, perhaps a method could be found to satisfy Austrian needs, "without literal compliance."

"Too bad this communication is not very interesting," Ali said to Zade after breakfast with a sigh.

"Except that it arrived on your desk."

"True. But next time I hope we find out what the Kaiser is saying to his cousin the Tsar," Ali ventured.

This gave Zade an idea.

"How well do you know the Russian Ambassador?'"

"There is none. There's only a chargé d'affaires. His name is

Arkadi Nikolaivich Bronevski. I know him well. A nice man. A man of the world."

"Do you know him well enough to take him into your confidence?"

"I think so."

"What about going to see him," Zade said, "to tell him about this, hm, misadventure. Take me along, introduce me. Tell him I am a special diplomatic envoy from Ouda. Find a way to suggest that I have a special mission. After all, he is trained to read between the lines. And suggest that, to help me carry it out, he send me directly to the Kaiser to tell him that personal communications between him and the Tsar were no longer secure."

"Splendid idea."

The Russian Embassy was on the Behrensstrasse at the corner of the Mauerstrasse, less than ten minutes walk from the Ouda embassy.

Bronevski reacted like all other normal males to Zade's spectacular charms. Ali had to be direct. He told him that she had come to Berlin all the way from Ouda to persuade the Kaiser to override his generals and declare himself on the side of peace. The question was how to construct a situation where she could be alone with him, if only for a few minutes. The Kaiser had not seen a beautiful woman for several weeks and could not help but be susceptible to the promise of ecstasy considerably more impressive than whatever was offered by Her Majesty.

"This is a form of diplomacy," he said earnestly, "of which I approve wholeheartedly. It is likely to be far more effective than all our strenuous efforts, which cost us so much hard work, and, at times like these, so many sleepless nights. Now tell me — please forgive me — where exactly is Ouda?"

Ali told him.

"Ah, yes, of course. Strange, I just had a visitor from Turkey who told me they were likely to side with the Germans. That really frightens me. We agreed what a tragedy it was that our secret arrangement with Austria of October 1908 could not be carried out."

> In October 1908, Russia was close to achieving her old objectives of obtaining access to the Dardanelles. Austria agreed to this, in return for permission to annex the formerly Ottoman provinces Bosnia and Herzegovina, which the Treaty of Berlin on 1878 had permitted her to occupy and administer. According to this treaty, such an arrangement required the consent of England and France.
>
> This was not given. During these negotiations Austria annexed Bosnia and Herzegovina anyway. This caused a grave crisis, leading to acute tension between Austria and Serbia, with the danger of Russian intervention, anticipating the events of July 1914.
>
> Source: Sebastian Haffner, Von Bismarck zu Hitler, Knaur, p. 101.

"Yes," Ali said. "The conspirators in Sarajevo seemed to have been Bosnians. But I suppose it was naive to think the British would ever agree to your gaining access to the Straits."

"A dream gone bad, like so many others," Bronevski said. "Now it seems to be not beyond human imagination that we will find ourselves on the same side as England, our old rival in Europe, in the Near East and the Far East. And that Turkey, in alliance with Germany, will attack us from the south. That, I must confess, is a very unpleasant prospect."

After a pause he turned to Zade.

"The more I think of it, the better I like your project, madame. Now, let me think how I can jump across the hundreds of barriers between me and the Kaiser. As you know, normally I would have to act through the Foreign Ministry."

"But times are not normal," Ali Hassan observed.

"Exactly. There is only way. I must act in the name of the Tsar."

❈ Two Cousins at Sea ❈

My noble king, when I sing the praises of Kaiser Wilhelm, by far the most admirable of living monarchs, in the hope that you will be inspired to emulate him I do so because I know that his ambitions for the future are, like yours, grounded in his profound respect for his predecessors. His model is Frederick the Great, who was born two hundred and two years ago and whose motto was suum quique, to each his own. What could be more fair and just, even if he was an infidel? He believed in austerity and self-discipline, the qualities that made Prussia great. How similar this is to Ouda's Bedouin ethos! Do we not also look back to heroic ancestors who were giants of courage, statesmanship, intellect and all the other qualities we think important? The difference between us and them is that in our Arab world the heroic age was timeless. In our desert, nothing has changed for thousands of years, whereas Frederick the Great would not recognize Wilhelm's Germany, suddenly a world power brimming over with exuberant energy. No, he would certainly not recognize it if he descended from Heaven today to take the salute at Wilhelm's side in front of the Neue Palais in Potsdam.

The story I want to tell you tonight shows Germany at the height of Wilhelm's power. The date was June 1905, the Chancellor the ever-optimistic Count Bernhard von Bülow, von Bethmann Hollweg's predecessor. During the recent crisis over Morocco, von Bülow had engineered a spectacular success for Kaiser Wilhelm, the greatest diplomatic success for Germany since the days of Bismarck. He had demonstrated to the French that England was useless as an ally. Uncle Edward VII was furious. On the day President Delcassé of France resigned, as a result of Bülow's clever manoevring, the grateful Kaiser made him Prince von Bülow. (Remember, Your Majesty, his grandfather Kaiser Wilhelm I had made Bismarck prince.) He was playing Weltpolitik — power politics on the world stage.

I must change the subject for a moment to tell you what life is like on the Kaiser's annual summer cruise to the Baltic. These Nordlandreisen are designed for him to recover from the strains of politics and court etiquette. So life is relaxed. But representatives from various sections of the government are invited not only because he considers them to be good company but also to coordinate the political work that must be done on board. All the guests are male, though at first Dona occasionally went along. But she was bored and felt out of place. She did not relish the frequent juvenile behaviour of her husband and his guests and their practical jokes. She told him she preferred to stay at home.

The day always starts with exercises on deck, conducted by His Majesty himself. The poor generals have to do knee-jerks and subject themselves to various agonizing tortures while His Majesty's eggs them on with digs in the ribs. On more than one occasion he cut a general's suspenders with a pen knife. Sometimes at midnight he chases old excellencies through the corridors to bed. His companions have to pretend, of course, that they are delighted by these imperial favours while they clench their fists in frustrated anger and embarrassment, and then later grumble about it among themselves. Some of them make entries in their diaries, which no doubt will one day be published. On Sunday mornings he delivers the sermon, which is sometimes printed. His shipmates amuse him with story telling, musical and outlandish theatrical performances, cards and other games. The guest list is virtually unchanged year after year, and many of the shipmates go along knowing they will suffer because it is impossible to make the insatiable Kaiser happy. Often he returns home more nervous and tired than he was when he left.

They sometimes anchor in Bergen, in Norway, and visit the German church there, surrounded by the graves of old Hanseatic traders. The composer Edward Grieg lived there until his death in 1907. On one occasion the Kaiser invited him to tea, or maybe to a glass of Aquavit, on the imperial yacht. They got together an orchestra and arranged a concert on board. They asked the famous man to conduct his Peer Gynt Suite. One of the generals attending sang Solveig's Lied, taking his tempo from Grieg. But it was too slow for the Kaiser's taste. Schneller, schneller!, he commanded. Quicker, quicker! So poor old Grieg had to speed it up.

In 1905, the cruise took them to the island of Björkö on the Swedish coast north of Stockholm, opposite the Russian province of Finland. As the yacht moored, the Kaiser seemed to some of his guests to be secretive and inscrutable, until he revealed his hand. He suddenly told them to change into parade uniform. "In two hours you will stand before the Tsar!" he announced. It appeared the Kaiser had contacted Nicky while he was nearby cruising in his Polar Star to invite him to dinner. The Tsar agreed. This made it possible for them to be able to converse freely, casually, cousin to cousin, monarch to monarch, without any ministers interfering.

The word "cousin" is not to be taken too literally, Your Majesty. There was a double relationship. The Tsar's mother was the Danish-born Queen Alexandra's sister, Dagmar, also known as Maria Fyodorovna Romanova, and the sister of Queen Alexandra (his uncle Edward VII's wife) — and the Tsarina Alexandra Fedorovna, née Princess of Hessen-Darmstadt, was a granddaughter of Queen Victoria, and the sister of Ella, Wilhelm's first love. They were second cousins.

Bülow had succeeded in making trouble between England and France. This was the Kaiser's chance, without any meddling by subordinates, to make trouble between England and Russia. Some people had said — so he had heard — that monarchs should never be allowed to discuss anything privately with each other except the weather. This would teach them a lesson!

It so happened that, in contrast to Wilhelm, who was jubilant after his Moroccan triumph, the Tsar most definitely needed cheering up. Remember, the date was 1905. Disturbing revolutionary turbulence was beginning to threaten his absolute authority. This was to lead to serious trouble in October and ultimately to substantial concessions to prevent a revolution. And the Japanese annihilation of his

Baltic fleet at Tsushima in May had left him with no alternative but to accept Wilhelm's advice and ask the Americans to mediate, a move that was to yield the 1906 Nobel Peace Prize to President Theodore Roosevelt.

On July 23, 1905, the Hohenzollern sailed into Björko and dropped anchor near the Polar Star. The Kaiser gave a dinner for the Tsar and his suite. Everybody was amazed how quickly the Tsar, normally a quiet and shy man, forgot his troubles. He seemed happy. Everyone spoke German. Both monarchs abused Edward VII. The Tsar called him a mischief-maker. The Kaiser wholeheartedly agreed.

Later that night Wilhelm telegraphed Berlin for the text of a treaty drafted by Bülow, which had been on the shelf for two months. (The treaty was a variation of Bismarck's secret Reinsurance Treaty Wilhelm had abrogated after he had dismissed Bismarck.) It had also been sent to Saint Petersburg. It was wired immediately. The next morning, the Kaiser, in a state of high excitement, rose early and copied it in his own hand. Later, he went on board the Polar Star and walked along the deck with Nicky. He mentioned the treaty. The Tsar said he remembered it well but unfortunately had forgotten the precise wording. Wilhelm happened to have it in his pocket. The treaty committed each country to help the other — the Kaiser had added the words "in Europe" because he did not wish to be fighting the British for Russia in the Far East — if either was attacked by a third European power. It was to come into force the moment a peace treaty was signed with Japan. The contents were only to be communicated to France on signature. It revived the German-Russian friendship that had existed at critical times in the days of Wilhelm's ancestors and had been the pillar of Bismarck's policies.

They went into the Tsar's salon. He read it and re-read it. "Would you like to sign it?" the Kaiser asked, his heart pounding. The Tsar sat down at his father's — Tsar Alexander III's — writing table. In front of him was the picture of his mother and other family photographs. The Kaiser opened the inkpot for him. The Tsar signed it with a firm hand — Nicholas. The Kaiser followed. They embraced.

What an achievement! As I have indicated, the Kaiser intended France to be invited later to join the new German-Russian alliance. A turning-point in the history of Europe. Perhaps this arrangement could become the core of a common European market. In due course, Japan might be induced to join, too. Proof that the world could be run dynastically, by monarch talking to monarch, without having to rely on inferiors.

But when the Chancellor von Bülow heard about it he was furious. He pounced on the words "in Europe" that the Kaiser had added on his own. The chief place where Germany would require Russian help was Asia, he objected vehemently. If Britain attacked Germany, Germany had to make sure that Russia counter-attacked in Afghanistan and India. Where else could the Russians help? Certainly not in Europe! The Kaiser argued that this argument made absolutely no sense. Russian help to Germany in Asia would be useless, he said. It would necessitate long preparations and enormous expense and

England would have plenty of time to take precautionary counter-measures.

Of course, he was absolutely right. But Bülow would not hear of it. This was a golden opportunity to exercise the sort of power Bismarck had wielded over his monarch. He simply said he could not take responsibility for the treaty and offered his resignation.

Poor Wilhelm! He was in shock. He felt betrayed. Bülow knew the Kaiser could not allow his Chancellor leave his government. After all, he was the man to whom he owed his recent triumph, the man he just made prince.

On the Russian side, too, there were difficulties. As it stood, the Tsar wrote to the Kaiser a little later — no doubt after his inferiors raised their objections — that the treaty seemed to conflict with Russia's obligations to France. Wilhelm responded that he hoped the French would join the treaty, and in any case it would only apply if France was to attack Germany, which it would never do except in conjunction with England. The fact, of course, was that the Russians were already negotiating with London, which was to lead to the Anglo-Russian Entente two years later.

Who can blame Wilhelm for feeling betrayed by his Chancellor and encircled by the mischief-maker weaving his suffocating net around him?

Chapter 12

Monday, July 27 (continued)

Five written messages awaited Ali and Zade when they returned from the Russian Embassy. The first — to Zade — was from Frau von Tiedemann in Hohenfinow, close to Chancellor von Bethmann Hollweg's estate, who wanted to know whether Zade was now ready to accept the temporary job as governess for her children. The answer Zade sent back was that unfortunately she had not yet been able to make a decision, but would do so as soon as possible. The second message — to Ali — was from Manfred von Kosenburg, his one reliable contact in the Hausmarschall's office at the Neue Palais in Potsdam, informing him that His Majesty was expected back in Potsdam any moment and asking him whether Zade was available to come to the palace at short notice any time on Wednesday or Thursday to submit to him the suggestion that neutral Ouda might be useful to Germany in case of war, as a source of intelligence and a possible base of operations in the Near East. To this the answer was yes, of course. The third message — again for Zade — was from Alphonse Picard to the effect that he had a better idea than trying to arrange a belly dance. He had taken the liberty of making arrangements for her to lay a wreath at the foot of the statue of the great hero of the War of Liberation, General Ludwig von Dansmarck, in the Lustgarten in Potsdam, just south of the Town Palace, in the name of the General's Egyptian descendants. Zade may not know that the General had married an Egyptian lady of high birth whom he had met while taking the cure in Baden-Baden. His Majesty was scheduled to attend the ceremony marking the centenary of General von Dansmarck's death at four forty-five o'clock in the afternoon on Thursday. The fourth message was for Ali from his two Turkish acquaintances, the gaunt Ismail Hazim and the stubby Fual Kamil, both advisers to Mouklat Pascha, the Turkish Ambassador. In view of the rapidly changing circumstances, they urgently requested another conversation, as soon as possible. Ali replied that he was of course prepared to see them but he was very busy at the moment and would let them know a suitable time by the middle of the week.

Ali knew, when he sent that reply, that the Turks were entirely justified to be concerned. It was generally feared that it was only a matter of days before war between Austria-Hungary and Serbia would be declared.

The fifth message was from an "anonymous well-wisher" advising Zade that Prince Otto was a confidence man from Riga who had just been arrested for impersonating a number of members of the highest aristocracy, and that therefore no invitation to mediate the Austro-Serbian crisis would be issued to Colonel Theodore Roosevelt.

At three o'clock, just as Manfred von Kosenburg had announced, Kaiser Wilhelm returned to Potsdam.

At exactly that moment Jonathan Lind appeared in the Ouda Embassy's main office.

THE SECOND JONATHAN LIND MONOLOGUE

I was ticked off by a considerable number of Old Etonians for being absent from Lord's during the last Eton-Harrow cricket match. I had a more important engagement the nature of which is nobody's business. Similarly, I am not mingling among the happy crowds in front of the Neue Palais in Potsdam cheering the All Highest as he returns to keep the forthcoming war local. Close observers have known for a long time that the last thing he wants is a war that spreads across the entire world.

My more important engagement at this moment is to give you

the unique privilege of hearing the profound thoughts with which I shall amuse my readers during the next few days. The most important of these is that the Kaiser's attempt to keep the war local will fail because on all sides it is assumed — even occasionally by the Kaiser himself — that war among the Great Powers is inevitable, and that the only question is when it will come and who can be blamed for it. The cause will be irrelevant. Even now that sad, pathetic, truly peace-loving Chancellor von Bethmann Hollweg is still desperately trying to keep it local — and, if that doesn't work and he can't prevent a larger conflict, to keep England out of it. And if, God forbid, that fails, then to try and achieve for Germany the best possible situation for launching it. Poor man!

And who can blame the Austrians for crying out to all the world during that last two weeks, "Will somebody please tell us — who is in charge in Berlin?" They keep receiving conflicting directives from the German generals and from von Bethmann Hollweg. From today on they can relax. It will be Wilhelm II.

Who can blame him for the age-old belief that war is the legitimate way to solve human conflicts, and that it is perfectly alright to kill hundreds of thousands of human beings for no purpose other than to preserve one's honour — a conveniently undefinable concept? Even the civilized Greeks loved war, not only the Spartans, as I was embarrassed to have to teach the boys at Eton. But not everybody loves war. Why doesn't somebody write a book about the hundreds of seemingly insoluble conflicts between nations that, during the last five thousands years or so, were resolved by rational men using reason, or that somehow evaporated without war, and without even the threat of war, merely because attention shifted elsewhere? Whoever does that will surely deserve the Nobel Peace Prize.

And let no one believe that it is internal tensions in Germany that are persuading the top people to seek their own salvation by provoking a little diversion. By no means. Compared to the other Great Powers, the social situation in Germany is stable. Internal tensions in Russia are far more explosive. France had the Dreyfus affair, which divided the nation in a way nothing ever divided Germany, and England is close to civil war about the Irish question, not to mention acute class tensions and many symptoms of galloping decline. No, I repeat, compared to them Germany is a happy country, delighted with its Kaiser and its spectacular achievements. Never mind the millions of workers and farmers who live under barely human conditions but obediently put up with them. They have no political voice.

Now I come to the really big point. The German General Staff has a strategic plan, the Schlieffen Plan. If I know about it, is it not overwhelming likely that the British Cabinet knows about it as well? What are spies for? Is it not also possible that even the German Chancellor von Bethmann Hollweg knows about it?

It is not merely possible. It is certain. But I have never heard of the Chancellor or any of the people near him objecting to it, privately. Of course, one of the characteristics of the Kaiser's regime is that military leaders only rarely talk to political leaders, and that the military take great pride in keeping their plans immune from impure political considerations. My question is this. If the German Army puts it into effect, which now seems highly likely, how is it conceivable that he thinks England can stay neutral?

> The Schlieffen Plan provides that, in the event of conflict with Russia, Germany would attack Russia's ally France immediately. Once France was defeated, which would not take very long, the German army would move east and take on the Russians. In the campaign against France, there would be an extensive outflanking movement by the Army's right wing through Luxembourg and Belgium, to evade the fortifications in the south. The violation of Belgian neutrality, guaranteed by the treaty of 1839, was an essential part of German strategy.

Even if the Belgian government agreed to the German army marching through its territory, which is highly unlikely, English intervention would be a virtual certainty. So for the Germans the only way to keep England out of the war, if one is coming, is to avoid — above all — a conflict with Russia.

In order to prevent a world war, therefore, the Kaiser must immediately put a brake on the German militants who cannot wait for war with Russia to start. Among these the Kaiser's oldest son, Crown Prince Wilhelm, is the most prominent. He is a mouthpiece for the General Staff, which firmly believes that the time for preventive war has at last come. There is no point, they say, in waiting for the Russians to finish the construction of their railways in western Russia to facilitate mobilization. We must act now.

How can the Crown Prince's father preserve the peace?

Very simple. By overruling the General Staff.

◆

"Oh, *madame*, by the way," Jonathan Lind said, "I understand you want to meet the Kaiser."

"Yes, I most certainly do."

"I think I can easily arrange that. I happen to know that my Ambassador will give a little dinner party for him tomorrow, or the day after. To talk things over. What about coming along? He likes beautiful women. And so do I."

"Nothing would give me greater pleasure," Zade replied.

The telephone rang the moment Jonathan Lind left.

Friedrich von Jensen, one of the equerries of Crown Prince Wilhelm, was on the line, speaking from the Crown Prince's residence, the Cäcilienhof. Was he the Ambassador? Yes, he was. His Imperial Highness wished to speak to him.

Ali felt he was expected to click his heels, a custom among German infidels he particularly disliked. He had never met the Crown Prince. He knew that his amorous adventures were a scandal to his mother and his political extremism repugnant to his father. In 1913, young Willy had dedicated his book *Deutschland in Waffen* to every able-bodied German who was "ready, sword in hand, gladly to risk his strength and his life for the honour and position of his country." The Crown Prince frequently called for Germany to expand its borders. He urged protection against cosmopolitan tendencies and against "aliens" on German soil, which was generally understood to mean Jews, and he admitted being in favour of "so-called chauvinism." The Crown Prince took exception to a recent speech made by the German Ambassador in London, Prince Karl Max von Lichnowsky, praising the role of commerce in promoting understanding between peoples, on the grounds that a forceful foreign policy, supported by the army and navy, was the best commercial policy. There were rumours, which may well have come to his father's ears, that he favoured a *coup d'état* in order to restore the effectiveness of the monarchy. Ali remembered that a few days earlier Manfred von Kosenburg had told him about the Kaiser's telegram from the *Hohenzollern* to his son ordering him to stop making inflammatory speeches. Starting with Frederick the Great's father, there had been an honoured tradition of father-son strife in the House of Hohenzollern.

"I have a note from His Majesty," the Crown Prince said in his clipped, parade-ground voice. "For some strange reason, he assumes I know you. I think he mixed me up with somebody else. It is not the first time I have to act as his messenger-boy."

"I am fortunate indeed, Your Highness," Ali said, demonstrating that the manners acquired at court in Ouda were considerably more refined than those of Potsdam, "that I am the beneficiary of this misunderstanding."

"That may well be so. His Majesty says your name was on the parcel of stories about him which was sent to Bergen, to be picked up by his couriers. I am told they may soon be published."

"Yes, Your Highness, that is our hope. I took the liberty of sending them to His Majesty, hoping that they would give him pleasure."

"It so happens they did." The Crown Prince's tone made it clear that his father's pleasure was of little interest to him. "He says he would like to help things along. He would like to meet the author, apparently a lady writer, as soon as possible. If she is still in Berlin. At a time like this, he says, it is of national importance that a favourable portrait of him reaches as wide an audience as possible, here and abroad."

"I will see to it," Ali replied, a grateful bow in his voice, "that this message is promptly conveyed to the lady writer. Yes, she is still in Berlin."

"All that is required is that you contact the Hausmarschall to make the necessary arrangements."

The Crown Prince hung up before Ali had a chance to express his appreciation to His Royal and Imperial Highness.

❊ The Nephew ❊

My revered king, you have heard me speak many times of Bismarck. But there were two men, not one, who are today revered as the Founding Fathers of United Germany, Bismarck and Field Marshall Helmuth von Moltke. The laconic Moltke was chief of staff during the three Prussian wars against Denmark in 1864, against Austria in 1866 and against France in 1870–1871. These wars were considered necessary for the unification of the country. (Please do not ask me whether I think they were actually necessary!) The only thing I need to say about Moltke is that he was known as Der Grosse Schweiger, which means the Great Mute. Since he knew German, Danish, English, French, Italian, Russian and Turkish, he was mute in seven languages.

But he is not my subject. His namesake and nephew is. Let me describe to you what happened in January 1905 when the Kaiser approached him to offer him the job of Chief of the General Staff, to succeed Count Alfred von Schlieffen. At seventy-two, the Count was considered too old for the job. Moltke was only fifty-six.

The nephew did not wish to accept the job, though he may very well have suspected a year earlier that the Kaiser had appointed him to the General Staff so that he could prepare himself to succeed Schlieffen. He did not think he had the temperament for it. "I lack the capacity for staking all on a single throw," he protested. This was the capacity, he said, that had made Frederick the Great,

Napoleon — and his uncle — born commanders. "Germany should not expect to win in the same lottery twice."

So the Kaiser invited Helmuth von Moltke to dinner at the Schloss, with the promise of a private interview first. Moltke had been His Majesty's personal adjutant and knew him well and was unreservedly loyal to him. While the Kaiser kept him waiting, he decided to tell him that he would accept the position only if His Majesty undertook to abstain from manipulating the annual war games in such a way that he would invariably win. No one had ever before had the courage to make such a request of the All Highest.

When at last the interview began, the Kaiser said he had consulted Count von Schlieffen, who was of the opinion that there was no better man for the job. Moreover, Moltke Senior, the uncle, had once said that the chief of staff did not have to be a genius but should have a character that would stand up to all challenges.

"I can tell you that I have full confidence in you," the Kaiser said. "Everyone admires and trusts you. As I do."

He went on to confess that in his early days as Kaiser he, too, sometimes thought he was not up to his responsibilities. But to his surprise he was. He never thought he would have the strength to dismiss Bismarck. But he did.

"When you confront the task," he said, "you will find in yourself the strength to do it."

Moltke made his request.

The Kaiser took it surprisingly well. He said he had no idea that at the war games each side did not fight on a level playing field with the same weapons. He gave his word he would in future comply with Moltke's request

The Kaiser then imposed his own condition. Moltke must give up spiritualism. It was known that his wife was a follower of Rudolf Steiner, the founder of anthroposophy, and that he, Moltke himself, was interested in it. In fact, in 1904 Moltke had met Steiner for the first time and they became friends.

Anthroposophy approached man's spiritual life scientifically. This included the possibility of communion with the dead. Please, Your Majesty, do not ask me to explain this. It is too far removed from our Muslim religion for Your Majesty and me to comprehend. I should add that in Germany anthroposophy is by no means considered particularly out-of-the-way or less than respectable among educated Christians, especially since much of it is based on an interpretation of the writings of the poet and nature-philosopher Goethe, whom Germans revere enormously. The Kaiser himself is interested in it. But at the time he approached Moltke he did not think that his top soldier should have séances with the dead. This might easily create misunderstandings, such as that he would take direction from the dead. Moltke fully understood this and agreed.

Among the military and civilian leaders who, for a variety of reasons, objected vehemently to the appointment but were overrruled was the chief of the Kaiser's military cabinet, Dietrich von Hülsen-

Haeseler, who, by reason of his position, was supposed to play a role in making military appointments. He wrote a memorandum to His Majesty, alleging that Moltke was a "religious phantast who believes in guardian angels, faith-healing and such nonsense," and threatened to resign. But in the end he did not.

In my view, it reflects favourably on Wilhelm that he appointed a thoroughly decent man, a man described as herzensgut, touchingly kind-hearted, for this crucial job anyway, even if he had to concede that those who objected could make a reasonably good case. Of course the resonant name of Moltke may also have had a lot to do with it.

Moltke was earnest and reflective, a quiet dreamer inclined to melancholy. He was entirely without any military bombast and was not comfortable on horseback, a serious flaw for the Chief of the General Staff. Nor did he really have the right training for the position. Under ordinary circumstances he might have risen to the rank of commanding officer of a brigade. He was not in good health. He had problems with his heart and liver and regularly went to Karlsbad for the cure. His God, he said, was not the God of Vengeance but the God of Penitent Sinners. He thought that in war man's noblest virtues came into play, and that without war the world would be swamped in materialism. He loved German and French poetry and never went to manoeuvres without a copy of Goethe's Faust in his pocket. He played the cello. He painted. He remained loyal to the Kaiser even when he was frustrated by the talkative Kaiser's indiscretions. In

1909, he said he was more afraid of the Kaiser than of the French and the Russians.

Among the books that had impressed Helmuth von Moltke deeply, even more deeply than Rudolf Steiner's The Philosophy of Freedom or any of his other mystical books, was The Foundations of the Twentieth Century by the Houston Stewart Chamberlain, who, as you know, had borrowed the term "Aryan" from the study of languages to describe the superiority of the Nordic "race."

There was one element in Chamberlain's message that was directly related to Moltke's function as Chief of the General Staff. History, Chamberlain had written, was a carousel in which various races rose and fell in relationship to one another. But the fittest survived. This idea was an adaptation of Darwin's biological discoveries. It was his job, Moltke thought, to prepare for the next war, which was to be a war between "Germandom" and "Slavdom." I suppose, Germandom had to demonstrate that it was fitter than Slavdom. According to Chamberlain, both Germans and Englishmen belonged to the same Aryan race, and a German-English alliance was, therefore, entirely natural and, in a way, pre-ordained.

My illustrious king, I must pause to tell you that I am as baffled as I am sure you must be by this idea of race that Chamberlain and others were always talking about at such length. He saw no contradiction between his views of the Jewish race as such and his friendship with many individual Jews whom he called wonderful people. What is this thing called race that these people seem to have taken over from the animal kingdom and from the world of plants? Is there such a thing as an Arabic race? The lands we Arabs inhabit don't even have a name. What matters to us is our Muslim religion, that is all. True, we have a language in common, and, I suppose, some sort of history — after all, everything has — but we don't have any sense of belonging together, So all this is incomprehensible to me.

Back to Moltke. Once he was appointed, he became more and more convinced that Time was not on Germany's side.

As Chief of Staff of the German Army and trusted friend of the Kaiser, this soft, decent, gloomy, fatalistic soldier with the magic name was by no means eager for war. He thought it would be a long war and after it was over the world would not be the same. However, like most members of his circle he thought it was inevitable. He thought it was by no means a foregone conclusion that Germany would win. However, he was in favour of taking a gamble and launching a war at a time when the chances seemed best, to prevent the enemy from striking first.

Chapter 13

Tuesday, July 28

What a coincidence! The official in the Hausmarschall's office whom Ali contacted by telephone on Tuesday morning, July 28, to follow up on his exhilarating conversation with the Crown Prince was none other than Manfred von Kosenburg! Manfred had not heard of Zade's stories. This would make all the difference, he said. To be quite honest, he'd had some doubts about the urgency of discussing Ouda with His Majesty at a critical time like this. Maybe next week, by which time matters might very well be resolved one way or another. But he had not the slightest doubt that His Majesty would see the author of these stories at the earliest conceivable opportunity.

"What is His Majesty's state of mind?" Ali asked.

"He is at his very best, Your Excellency. My brother saw him last night and was very reassured by his condition." The neurologist Hermann von Kosenburg was one of the Kaiser's doctors. "'Completely clear-headed,' he told me. Well, he'd better be! You see, as you know, both the Chancellor and the military tried to keep the Kaiser away as long as possible, to prevent him from interfering. And now he is back, in excellent condition, as I say, and the first thing he does, naturally, is interfere!"

"In what way, if I may ask?"

"I'll tell you in a minute. You have to understand that the military are convinced this is the most favourable time for them to strike. Their main concern is to put Russia in the wrong. Things are going their way because reports have reached Berlin that Russia has already decided on partial mobilization, to get their steamroller going. Like everybody in Berlin, they expect Austria to declare war on Serbia today. The Austrians have already mobilized their troops along the Russian border and they will probably begin hostilities by artillery-shelling Belgrad. As to the Chancellor, he is convinced of our need to support Austria-Hungary to the fullest in order to maintain their position as a world power. That is why he is very reluctant to bully Vienna into accepting Grey's mediation."

"So in what way did the Kaiser interfere?" Ali asked.

"In this way."

And he explained.

> Extracts from a note dated July 28 the Kaiser wrote by hand to Foreign Minister Gottlieb von Jagow:
>
> After reading over the Serbian reply, which I received this morning, I am convinced that on the whole the wishes of the Danube Monarchy have been acceded to. The few reservations that Serbia makes in regard to individual points could, according to my opinion, be settled by negotiation. But it contains the announcement orbi et urbi of a capitulation of the most humiliating kind, and, as a result, every cause for war falls to the ground.
>
> Nevertheless, the piece of paper, like its contents, can be considered of little value as long as it is not translated into deeds. The Serbs are Orientals, therefore liars, tricksters and masters of evasion. In order that these beautiful promises may be turned to truth and facts, a douce violence must be exercised. This should be so arranged that Austria would receive a hostage (Belgrad), as a guarantee for the enforcement of the promises, and should occupy it until the petita had actually been complied with. This is also necessary in order to give the army, now unnecessarily mobilized for the third time, the external satisfaction d'honneur of an ostensible success in the eyes of the world, and make it feel that it had at least stood on foreign soil ... In case Your Excellency shares my views, I propose that we say to Austria: Serbia has been forced to retreat in a very humiliating manner, and we offer our congratulations. Naturally, as a result, every cause for war has vanished. But a guarantee that the promises will be carried out is unquestionably necessary. That could be secured by means of a temporary military occupation of a portion of Serbia, similar to the way we kept out troops in France in 1871 until the billions were paid. On this basis, I am ready to mediate for peace with Austria. This I will do in my own way and as sparingly of Austria's

> nationalistic feeling and of the honour of her arms as possible ... I have had Plessen [Hans von Plessen, the Kaiser's aide-de-camp] write along the lines indicated above to the Chief of the General Staff, who is entirely in accord with my views. [Italics in the original].
>
> Source: Imanuel Geiss, July 1914, Selected Documents, New York: Scribner 1967, p. 256.

It took Ali a minute to think this through.

"Do you think Moltke was really in accord with his views?"

"He may have thought it prudent to suggest to His Majesty that he did, knowing very well that events were bound to overtake this — for Moltke — irritating, annoying and unnecessary — imperial initiative. The Kaiser, it seemed to those around him, was out of touch, and interferences like these could safely be ignored. Later, I understand the Kaiser made a number of remarks leaving a clear impression that he no longer wanted war, that he was determined to avoid it, even if it meant leaving Austria-Hungary in the lurch. Betrayal of one kind or another seems to be in the air. I have no doubt that the Kaiser's views are not being passed on to Vienna in time to stop them from declaring war on Serbia. For those who control the levers of power, there have always been ways to outwit the imperial master.

In any case, for the moment, all eyes are on London, not on Potsdam. On the one hand, Ambassador Lichnowsky reports that the mood there has changed for the worse during the last two days. He says people there are getting fed up with us for not doing enough to support Grey's attempt at mediation. Grey himself has warned us against believing that the war between Austria and Serbia can remain a local war. On the other hand, the Kaiser's brother Prince Henry was in Windsor last week and talked to King George who gave him assurances that Britain would keep aloof. Naturally, the Kaiser was elated when he heard this because nothing means more to him that one monarch speaking to another, even if it's only through his brother."

"And then His Majesty's great friend Albert Ballin came back from London with another optimistic report. He had gone there at Bethmann Hollweg's request, but strictly in private. Perhaps the Kaiser himself had suggested the mission."

"I had not heard of it."

"Your Excellency was not supposed to. He returned on Monday to his home in Hamburg, with a fever and a bad cold."

Ballin had been dispatched to London, Manfred explained, because it was hoped that, building on his previous hard work in the cause if German-British friendship, he could thwart the Anglo-Russian naval talks that apparently were about to take place. He is close to Sir Ernest Cassel, who was in Berlin two and a half years ago to pave the way for Lord Haldane.

> Reports about the secret Anglo-Russian talks had been conveyed to Berlin by the German spy Benno von Siebert, who had been strategically placed in the Russian Embassy in London where he held the position of Second Secretary.

Sir Edward Grey had repeatedly given assurances to Lichnowsky that under no circumstances would any agreement emerging from such conversations commit England to any action in the event of war. These assurances conflicted with Siebert's coded messages, which were alarming.

Last Thursday, the day of Austria's ultimatum to Serbia," Manfred continued, "Ballin was Lord Haldane's guest for dinner, together with Sir Edward Grey. Ballin understood them to state quite clearly that England had no contractual obligations of any sort to Russia or France. However, Sir Edward Grey had told Lichnowsky that under no circumstances would Britain remain neutral if Germany attacked France. And, of course, there had been a number of public declarations by British statesmen to the effect that Britain would never tolerate France being crushed. But what did being crushed mean? On Saturday, Ballin dined with the First Lord of Admiralty, Winston Churchill. Ballin asked him what England would do if Germany gave guarantees that, in case of victory in a war with France, it would not annex a single inch of territory, so the balance of power would not be disturbed. Ballin understood Churchill to answer that such guarantees might indeed make a difference. This answer made Ballin quite optimistic about the possibility of British neutrality. He quoted Churchill as saying as well that England would judge events as they arose but naturally that it would be a mistake to assume that England would stay out whatever happened. When they parted, Churchill said to him, 'My dear friend, do not let us go to war'.

So you can see," Manfred concluded his report, "that there is considerable confusion among the diplomats. No doubt the terms of the British-French entente are deliberately vague. So are the terms of the entente with Russia. An entente is not an alliance. But there is no ambiguity in the agreement between the French and the Russians. That is an alliance. But even so, to avoid any conceivable misunderstanding, it seems the French have just now once again given the Russians a clear assurance that they will definitely live up to the terms of their alliance. By the way, Poincaré and Viviani left Kronstadt on Thursday and were isolated at sea during the six-day voyage and diplomatically impotent. But they have now cancelled their visits to Copenhagen and Oslo and are on their way home without delay. We understand that before they left Saint Petersburg they asked the Russians to do their best to avoid any provocations on the Austrian front and on the German front. The slightest imprudence — meaning anything that could be interpreted as an act of aggression — could easily cost them the help of England. So their eyes, too, are on London." He lowered his voice. "But not the eyes of our generals. They do not care. They have their eyes fixed on their prepared strategic plans. They can hardly wait for the go-ahead to march. His Majesty will have the greatest difficulties restraining them. They demand an order for general mobilization today and they think it hardly matters what London does, since they will be in Paris before any British troops can land in France anyway."

"I can see," Ali said with slow deliberation, "that the future of the world now rests in the Kaiser's hands."

"So it seems. But I am sure, Your Excellency, even so he will take time off to see the author of those stories as soon as possible. He is very much concerned what the world thinks of him."

Arabian Nights, 1914

❁ *The Interview* ❁

My noble Lord, you asked me to tell you what it is to be a "modern monarch." What, in short, makes Wilhelm II modern, you ask. My reply is he must grasp the spirit of the times. He must understand the importance of cultivating the magical image of a great leader, to use the press for this purpose and for whatever other purposes he chooses; he must understand the need to discard obsolete old practices, to be aware of the requirements of the new industrial age, of extraordinary new technologies — Zeppelins for example — of the crucial importance of lower and higher education, of communications, of scientific research and scholarship, of the uplifting function of the arts. A modern monarch must always think of the future but he must respect the past and understand that only certain old traditions must be maintained, by no means all. He must be popular. He must identify with his people, not merely represent them, he must, so to speak, be his people's incarnation, and he must grasp intuitively what they need and want and he must be seen as trying to give it to them. He must understand that unless they happily support him, he cannot achieve anything. Therefore, he must know how to shape and influence public opinion. He must honour the religion of others even if to him they are infidels, and he must be tolerant of people who do not agree with him. A modern monarch must have the ambition to lead his country to be the best, the most respected, the most progressive in the world. Kaiser Wilhelm does.

Do not worry, Your Majesty, to be a modern monarch does not mean that his role is merely ceremonial. Nor does it mean that he is to be a mere servant of some sort of parliament. A modern monarch has a constitution that tells him what he must do himself and what he must leave to his chancellor and to others.

Kaiser Wilhelm knows this. But does the Chancellor know it? Do his subordinates know it?

Listen, my noble Lord, to the story I must tell you tonight.

In the summer of 1908, an English admirer of Wilhelm's, Colonel Edward Stuart-Wortley, attended German army manoeuvres in Alsace. He and Wilhelm had long talks. The colonel went back home and, with the help of a friend, drafted an article for the Daily Telegraph whose proprietor, Lord Burnham, was a friend of his. The article was written in the form of an interview, based on these conversations. The Colonel's purpose was, as he put it to the Kaiser, to correct "the stupid impressions concerning Your Majesty's feelings towards this country." He insisted a draft of the article be sent to Wilhelm for approval. Wilhelm looked at it, recognized his own words but, realizing that he was vulnerable to criticism that he was sometimes imprudent, sent it to his Chancellor, Bernhard von Bülow, asking him to for his opinion and, if he thought it was acceptable, to authorize publication. The constitution did not require this. The Kaiser often made speeches and gave interviews on matters of policy without consulting the Chancellor first.

Bülow's conduct in this matter was indefensible. He was on holidays in Norderney, on the Dutch coast, going for long walks along the dunes with his poodle Mohrchen. He glanced at the draft but, after all, he was on holidays and was not in the mood for serious work. So he sent it to the ministry in the Wilhelmstrasse to have the piece scrutinized. There, senior officials were also on holidays, so junior bureaucrats took over. They corrected a few passages and sent it back to Bülow. He may or may not have glanced at it. In any case, he authorized publication.

In the article, Wilhelm declared his navy was not intended for use against England but for the protection of German trade in the Far East. Germany was a young and growing Empire. She had worldwide commerce that was rapidly expanding. In the light of Japanese development and the Chinese national awakening, the day would soon come when Britain would be only too glad of the German fleet. His heart was set on peace. The British were "mad as March hares" to think otherwise. As to the recent Boer War, he said he had given his grandmother Queen Victoria tips on how to win it. In fact, he had instructed his General Staff to work out a plan, subsequently used by Lord Roberts successfully, on how to defeat the Boers. Not only that, but during the war he had refused French and Russian suggestions to join in a continental alliance against Britain. It was understood that this position had required considerable courage at a time when large sections of German opinion were not on the English side, as he had been, but on the side of the

Boers. There was no need to mention the Kruger telegram, which he had sent at a time when he, too, had sympathized with the cause of the Boers.

As soon as the interview was published, the roof fell in.

Now, Your Majesty, what was wrong with it? Can you understand it? The Kaiser spoke honestly and clearly meant what he said. Why then all the fuss? Why the amused contempt in England? Why did the English raise their eyes to Heaven about his protestations of friendship and his claims about his role in the Boer War? Can they not take the truth? When all was said and done, what was so terrible about a close relative of their own royal family speaking his mind?

The only answer I have is that the British nation, which pretends to believe in fair play, was being unfairly prejudiced against him. This, however, was nothing compared to the reception the interview received at home in Germany. The Germans behaved in a manner I find totally incomprehensible. What the Kaiser had said was no worse than many of the things he had said many times in the past. Maybe one day I will understand it. The Kaiser had recently suffered a humiliating diplomatic setback in the Morocco crisis; maybe that had something to do with it. And relations with Chancellor von Bülow had become increasingly strained, so he made no effort to protect the Kaiser. On the contrary, in fact. Bülow may have taken mischievous delight in Wilhelm's embarrassment. Let us also remember that it was Bülow who had raised fatal objections to the treaty the Kaiser had recently concluded with the Tsar off the Island of Björkö, because the Kaiser had unilaterally altered the text of the original draft. Also, unpleasant things had recently happened to one or two close friends of his that had suggested that there was something questionable about the Kaiser's entourage. Wilhelm's popularity had sunk to a low point.

However, I must not do Bülow an injustice. He was quite willing to admit that he had not read the text of the interview. Had he read it, he said he would have advised against publication. He accepted full constitutional responsibility and offered to atone for his omission by submitting his resignation. The Kaiser refused to accept it. If the world wanted to call this a serious constitutional crisis, he thought, then let it. But he certainly would never agree that the constitution did not allow him to say to the press at home or abroad, or to anybody else, whatever he wanted to say. He did not state this explicitly but I have no doubt he thought that, if indeed he was indiscreet, it was his constitutional right to be indiscreet. Nor did he refrain in the years since from acting on his own authority when he felt it advisable to do so. Incidentally, during this crisis the American Century published an interview with the Kaiser conducted by the prominent pro-German, anti-British American journalist William Hale in which the Kaiser said he hated England and hoped that, after the British Empire was demolished by the Indians and the Chinese, the Americans and Germans should jointly liquidate it.

One aspect of the Daily Telegraph affair was that the Kaiser was suddenly cast as an anglophile while his people were in an anglophobe mood. Germany was a late-comer among the Great Powers and Germans were sensitive about their international reputation, aware that their rapid rise in the world was producing distrust rather than admiration. Now they felt that the Kaiser's irresponsible indiscretions were making things worse. They were attracting disrespect, they felt. They wanted him to stop embarrassing them. But they most certainly didn't want any harm to come to him.

Bülow, with great skill, tried to deflect the major blame for the affair to the Kaiser. There was a debate in the Reichstag. Many speakers from all parties expressed their dismay at Wilhelm's "personal government." The princes were going to act if the politicians did not. What was demanded was not parliamentary government, people said, — Germany remained fundamentally monarchist — but constitutional government. Already Bismarck has said that the time for absolutism had gone. Bülow intervened in the debate only once. He said His Majesty recognized with profound disquiet and pained regret that the interview had caused so much concern in Germany. In future His Majesty undertook to exercise restraint even in his private conversations. Neither he, the Chancellor, nor his successors would be able to perform their duties unless the Kaiser adhered to this principle. Incidentally, in the middle of the speech Bülow fainted and had to be carried out.

When Wilhelm heard what the Chancellor had said, he was profoundly shaken. He asked the people around him, "What is going on here? What is the meaning of all this?" But he was not so profoundly shaken as to be unable to receive Count Zeppelin, that very same day, to award him the Order of the Black Eagle, calling him the greatest German of the twentieth century, and observing that the arrival of the first airship was one of the great moments in the development of human culture.

Bülow had advised the Kaiser to stay away from Berlin while the debate took place. Therefore, His Majesty accepted an invitation to attend a hunting party in Donaueschingen on the estate of his friend Prince Max Egon zu Fürstenberg. A fellow guest remarked that the Kaiser seemed to him like a man who was looking with astonishment on the world as it really was for the first time in his life. He impressed another guest, Princess Norah Fugger, with what she called his indefatigable loquacity. During his stay in Donaueschingen he suffered another shock, a death under unusual circumstances, which will be the subject of another story.

That year, 1908, was the worst of Wilhelm II's reign — so far.

He had good reason to feel Bülow had betrayed him. He never forgave him. He once cut him dead in the Neue Palais. (Bülow had to resign six months later to make way for Bethmann Hollweg.) Voices were raised demanding the Kaiser's abdication and, for all I know, he may even have considered it himself, in his son's favour. Questions were asked about his sanity. The series of blows he had had to endure in the end led to a nervous breakdown, a mental collapse. He was no longer capable of making ordinary conversation with the adjutants who accompanied him on his morning walks. For a few days the Crown Prince acted on his behalf.

But in the end, his sense of duty towards the causes he served as a modern monarch prevailed.

Chapter 14

Tuesday, July 28 (First Continuation)

Ali had nearly forgotten that at eleven he had an appointment with the gaunt Captain Ismail Hazim and the stubby Captain Fual Kamil, the two advisors to the Turkish ambassador Mouktar Pascha. Once again, he invited Zade to be present.

Ali and Zade had heard — and no doubt his two visitors had also heard — that last Friday the Kaiser personally overruled Baron Hans von Wangenheim, his Ambassador in Constantinople, and ordered that a Turkish offer of an alliance be explored. As late as at the end of May, two months ago, the Kaiser had given up on the Turks and their promises, denouncing their dishonesty and shallowness, and was prepared to have them join the Russian-French camp that was apparently prepared to put up more money for their reforms — that is, for their attempts to convert Turkey into a modern Muslim state — than Germany could afford. Moreover, in the Turkish quarrel with Greece over the Aegean Islands, his sympathies were with the Greeks.

Now the situation had changed. Unless something went unexpectedly wrong in the forthcoming negotiations, it could safely be assumed that Turkey was to be on Germany's side in the coming conflict. Before arriving at the Ouda Embassy, Hazim and Kamil had discussed the various ramifications of this development with Baron Edgar von Toplitz, the banker in whose sumptuous Villa Suleika near the Tiergarten Ali Hassan had first met them.

"Congratulations, gentlemen!" Zade gave them a smile neither of them was likely to forget for a while. "I suppose you will be very much involved in whatever comes next."

"We hope so," Hazim said.

"The only country that will be able to remain neutral in the Near East will be Ouda," Kamil added. "I hope you lucky people will make the best of it."

"We will try," Ali assured him.

"But better make sure you don't become too rich," Hazim observed. "Otherwise we will eat you up. If we don't somebody else will."

"We will take your advice to heart," Ali nodded solemnly. "Tell us what happened."

"During the last month," Ismail Hazim began, "our people became more and more desperate. Almost hysterical, you might say. After we were rebuffed by England, France and Russia, our leaders conferred at the villa of the Grand Vizier. That is when it was decided not to wait any longer for a direct approach by Germany for which they had hoped. So they authorized Enver to take the bull by the horns and talk to the German Ambassador, Baron Hans von Wangenheim. Enver told him that the domestic reforms planned by the C.U.P. could only be carried out if the Ottoman Empire was secure against outside attacks. Such security could only be given by one of the Great Powers. He suggested that power be Germany.

This approach was made last Wednesday. Wangenheim turned him down. He did not think that such an undertaking, which was clearly designed to lead to the alliance that clearly was the C.U.P.'s eventual objective, would yield sufficient value to Germany to be worthwhile. I am told many Germans share his views. With that rejection our diplomatic isolation was complete."

"If anybody in London, Paris or Saint Petersburg thought about your people at all during the last two days," Ali said, "they no doubt thought the entire German government and military, not just the Kaiser, would do everything possible to win you Turks over as allies, at this critical moment. I am sure nobody thought it would be the other way round and that you would take the initiative to win over the Germans."

"Exactly," Kamil agreed. "Until the Kaiser overruled his Ambassador and broke the isolation, we had nowhere to go. But the Kaiser grasped our critical strategic importance to Germany at this very moment — against the British and the Russians. The people around him probably still agree with Wangenheim. The Kaiser is ahead of them all."

"Absolutely," Hazim exclaimed. "The Kaiser is our saviour!"

Ali and Zade could not help but share their joy and their relief.

"Now we face tremendous problems," Fuad Kamil said. "One of them is the question how the Arabs can be mobilized against the entente. Being Arabs yourselves, you may have some ideas about that."

The first image that came to Ali's mind was that of the remarkable Ned Lawrence, the Oxford student of archaeology he had met a year or two ago, helping to excavate the Hittite city of Crachemish, on the Euphrates. He was a born leader and just the man to arouse the Arabs. He loved the desert. But how could he rally Arabs for the Turks when most Arabs hated them? Ali did not know the answer. So he left it to Zade to deal with the question.

"There is only one way," she said. "The Germans must use their influence on the C.U.P. government to make them change their ways, stop centralizing and give a few key positions to Arabs. For one thing, the Caliph should be an Arab, not the Turkish Sultan. The Prophet Mohammed was an Arab."

The two Turks frowned.

"We know that there are some people in German universities who are thinking along those lines," Hazim said. "But I don't think they have had much impact on the Berlin government, and even less on the government in Constantinople."

"I know what the Kaiser thinks," Ali said.

"You do?"

'He has made it very clear during his second visit to the Holy Land in 1898. Don't you remember his speech in Damascus when he assured the Sultan and three hundred million Muslims that he would always be their friend? He practically declared himself their protector."

"To put these ideas into practice, he would need strong allies among the Arab emirs," Kamil said. "Men like Hussein, the ruler of Mecca, would have to be wooed. I understand his favourite son, Abdulla, has visited Lord Kitchener at least once, in Cairo. Men like that will go anywhere if they think they will be rewarded after the war. The Germans will have to outbid the British."

"The Kaiser has to learn," Ali said, "that the British have an entirely wrong idea about Islam. They think that if they can control the person at the top, the Caliph, they've won the battle. That's how they always operate, going to the top. But Islam is divided into hundreds of factions. It would do the Kaiser no good wasting his time on the Caliph, whether he's a Turk or an Arab, thinking he can get anywhere through him, for example by having him declare a holy war. Nobody would be swayed. No, there is only one way he can win the Arabs, and that is by persuading the people in Constantinople to make them their partners in running the Ottoman empire. Which is not to say that German agents couldn't make a lot of trouble for the British in Egypt and in the Sudan. And of course in India. But that has little to do with your immediate problem."

"Our immediate problem," Hazim said with a sigh, "is to have the Germans help us protect Constantinople from the Russians."

"On that subject," Ali raised his hand, "I have nothing to say. No doubt your military people are in touch with their counterparts here. But now that the Russians and the British will be on the same side, for the first time ever, the British don't have to worry about their old nightmare — the Russians taking India away from them."

"Not until the war is over." Hazim smiled. "Whoever wins."

The two Turkish visitors rose.

"No doubt you have heard," Zade said, as she accompanied them to the door, "what I'm told the Kaiser said the other day. 'Our agents in India,' he said, 'must get a conflagration going throughout the whole Muslim world against the English, this hated, unscrupulous, dishonest nation of shopkeepers. If we are going to bleed to death, England must at least lose India!'"

Holy War — Made in Germany?

You must forgive me, my gracious Lord, if I jump ahead a little. I have been telling you stories about our model monarch in more or less chronological order. We have now reached the year 1908, the year of the Daily Telegraph affair, which threw Wilhelm so much off balance that he even considered abdication. There is one more story to tell related to that affair about another terrible thing that happened to him immediately after Bülow's self-serving speech in the Reichstag, when he said that His Majesty recognized with profound disquiet and pained regret that the interview had caused so much concern. For this other story I am afraid Your Majesty will have to wait.

In the last few years, as I have told Your Majesty, many Germans, especially in the military, thought a war with Russia and France was inevitable. So it was not surprising that the question was frequently discussed, mainly by experts in universities and research institutes, what role, if any, Turkey might play in such a war.

In 1908 the Young Turks took over in Constantinople, removing the Kaiser's friend, the "blood-drinking" Sultan Abdul Hamid II from his throne and replacing him with Mehmed Reshad who was their man. How would this new revolutionary regime behave?

Germans have no experience of fighting a war with Muslim allies, who only know one kind of war — holy wars, wars to crush infidels who enslaved Muslims and robbed Islam of its splendours. Similarly, as far as I know, the Turks have never fought a war as the allies of infidels. So this would be a new situation for both. We Muslims, I repeat, do not know any wars other than holy wars, jihads. All the wars the Ottoman Empire fought under Sultan Abul Hamid II against Russia and Greece were, of course, jihads. So were all their previous wars against Austria-Hungary in the Balkans. Modern Europeans, of course, don't think religious wars make any sense at all, perhaps because in their history they had so many of them and they don't want to be reminded.

Now, in 1908, the secular Young Turks took over with the slogans of the French Revolution — Liberty, Equality, Fraternity — and declared their intention to establish a modern constitutional state. They retained Islam as the state religion while, in the spirit of modern times, guaranteeing adherents of other faiths equal rights, though no doubt in the minds of True Believers it is absurd to think of infidels as equals. Most of their leader were freethinkers who had been educated in the west, mainly in Paris. They had no use for Kaiser Wilhelm II, who had been the tyrant's friend and whom they considered an old-fashioned autocrat. Nor did it help Germany's prestige that, three months after the Young Turks' revolution, Germany's allies, the Austrians, annexed Bosnia and Herzegovina, both parts of the Ottoman Empire. In their anger with Germany, they even invited the British and the French to participate more fully in the building of the Baghdad Railway.

However, when the new government in Constantinople revived pan-Islamism as a political movement in the years since 1908 and stirred up nationalist trouble for the British in India and Egypt and for the French in Tunis, Algeria and Morocco, London and Paris soon became disenchanted. For Germany, Turkish nationalism was not threatening in the least, and very soon the Kaiser emerged as leading candidate for the position of the Young Turks' only foreign friend. And they certainly needed such a friend since things were not going at all well for them. Many, if not most, of their programs had to be put aside, while among the people at large the old Muslim beliefs remained as strong as ever.

In Germany, there are many military thinkers who were delighted that the C.U.P. — the Committee of Unity and Progress — failed to undermine the old Muslim faith. They believed that, when the time comes, holy wars against Russia, England and France will be immensely useful to German strategies in the Middle East. All that would be required is that their leaders, even if they are free thinkers, have their Caliph declare a holy war against England, Russia and France, and call on the millions of fellow Muslims languishing in their enemies' vast territories in Asia and Africa to do Allah's will and rise up against the tyrants. The mercy of Allah and the support of the Prophet, the Caliph would assure all True Believers, would bring victory in the war against the enemies of Islam.

Wilhelm may be a modern monarch but he is a Christian. He thinks his god is on his side, on the side of his holy fatherland. As we True Believers look down on infidels, they, the Christians, of course, look down on us. Your Majesty will readily understand that as a Christian Wilhelm will find it somewhat strange to become a party to a Muslim holy war. He must also remember that there are a few thousand Muslims languishing in Germany's colonies who may be aroused against his regime. No doubt Wilhelm also knows that in the past there has been a good deal of, as some put it, "predatory murder on the path of Allah." It may not be easy to prevent the German press from reporting crimes committed by their ally, even in wartime. Also, the Young Turks may continue what the Old Turks used to do from time to time — massacre Armenians, who are close to the Russians.

I doubt whether at the outset Wilhelm will worry too much about such possibilities. He will remind the world of his speech in Damascus in 1898, on the grave of Salah a-Din, when he declared himself a friend of the Sultan and protector of three hundred million Muslims. And he will announce that Turkey and Germany will jointly lead three hundred Muslim to freedom. He will believe this no less than he will believe that Germany will win the war. And he will see nothing incompatible in such a declaration with his view that after victory has been achieved Germany may have to establish a protectorate over the Ottomans until they have get rid of the corruption that had eroded their power during the last two centuries.

One of Wilhelm's most impressive characteristics is his sense of reality. It was the most valuable lesson he learned from Bismarck. When he was a friend of Sultan Abdul Hamid II, he realized he was dealing with a despot, but he did so in the interest of Germany. He saw no reason to open Germany's doors to liberal refugees from the Sultan's despotism.

And, similarly, when in 1908 the Young Turks replaced the old Sultan with a new one who would comply with the new revolutionary spirit, he sent him a message of friendship and assured him that nothing had changed, or would change, in his well-established feelings of friendship for Turkey.

That, Your Majesty, is how a modern monarch must behave.

Chapter 15

Tuesday, July 28 (Second Continuation)

When the Austrians mobilized their troops along the Russian frontier, thousands of people gathered outside the Austrian Embassy in Berlin shouting "hurray" until late in the night and sang patriotic songs. "It was," Helmuth von Moltke noted in a letter to his wife, "as though we ourselves had mobilized. Enjoy whatever is beautiful in the world while you can."

After Ismail Hazim and Fuad Kamil left the Ouda Embassy's office — elated now that Turkey's fate as Germany's ally was almost settled — and Ali and Zade had a brief lunch, Zade called Frau von Tiedemann in Hohenfinow. She did not think it fair to keep her waiting any longer. They had a long talk.

Each of the three opportunities for history-making pillow talk with the All Highest held greater promise than an erotic trap to be laid by her as governess of the Tiedemann children in Hohenfinow.

These three opportunites were:

1) the interview Manfred von Kosenburg had undertaken to organize;

2) Jonathan Lind's projected dinner at the British Ambassador's;

3) the wreath-laying ceremony in the Lustgarten planned for Thursday, July 30, which Alphonse Picard had arranged.

Frau von Tiedemann was gravely disappointed.

"You did the right thing," Ali said. "It would have been a waste of time."

"Who knows? The Kaiser can't make any peace-or-war decisions without the Chancellor," Zade retorted. "The constitution won't allow it. Everybody has been telling me the Kaiser is unpredictable. Remember what Manfred von Kosenburg has just told us: he has the bit in his teeth. The 'Stop at Belgrad' proposal was all his own."

"You're right. He may be in one of his Frederick the Great phases. He may even take on the General Staff. I am told he is going to send another telegrams to the Tsar, addressed, as usual, to 'Dear Nicky,' imploring him not to mobilize and to talk to the Austrians directly. But something unexpected has happened a couple of days ago that for a moment gave some hope. Sergei Sazonov, the Russian Foreign Minister, was trying out a new idea. He thought the Germans were perhaps having second thoughts about their blank cheque to an empire on the brink. He hinted to the Germans that if they would abandon the Austrians, the Russians were prepared to drop their French allies. And for a day or two this titillating idea of a double betrayal to save the peace must have seemed immensely tempting even to such an honorable man as Bethmann Hollweg. A philosophical mind like his could always rationalize that ends justify means. After all, he has always dreamed of splitting the entente. This certainly would do it. Furthermore, a German-Russian alliance in Bismarck's spirit — what could be more alluring?

"But of course it was too good to be true. Or rather, too good to be sensible. Germany would exchange one ally who was merely decadent for another who had chosen pan-Slavism to stave off revolution at home. The Austrians, even if they had their backs to the wall, were a better risk after all. However infuriating, they could still be propped up by their stronger, more vigorous ally. By the way, I doubt whether the Kaiser ever heard of Sazonov's scheme."

"My hope," Zade said with a slightly mischievous smile, "is that he will do anything to preserve the peace."

Ali did not have to be told what she had in mind.

"Did you ask Frau von Tiedemann what Bethmann Hollweg has to say about the latest developments? After all, by now she knows that you are not meant to be a governess."

"Yes. She seemed to want to talk to me. The Chancellor is profoundly pessimistic, she says, and has premonitions of disaster. But he has an overwhelmingly strong sense of responsibility and feels he must do everything he can to maintain the German position in Europe, in keeping with her vitality and economic strength, and to achieve that Austria must remain strong. He certainly does not think in terms of Germany becoming master of Europe. No, he is guided not by ambition but by fear. He is terrified of rapidly industrializing Russia, with its huge population, and is haunted by the spectacle of an expansionist Russia allied with England and France, strangling Germany. Things are going badly, for him and for everybody else."

"Have you heard the rumour that the Russians have ordered the mobilization of their four western districts, Odessa, Kiev, Moscow and Kazan?"

"No," Zade replied. "I have not heard that. Isn't that the same as a declaration of war — against both Austria and Germany?"

"Oh yes. At any rate, so the Germans say. Of course we don't know how the Tsar will respond to the Kaiser's latest telegram. But it seems, if this rumour is true, Russia has now put itself in the wrong in the eyes of the world, by acting prematurely. By the way, there seems to be no real difference between ordering partial and general mobilization. Naturally, the Germans will be delighted, if this is true, both the generals and the Chancellor. The generals will want to mobilize immediately. The Chancellor will want to wait to see whether London will make one final effort. For the generals on both sides, time is of the essence. In any case, once you order mobilization, there is no easy way back."

Zade was thinking of her dinner with the Kaiser and the British Ambassador tomorrow.

"Surely the Kaiser, too, will have some ideas," Zade said.

"No doubt. He will say to the British if there was a war with

France, he could promise that Germany would seek no territorial gains in Europe. Therefore, England should stop worrying about the balance of power. As to the touchy, possibly crucial matter of Belgium, he will say that there was always the possibility he might be able to persuade King Albert to permit German troops to march through Belgian territory. After all, the King's mother belonged to the Hohenzollern-Sigmaringen branch of the family. There was always the possibility that a quiet, family, monarch-to-monarch approach might work. But if it didn't and if hostilities began, everything depended on the countermeasures the French took. If the Germans could argue that they were being attacked …"

"That won't be so easy, under the circumstances," Zade observed. "Now let me ask again. I am curious about Bethmann Hollweg. Does he really think Germany has a chance?"

"He believes a quick war in the west would keep the Russians at bay and shake up the status quo. He imagines young people would consider it a kind of liberation, a great adventure. He knows a long war does not bear thinking about. He is convinced the present arrangements can't last anyway unless there is a real shake-up."

"A shake-up? You mean a revolution?"

"No one ever uses that word. Everybody thinks about it. I am sure the Kaiser does. He is not stupid. The Tsar has nightmares about it. The one great service Bethmann Hollweg can still render the Kaiser is to keep the Social Democrats on board. He is having secret talks with them, possibly at this very moment. No one else in the government can do that. Or wishes to do that. The generals would despise him for it if they knew about it. They want to shoot all the leaders, the day war breaks out. What he is doing takes a lot of courage, true patriotism. Of course it's an open question whether it wouldn't be better for the world if the Social Democrats in Germany would not be kept on board and, together with their brothers in France and possibly England, refused to fight. There are a lot of them, here and elsewhere. You can't have an army without them. If they all went on strike there would be no war."

"Ali Hassan," Zade cried, "you are dreaming."

"I know. In London the socialists demonstrate every day. They don't want to fight at all, and they certainly don't want to fight on the same side as Russia, a despotic, expansionist slave state that has designs on British India and threatens British interests in Persia. There are meetings opposing a war everywhere in Europe, in all the big towns. And here in Germany — if only the military did not have the system so firmly in its grip! If only they allowed the huge civilian opposition to have a voice! Most people aren't militarists at all. They're obedient and intimidated. That's not the same thing at all. Those who are militarists have the power and make all the noise. There is a revolutionary leader called Karl Liebknecht, an ardent anti-militarist. His father, Wilhelm, was a friend of Karl Marx. You may have heard of Marx, though few people in Ouda have. Liebknecht's son, Karl, was elected to the Reichstag while he was in prison for having urged that young boys be taught how to avoid military service."

"What is this I hear?" The door must have been open, allowing Jonathan Lind to make his way silently into Ali's office, after climbing the stairs from the floor below. "Karl Marx? Revolution? Good thing, my friend," he laughed, addressing Ali, "you have diplomatic immunity!"

He looked at Zade, dazed once again by her beauty.

"Madame," he bowed to her, "I have good news for you and especially for me. The Kaiser has agreed to attend a small working-dinner at the British Embassy tomorrow evening. No one is to know. The press is not invited. I am allowed to pose as a diplomatic adviser. Will you come with me?"

Zade was no flirt. She looked him straight in the eye.

"I would be honoured," she said. "I know how to behave with monarchs. I am on excellent terms with His Majesty King Shahriyar of Ouda."

Jonathan Lind laughed.

"But do they know how to behave with you?"

"So far my experience has been entirely positive."

"Good. Now, I have more good news. My sources in London tell me that if Grey goes on saying to one and all that England will automatically come to France's aid if Germany attacks there may be a split in the British Cabinet."

"You mean," Ali asked, "the government may fall?"

"That is what I mean."

> Three quarters of Britain's governing Liberal parliamentary party were for "absolute non-interference at any price." Twenty-two Liberal members of the back-bench Foreign Affairs Committee indicated that they may withdraw their support from the government if there was a commitment to go to war. A third of the cabinet, nineteen members, were in favour of neutrality, another third had not made up their minds and only a third was in favour of a commitment to France.
>
> Source: Niall Ferguson, The Pity of War, Basic Books 1999.

"So there will be a good deal to talk about at the dinner tomorrow," Zade smiled. "Such as the question why Sir Edward Grey has so few friends."

"I have my own views on that," Lind said. "We Englishmen prefer the virile Germans to the decadent French. Grey's critics think he's just anti-German, that's all. There is not much sympathy for the French, anyway, because all they want is revenge, which we don't think is a great virtue. Also, they are our rivals in Africa and the Near East. What would be so terrible about the Germans defeating the French, people ask themselves, which was overwhelmingly likely if they were allowed to fight it out by themselves? As for the Russian alliance, the less said the better. No one likes it. Besides, we remember how popular Wilhelm was when he came over only thirteen years ago, when Queen Victoria was dying, and again three years ago at Edward VII's funeral. In a curious way, we are quite fond of the Kaiser. I am told he is a good cricket player, but I haven't seen him play myself. People don't really mind his sabre-rattling. We find it entertaining. We believe that if things get tough, he will behave like a lamb. Anyhow, we are the nation of Shakespeare. We like Theatre and Pomp and Circumstance. Not only that, but we think men such as Haldane and Grey could have come to an agreement with him if they had been a little more generous and broad-minded. After all, we've got a huge empire and the Kaiser is a newcomer. We believe in fair play, or at least so we say. And when he complains about being encircled, we look at the map and read the newspapers and say, 'True, he is being encircled. He's absolutely right about that.' And we think all that talk about the balance of power is hogwash and a mere pretence for keeping him down."

"So you think it's possible," Ali said, scratching the back of his neck, "that Sir Edward Grey and those who agree with him may be pushed out?"

"It is entirely possible," Jonathan Lind nodded.

"I understand," Zade said thoughtfully, "that Bethmann Hollweg believes the Germans are not virile at all but are suffering rapid cultural decline. I suppose the British don't agree with him."

"Oh no," Jonathan Lind laughed. "They've never heard of a single decadent German!"

The Dance

My exalted King, the time has come for me at last to tell you the painful story I promised you about the shock Wilhelm suffered immediately after the Daily Telegraph affair, which had already shaken his self-confidence to the core.

To prevent demonstrations against him, he was advised not to be in Berlin during debate in the Reichstag, on November 10 and 11 in 1908. To comply with this request he attended a fox cull on the estate of his wealthy friend Prince Max Egon zu Fürstenberg in Donaueschingen in the Black Forest, just north of the Swiss border. Born and raised in Bohemia, the Prince was one of the largest landowners in Austria-Hungary, and also, by inheritance, of large estates in southern Germany. He was a member of the upper houses of Austria-Hungary, Prussia, Baden and Württemberg.

Wilhelm was very fond of the Prince but his friendship never reached quite the same emotional intensity as that with Philipp von Eulenburg-Hertefeld. They had met in Vienna in 1893 and became close only after the Kaiser's first visit to Donaueschingen in April 1900. By October, Wilhelm sent him birthday greetings in verse. The next year he became one of the very few with whom he was on the familiar du basis. The Prince's upbeat personality had a beneficial effect on his own. He was an incurable optimist, had the temperament of a gambler and was known for taking risks in the financial world as well. Years later, when a large enterprise in which he was deeply involved went bankrupt, the Austrian Ambassador tactfully noted that mere dilettantism was perhaps not quite sufficient to manage large operations in the capitalist world.

For Wilhelm, Donaueschingen was different from Liebenberg. The Prince was a Catholic, unusual in the Kaiser's circle. Moreover, among his friends suggestions of social reform were by no means taboo, as they were in Liebenberg. For these reasons perhaps it was not surprising that the Prince never belonged to the Kaiser's inner circle. Still, the hunts every November and what Wilhelm called the skillfully matched company and the unrestrained conversation were for him highlights of the year.

This autumn, perhaps to cheer himself up, His Majesty was unusually well equipped sartorially. For the hunts he wore the heavy gold cords of an adjutant general, and at the opening of his collar a golden cross he had designed himself, a combination of the Order of Saint John and that of the Knights of the Teutonic Order. His boots were made of shiny yellow leather and were equipped with gold spurs. In this costume, he notched up eighty-four out of a total hundred and thirty-four foxes, which Prince zu Fürstenberg had either bred or bought in sufficient numbers to please His Majesty. In the evening, the All Highest wore a green hunting coat, below his knee the English Order of the Garter, across his chest the ribbon of the Order of the Black Eagle and around his neck the Spanish Golden Fleece.

Usually, the guests were members of the highest Austrian and German nobility but also included the owners of neighbouring estates and their families. Children were invited to some of the entertainment, and the older ones were allowed to stay up for the fireworks, the theatrical presentations and the jokes and amusements, often performed by visiting cabaret artists from Berlin.

The ladies set the tone of the meticulously planned festivities. Wilhelm was delighted that Dona got on so well with their hostess, the Austrian-born Princess Irma zu Fürstenberg, née Countess von Schönberg-Buchheim.

This year the party was particularly glittering. At the dinners, His Majesty was in top form, and several later remarked on the brilliance of his conversation. Among his many subjects was that of wireless telegraphy, which he explained so clearly, so I was told, that a university professor could not have done better. At some time during the weekend he had a tête-à-tête with the Countess Salm, who later reported that he lectured her on Protestantism.

One of the guests at the table was a friend for whom the Kaiser had particularly warm feelings and great respect, Count Dietrich von Hülsen-Haeseler, the chief of his Military Cabinet. He was often one of the Kaiser's most entertaining guests on his annual summer cruises in the North Sea. The Count knew how to criticize the All Highest without offending him, usually by couching his criticism in the form of Berlin jokes. You may remember that I mentioned him a few weeks ago, in connection with the appointment of Count Helmuth von Moltke to the position of Chief of the General Staff, to which he objected.

Dietrich von Hülsen-Haeseler was more than six feet tall and had a commanding military presence, manly and aggressive — a type very different from Eulenburg, whom he detested. He had married money and therefore did not depend on his position at Court. Unlike some other members of the officer corps, he firmly opposed any tendencies to make the army more democratic. There was theatrical talent in the family — his brother Georg ran the imperial theatre in Wiesbaden. Unlike Dietrich who, as I said, was an adversary of Eulenburg, Georg had been a frequent guest at Liebenberg and, after dinner there, often put on dramatic sketches for the entertainment of the guests. On this occasion, Dietrich rendered a similar service in Donaueschingen. However, he had found the limitations of the male cast imposed on him unduly restrictive. Therefore, he often demanded female impersonations, of which he provided some himself.

Now, it so happened that Wilhelm, like many Germans, found men pretending to be women on the stage — sometimes men performing solo dances dressed only in a tutu — a particularly hilarious source of amusement. The more unlikely and incongruous, the better. There was nothing in the least scandalous or depraved about cross-dressing on the stage, though I doubt whether similar entertainments were presented very frequently on the estates of his grandmother Queen Victoria's friends. Not only Wilhelm and other men enjoyed watching these performances, but apparently so did the ladies. Perhaps they only pretended to, to please the Kaiser. I don't know.

Dietrich von Hülsen-Haeseler did a solo dance one evening after dinner, in one of Princess Irma's ballgowns, complete with feathered hat and fan. It was a flirtatious little dance. He blew kisses to the audience, among laughter and applause. The Count was a wonderful, graceful dancer. The pianist who accompanied him was excellent. No doubt there was something special about seeing the tall, virile Chief of the Military Cabinet on the stage, in His Majesty's presence.

After the dance was over, the Count disappeared through a side door. Then he stumbled and fell. Everyone heard it, even though the piano-playing continued. The pianist did not stop playing until after a doctor who was quickly summoned had established that the Count had just died of a heart attack.

Chapter 16

Wednesday, July 29

On Wednesday morning, the Hausmeister collecting the garbage at Luisenstrasse 16, around the corner from the Wilhelmstrasse, sniffed the air and said quite calmly, to nobody in particular, "I smell gunpowder." He was not the only one. The smell pervaded the entirely landscape, particularly the air surrounding the generals and diplomats all over Europe, and of the socialists and pacifists trying desperately to save the peace. However, many of the bored, adventure-seeking young men could not wait for the shooting to start, to give their lives meaning at last.

There were excellent reasons to assume that this evening at dinner in the British Embassy Zade would come face to face with the Kaiser and therefore achieve her history-making objective and clear the air of the smell of gunpowder. Then the next two other events planned for her to conquer the Kaiser, the wreath-making ceremony in the Lustgarten in Potsdam scheduled for tomorrow, Thursday, and the encounter Manfred von Kosenburg was arranging in the Neue Schloss, at any time at short notice, would turn out to be superfluous.

Her course of action was clear. Having written her stories about the Kaiser, and having concentrated on him with great intensity during the last three weeks, she knew more about him than (almost) anybody else. Only Ali was privy to her intentions and shared her conviction that she was bound to succeed. There was no need for them to talk about it. She did not allow herself a moment's doubt that once she and the All Highest had looked into each other's eyes, he would be hers. She had worked out in her mind precisely what to say to him post coitu.

This was the day on which the Kaiser sent his second pleading "Dear Nicky" telegram to the vacillating Tsar who, so it seemed from the outside, was being increasingly pushed aside by his generals, the day on which the Russians, after a series of meetings and hysterical telephone conversations, were once again reported to begin mobilizing in the districts of Odessa, Kiev, Moscow and Kazan. This, however, they assured the German Ambassador, did not by any necessarily mean war. It was the day on which Moltke again demanded general mobilization, not only against the Russians but also against the French, the day on which in London Sir Edward Grey categorically told the German Ambassador Prince Karl Max von Lichnowsky that England would not remain neutral in case of a continental war, a statement that Bethmann Hollweg would not accept as London's final word, the day when in Paris …

"You want to know the latest news from Paris?" Alphonse Picard, looking more than ever like the impish dwarf Henri de Toulouse-Lautrec, asked breathlessly when he burst into the Ouda Embassy, just after Ali and Zade had said their prayers. "Yesterday, the lawyers' summation began. After eight days!"

He was speaking, of course, of the Affaire Caillaux, the crime passionel that was making headlines all over Europe and that Germans saw as a perfect example of French frivolity. In Paris even today, on July 29th, 1914, papers as important as Le Temps and Le Petit Journal were devoting more space to the "the trial of the century" than to the momentous news that normally would have monopolized the front pages. The reason was that a decaying regime was on trial and that the press itself, by its outspoken, passionate partisanship, was being accused of having been a major factor in causing the cold-blooded murder of a celebrity. The trial highlighted the changing role of women in relation to their husbands and lovers. It was, moreover, the first case in the history of France to feature depositions by a president of France and by many of the most powerful members of French society. Two of the lawyers who had become famous in the Dreyfus affair were once again in the limelight. The novelist Marcel Proust had dedicated Swann's Way to Gaston Calmette, the murdered editor of the conservative Le Figaro.

> Gaston Calmette had conducted a campaign of libel and character assassination against Joseph Caillaux, the Minister of Finance and head of the left-leaning Radical Party, a campaign excessive even by the tolerant standards of the Third Republic. Calmette had gone as far as to publish Caillaux's love letters to Berthe Gueydan, later Caillaux's first wife, written thirteen years ago when she was still only his mistress. Berthe was a married woman. The paper also promised to reveal more love letters of Caillaux's, presumably between him and his second wife, Henriette. This had been unheard of in French journalism. Henriette felt her husband should have challenged the editor to a duel. She put that to him but he chose not to oblige. So she took matters into her own hand. During a late afternoon visit to his office on March 16, wearing a fur coat over a strangely formal gown, Henriette asked him, after being ushered in, whether he knew why she had come. 'Not at all, madame,' he responded, offering her a seat. Whereupon she pulled out a Browning automatic hidden in her muff and shot him point blank six times.

"Oh, come off it, Alphonse," Ali laughed, "surely on the day that Poincaré and Viviani are returning to Paris and taking charge, more important things must be going on."

Picard raised his right hand in mock horror.

"Please do not try to deflect me," he said. "All you need to know about those two is that while they were being toasted in Saint Petersburg, they pledged a hundred times to rush to Russia's aid, if necessary. And you also need to know that they will do nothing to provoke the Germans, in order not to give the British any excuse to leave them in the lurch. No Frenchman ever trusts an Englishman. What else is there to be said? That we may be at war next week? But everybody knows that!"

"Not everybody!" Ali replied with heat. "All kinds of things can happen that may prove everybody wrong. If the Russians, who — remember! — are not being attacked, occupy the Austrian province of Galicia to help the Serbs, do the French necessarily have to cross the Rhine?"

"Oh, I don't know," Picard said irritably. "All you're trying to do is stop me from giving you the latest news from Paris. Listen." He pulled out a telegram from his coat pocket. "I've just heard what Henriette Caillaux's lawyer told the court. 'Madame Caillaux's act was a tragic result of unbridled female passion. It was governed, according to a most eminent specialist from the Paris Faculty of Medicine, by a subconscious impulse that resulted in a split personality.' Do you think the court will believe that?"

His two listeners shrugged. A sudden idea occurred to Alphonse Picard.

"Tomorrow you will be in the Lustgarten in Potsdam," he said to Zade, "and for the first time you will be in close proximity of the Kaiser. Why are you so keen to see him? Are you in the throes of unbridled female passion? Are you going to murder him?"

"No," Zade said, as though she had been waiting for the question. "But you're almost right. I am going to seduce him."

Alphonse Picard burst into uproarious laughter.

"Bonne chance!" he cried.

·

At six o'clock, Jonathan Lind and Zade walked to the British Embassy on Wilhelmstrasse 70, less than ten minutes' away, where they hoped dinner with the Kaiser was waiting for them. It was still very warm. Zade wore an elegant dark blue dress with a high collar, very tight at the waist, and a silver Oudanian necklace, and Lind a dark grey suit and his Etonian school tie. On the way, he told her the latest news.

"It seems the Russians are having bilateral talks with the Austrians after all," he said. "This is what Grey had been hoping for. Of course, talking to the Russians was the last thing the Austrians wanted to do, but Bethmann Hollweg put a lot of pressure on them. He actually threatened them that the alliance was at stake. He knows how important Grey thinks this is. England can still stay out, Bethmann Hollweg thinks, if either Russia or France committed acts of aggression, or if France broke her pledges to Russia and remained neutral, or at least promised to keep her troops on her own territory, in the event of a war between Germany and Russia. The Russians are shifting their position all the time. The Germans, too, are far from clear. As I say, Bethmann Hollweg and other civilians still hope against hope that the war can remain localized and Britain neutral. The military don't care what the British say. They want to mobilize immediately and proceed to the offensive."

"And the Kaiser?" Zade asked. "Where does he stand?"

"We may find out tonight," Jonathan Lind said. "My guess is the same may happen to him as what's no doubt happening to the Tsar at this very moment."

"What's that?"

"It won't matter where he stands because the generals will ignore him."

They arrived at the British Embassy. There were no crowds at the gate, no police, no soldiers. A bad sign. Obviously, the Kaiser had not shown up. And was not going to show up.

They were shepherded to a room in the back. In the corridor, they nearly stumbled over a suitcase. Diplomats were evidently preparing to leave Berlin. Jonathan Lind, thanks to his father, had German nationality and was therefore not a candidate for internment as an enemy alien. He had no intention to leave in case of war.

A smiling man rushed in, Gerald Muirhead, who had been in the same First Eleven with Lind at Eton. He was now First Secretary at the Embassy and had been a useful source of information to Lind since he arrived in the spring.

Muirhead saw Zade and was stunned.

"Tough luck, old boy," he announced. "Dinner has been cancelled. Anyway, you get better food at Borchard's. Take your lady there."

"What's going on, Gerald?"

"The All Highest is livid. He won't see anybody. The Berliner Lokalanzeiger brought out a special issue saying the Tsar had ordered total mobilization. The information came from an anonymous, highly placed, absolutely reliable source, they said. But the whole town knows who it was. Including — by now — His Majesty. Guess who."

"The Crown Prince," Zade said without a moment's hesitation.

"How did you know that, madame?" Muirhead was even more stunned. "And do you know," he went on, "what King George said to somebody last week? He said, 'I don't think William wants war. But he's afraid of his son's popularity. His son and his party will make war.'"

How to Handle the British

My honoured King, I know you will not misunderstand me if I say that it is a characteristic of monarchs, True Believers and infidels alike, to feel that they can do things better than their viziers and ministers. If only they were left alone to do things the way they think they should be done! I know, Your Majesty, you are an exception. I have never heard you utter a single word of criticism of my father.

But poor Kaiser Wilhelm! There was a moment in January 1912 that he felt presented a unique opportunity of the kind that happens once in a lifetime, a turning point. He believed that this time there was a real possibility at last of a comprehensive agreement with England that would lead to a commitment of English neutrality in case of war with France. That moment was the sudden arrival in Berlin — without any previous announcement through diplomatic channels — of an informal emissary of Sir Edward Grey (the Foreign Secretary), Winston Churchill (the First Lord of the Admiralty) and Lloyd George (the Chancellor of the Exchequer). The emissary's mission was to sound him out whether perhaps the time had come for a British minister to come to the German capital and have discussions with individual members of the German government.

The Kaiser was in the highest state of excitement. This was exactly the event for which he had been praying. The initiative came from three of the leading figures in the British government. The emissary,

Sir Ernest Cassel, could not have been chosen with greater care. Originally Winston Churchill was to have been sent, because he was considered very clever, but it was thought that Sir Ernest, whose native language was German and who was one of the City's great bankers, was more likely to impress the Kaiser. Sir Ernest was an immensely rich, self-made man who had been an intimate friend of Uncle Edward, and a man who sat on innumerable boards including that of the Turkish Petroleum Company. He was a native of Cologne, a naturalized British subject, originally Jewish but now baptized. Ostensibly he was on a private mission, in connection with the business of a university committee. He brought with him a note outlining the conditions under which talks might take place. Germany would have to recognize Britain's superiority on the sea and agree not to expand the present shipbuilding program. In return, London would support Germany's colonial ambitions and would welcome reciprocal assurances precluding either party from joining coalitions to commit aggressions against the other.

The Kaiser immediately summoned Chancellor von Bethmann Hollweg and the Secretary to the Navy, Admiral von Tirpitz. Although he had appointed them both and in theory demanded total subservience, in practice he had to hammer out, together with them, a common position. It was decided to draft answers to the note immediately, in English, to avoid any misunderstanding. Wilhelm's English was better than theirs. He sat down at his desk, the two ministers stood beside him. He drafted a sentence. He then read it out to his two ministers. To one it was too conciliatory, to the other too tough. It was then trimmed and shaped. Then the second and then the third sentence. This took hours.

In February there was the follow-up. Lord Richard Burdon Haldane arrived, the British Secretary of State for War. He was a Scottish lawyer who had studied law in Göttingen and had a taste for German philosophy. As a Liberal member of Parliament he had advocated reforms to the educational system along German lines. Once in office, he had reorganized the reserve system of the British Army, thereby in effect doubling its size, a task that had eluded his predecessors. The British army was still pitifully small, by European standards.

If only the situation had allowed Lord Haldane to negotiate alone with the Kaiser! On the eve of his mission, the Reichstag had passed Tirpitz's navy bill with the proposal, among others, to build three new battleships at two-year intervals from 1912 onwards. It had been strongly supported by the Kaiser who needed a strong bargaining position in the forthcoming negotiations. It required extraordinary skill to move the British from their position, if that was at all possible. Supremacy on the sea meant to them in effect that their navy was to be superior to the next two navies put together. Furthermore, he knew that the aim of British policy was not only to limit German shipbuilding, but also to preserve the balance of power in Europe, as though it had not already been upset by Germany emerging, within the last two decades, as economically very much in the lead, especially in developing important new industries. It was not clear whether

Lord Haldane knew that on one occasion the Kaiser had publicly declared that he was "the balance of power in Europe". What he meant was that, in a sense, Germany dominated Europe even without a military victory over France, which the British seemed to be trying to avoid at all costs. On the issue of neutrality it was reasonable to expect that England was not likely to be in a giving mood.

So on both sides there was little room for compromise. But if Lord Haldane had been able to negotiate with the Kaiser alone, there would have been at least a remote chance they might have come to some sort of an understanding.

But they could not negotiate alone. The constitution did not allow the Kaiser to function as an absolute ruler, like the Sultan.

Everything went wrong. Lord Haldane found himself talking to two separate German governments, to Bethmann Hollweg on the one side, to the Kaiser and Tirpitz on the other. Neither wanted to make substantial concessions unless the other side made them first. But in the end there was some real bargaining. There was talk about a British agreement to the purchase by Germany of colonial territories from Portugal and Belgium, in return for the curtailment of German naval estimates. This seemed to indicate at least the remote possibility a meaningful resolution. In fact, in the end Lord Haldane made a conditional offer.

But after he returned home, British experts analyzed Tirpitz's figures. They found the concessions offered to be ludicrously small. The British Cabinet met. Haldane's offer was slightly modified, but it made no difference. The negotiations collapsed. What had happened was the exact opposite from what the Germans had hoped for. British squadrons previously stationed in the Mediterranean were moved to the North Sea and French ships were moved south to replace them. This was a clear indication that in case of a war between Germany and France, the British were prepared to defend the French channel coast.

 The Kaiser said later he knew better than his diplomats how to handle the British. Who can blame him?

Chapter 17

Wednesday, July 29 (continued)

In the afternoon before the dinner in the British Embassy Zade had gone to the Kaiser Friedrich Museum on the Museum Island to think about something other than what to say to the Kaiser in the Moment of Truth. On the ground floor, in Rooms Nine and Ten, there was a collection of Persian and Arabian art, and particularly three Persian carpets that she had admired once before. She asked a guard whether they also had some Oudanian carpets on display to which the answer was, regrettably, no. The exchange was overheard by an affluent-looking Turkish gentleman whose name was Mehmed Bey.

"Ah, Ouda," he sighed. "The last time I was there I bought myself a fifteenth-century carpet, one of the best in my collection."

One thing led to another. They went to a restaurant to have a coffee. He was too well brought up to ask what a stunning beauty from Ouda in western clothes was doing alone in Berlin, but he was not too discreet to tell her why the C.U.P. had sent him, a distant cousin of the Sultan, to Berlin to explore ways in which Turkish industry could benefit from the work that was being done in German scientific institutions.

"We need closer ties with Germany," he said. "There's going to be a war. I studied engineering here. I hope there will be an alliance."

"It looks very much like it," Zade observed.

"So I understand. All the other powers are waiting to cut us up and pick up the pieces," he went on. "And whatever help they give us they use to strengthen the hold they have on us already. I've had something to do with trying to install a telephone system in Constantinople. You have no idea of the obstacles I ran into. And the few railway systems we have are all in foreign hands. The Germans are the least objectionable. And even though we are poor, we are buying more from them, and less from England and France. But sometimes I think we should stick to caravans. At least they are our own. I know that railways are ten times faster, never mind that they are ten times more expensive. But for us, as things are now, to modernize means to sell out. You people in Ouda must understand what I'm talking about."

> German investments in Turkey rose from 40 million marks in 1880 to more than 600 million in 1914, the bulk being invested in the Baghdad Railway. From 1897 to 1910, Turkey's imports from Germany rose from 6 percent to 21 percent, while over the same period its imports from Britain fell from 60 percent to 35 percent and those from France from 18 percent to 11 percent.
>
> Source: Fischer, p. 299.

"I happen to know that King Shahriyar is very much aware of the dilemma," Zade said.

"I have no doubt. I just hope that the coming war will create such turmoil that none of the old rules will apply at the end of it. The question is — will we survive until then? Well, as I was saying, if we have any sense, we will convince the Germans now that we can help them in their coming campaigns against the Russians and the British. In return they should help us establish scientific institutes like the ones they have here. I'm convinced we'll never be able to industrialize without proper scientific education and research. Do you know anything about the Kaiser Wilhelm Institutes?"

"As a matter of fact, I do," Zade said. No wonder she did — last year she had told King Shahriyar a story about them.

"You do? Have you heard of their new genius, Albert Einstein?"

"The gypsy?" she asked, laughing.

"That's the one." Mehmed Bey joined in her laughter. "I'm going to have dinner with him tonight. Why don't you come along?"

"I wish I could," she responded. "But I'm having dinner with His Majesty Kaiser Wilhelm II."

✺ The Gypsy ✺

Hail to Thee, my noble King! One day you, too, will be a model modern monarch like my Wilhelm! Like him, you will create your role out of the ingredients that are specifically your own and combine them with those you admire in others.

Tonight I want to tell you how Wilhelm proceeded to establish centres of scientific research in a manner that reflects the concept he has of his own role in the world. He sees himself as a traditional monarch who refuses to go along with the liberal, and in his view profoundly un-German fashion of democratic government. At the same time, he regards himself as a man of the future. He uses modern techniques to be seen by his people — trains, motorcars, photographs — in a way that none of his predecessors ever had. He promotes all the newest inventions in industry, manufacture and transportation. As Your Majesty knows by now, he understands that the new technologies are based on pure research, that military prowess and excellence in basic science are the two pillars of German greatness. He is glowing with pride that in the area of technology Germany is the undisputed leader in Europe, and he understands you can't be that without first having basic research. The British are very much aware that much of their artillery is using gun sights made in Berlin.

In recent decades, a number of giants in scientific discovery, invention and innovation have drawn the world's attention to Germany. People are talking about the second age of German genius — the first being the age of Goethe, Schiller and Beethoven a hundred years ago. To support their work, large, prestigious institutions for basic research were required. In 1911, the Kaiser gave his blessing to the establishment of research institutes outside the universities, modelled on American organizations like the Carnegie Institute. They were to be built in Dahlem, a suburb of Berlin, on a site near the end of the new underground. He would graciously allow them to be called Kaiser Wilhelm Institutes. They would have a mixed paternity: the state plus a semi-autonomous foundation in which scientists, industrialists and government bureaucrats would be represented. The foundation would conduct a massive effort at fundraising and the largest donors would be rewarded with the title of "senator," which gave them the right to wear senatorial gowns on ceremonial occasions. They would also receive a medal with the Kaiser's portrait on it. Moreover, they would have the honour to be invited to an annual reception in the Schloss.

In 1912, the Institute for Physical Chemistry and Electrochemistry was opened, headed by the renowned scientist-entrepreneur Fritz Haber, who was expected to receive the Nobel Prize for the fixation of nitrogen. To head the Institute for Physics, to be opened the following year, Haber suggested a uniquely gifted, in fact an amazing, German-born, theoretical physicist, thirty-four years old, whom he had known for two years. His name was Albert Einstein.

Einstein was an unlikely candidate. For one thing, he was a convinced pacifist. For another, he had left

Munich when he was fifteen because the autocratic militarist spirit of Wilhelmian Germany was profoundly distasteful to him. He followed his parents to Italy. Already at fifteen he disdained the idea of patriotism, any patriotism, and said he owed allegiance only to humanity. A year later he went to Switzerland to continue his education. Two years later he renounced his German citizenship to become Swiss. He seemed more like an artist than a scientist and his solitary, unconventional, humourous, highly original personality seemed to be that of a Bohemian. In fact, he told everybody he wanted to live like a gypsy. So people naturally called him "the gypsy." They even thought he looked like one. He never wears socks. He says that when, as a little boy, he did wear them, his big toe always made holes in them, so he gave them up. Most Prussians to him are philistines. He plays the violin and is Jewish, in a non-religious, free-thinking way. For that matter, Haber is also Jewish and so are many of the financial backers of the Institutes. In fact, thirty-five percent of the original contributions came from Jews. They were anxious to demonstrate their German patriotism and their faith in rationalism and science.

In 1905, when he was twenty-six years old, while working in the Patent Office in Berne, Albert Einstein had published five papers that physicists considered the work of a new Copernicus, the Polish astronomer in the early sixteenth century who turned current thinking upside down when he declared the sun, and not the earth, was the centre of the universe. One of Einstein's theories — I am quoting — "amalgamated space, time and matter into one fundamental unity." It overthrew all the axioms held sacrosanct by the experts and became known as the special theory of relativity. Please, Your Majesty, don't ask me to explain it.

In the summer of 1913, two of Germany's most renowned scientists — the aloof, tall Max Planck, who had developed a theory of his own, the quantum theory, and the jolly, plump chemist Walter Nernst — went to Zürich to sound out Einstein whether he might be willing to take over the new Institute for Physics if it was offered to him. Einstein knew both of them. The terms were extraordinarily attractive, quite unprecedented in fact. He would be working in the company of the most advanced, most imaginative scientists in the world, and he would not have to teach. A little later the story did the rounds that they persuaded him to accept the offer by telling him only a dozen people in the whole world understood the theory of relativity, and eight of them lived in Berlin.

However, going to Germany meant returning to an atmosphere he had found repulsive when he was a teenager, and that, from everything he had heard, was worse now. He certainly was not prepared to give up his Swiss nationality to become a German again. They told him it was no problem, he could retain his Swiss nationality. And the prospect of working with men such as Planck and Nernst and his friend Haber was very, very tempting. The conditions offered would give him full professorial status but left him completely free to do his research, unencumbered by worries about money and administrative duties.

Einstein said he needed a few hours to think it over. Whereupon, to make the best possible use of their time, they did what many tourists do: they took the train and the funicular up the Rigi Mountain. Before they left he told them he would meet them at the station on their return. They would be able to see right away, when they stepped down from their carriage, what he had decided. If the answer was yes, he would be carrying a red rose. If no, a white one.

He carried a red rose.

Now he is in Berlin, while the new Institute is being set up, living in an apartment in Dahlem, travelling each morning to his office in the Prussian Academy of Science, which is still housed in the Prussian State Library on Unter den Linden. When requested to tell the authorities what his needs were, he replied they consisted only of pencils and paper and he could buy those himself. He is determined to have nothing to do with bureaucracy.

Einstein was in a playful mood when he was asked the other day how a foreigner could become a full professor in Germany, which had always been considered absolutely impossible. Professors in Germany are civil servants. (Let us forget for a moment that membership in Prussian Academy, which came with the job, made him a Prussian citizen automatically.) To reply, he made up a story. He said one morning the Kaiser arrived at the Academy and asked to be introduced to Professor Einstein. He was brought forward. The Kaiser called him Professor. So he had to be professor.

Of course, as I say, the story is not true.
Albert Einstein has never met the Kaiser.

Chapter 18

Thursday, July 30

The one event that would make a general war, not merely a local war, irrevocable, so everybody had been told for weeks, was mobilization in Russia. As we have noted, according to a special issue of the Berliner Lokalanzeiger of Wednesday, July 29, yesterday, quoting a highly placed source — the Crown Prince himself, as everybody knew — this had already occurred. So, that seemed to be it. War with Russia was a certainty. But it still had to become official.

The time for Zade to make the irrevocable revocable was getting tight. The wreath-laying ceremony was to take place at four forty-five this afternoon. She was to report at four to the office of the Ober-Zeremonienmeister, the senior master of ceremonies, at the back of the Neue Schloss in Potsdam, to receive her instructions and to be given a wreath with a correctly inscribed white-and-black ribbon. (White and black — the colours of Prussia). And Manfred von Kosenburg had arranged the interview with His Majesty for tomorrow afternoon in the Neue Schloss, also at four forty-five. If neither of these two occasions yielded the requisite result and no deus ex machina turned up at the last minute out of the blue, she had come to Berlin for nothing and the match would finally be put to the cinder box. Her self-confidence remained unshaken. She was doing Allah's work. Allah did not want a world war.

The bell rang. Alois Penner came in with a letter in his hand addressed to His Excellency Ali Hassan, Ambassador of Ouda. The postman had mistakenly delivered it to the office of the Double Eagle on the third floor. The letter was of no interest. Penner's grey Franz-Joseph-Backenbart was dishevelled and he was clearly in need of company. Also, it was evident that the sight of a dazzling beauty from the Morgenland was balm for his deeply melancholy soul at a time of extreme stress.

Ali asked him to sit down.

"I think I have discovered what it is that is making everybody stupid and is about to push the world into the abyss." Penner lit a cigar. "It is that everybody wants to be as virile as that nauseatingly dashing Kaiser of the Sau-preussen, the piggish Prussians, over there." He pointed vaguely in the direction of the Schloss. "There is only one thing that can still save the world. And," he addressed himself to Ali — "only Your Excellency can do it. No one else."

"Yes?"

"You can organize a harem for him right away. Immediately. Straight out of the Morgenland. You know how to do it, you people have done it for centuries. Let him work off his virility. Three or four ladies a night. That would do it. The General Staff will follow, and we will have peace for ever. There's a doctor in my hometown of Vienna who knows exactly how the human mind works. He would approve of this prescription wholeheartedly."

He looked admiringly at Zade but he was too shy and too civilized to say anything.

"I think that is a very useful idea," Ali said solemnly. "I will study your proposal and see how it can be implemented."

"Oh, the Prussian Kaiser," Penner continued his lament, shaking his head in despair, "and his accursed, absolutely fatal Schneidigkeit. To be schlaff — do you know the word? It means slack — is an act of high treason, nearly as bad as being civilian. For being schlaff one is be put against the wall, blind-folded and shot. That's what will probably happen to that poor, miserable Chancellor of his, Bethmann-Hollweg, whom the Crown Prince and the generals loathe so much. Mind you, my Kaiser and his generals are no better. But we Austrians at least have the excuse of being in a state of galloping decay. Oh, the stupidity of it all!

I understand they've already bombarded Belgrad. Do they really think that by occupying Serbia they can prevent the Serbs and all the other nauseating minorities from tearing the empire apart, even if they first set fire to the world?"

Ali took this to be a rhetorical question.

"The Prussians up here are getting everything wrong. They think the Russians and the French are not prepared. Well, they are — as they will find out soon enough. They think everybody in Europe is still outraged by Sarajevo. Wrong. Only a few blood relatives of Franz Ferdinand and a dozen journalists in their pay still remember it. They think the English want peace above all. Well, they don't. They would not be sitting on a quarter of the world if they didn't love fighting. They're determined to crush Germany. The Sau-Preussen think it's worth risking a world war to save the Austro-Hungarian Empire as a Great Power, which is the greatest illusion of them all. Everybody in Vienna knows our multinational empire is too good to survive in an age of nationalist idiocy. Even the ancient Emperor knows it and nobody has ever accused him of having any brains. But we Austrians have honour. We think it is honourable to go down fighting. We think we've inherited this virtue from the Greeks and the Romans. Am I the only person on earth who thinks that this is stupid? Don't you people in Ouda also think it is stupid?"

"We certainly do," Ali laughed. "And we should know. We are so intelligent that we have been going down happily for centuries without firing a shot."

◆

The crowd had been waiting for His Majesty in the Lustgarten in Potsdam, next to the parade grounds, for more than two hours, while a band entertained them with military marches. The occasion was the ceremony honouring the memory of General Ludwig von Dansmarck, a hero of the Wars of Liberation against Napoleon, who had died exactly one hundred years ago. His statue was close to that of Field Marshal von Blücher and other war heroes, and not far from that of Friedrich Wilhelm I, the father of Frederick the Great.

The All Highest arrived with his retinue fifteen minutes late, at five o'clock, accompanied by the Zeremonienmeister and half a dozen uniformed officials, among them the distinguished neurologist Professor Hermann von Kosenburg in the uniform of the famous Lützow Grenadiers, a man with a remarkably amiable, sympathetic face and a white goatee. The crowd greeted His Majesty with excited cries of Hurra! and a joyous rendering of the imperial hymn Heil Dir im Siegerkranz, which has the same melody as God Save the King.

Wilhelm had been told that before he was to deliver a short speech from the ramp built for the occasion in front of the statue of Dansmarck, an Egyptian descendant of the general was to be presented to him. He was also informed that the lady was escorted by His Excellency Ali Hassan, the Ambassador of Ouda. His Majesty was to exchange of few private words with her. After that, the Zeremonienmeister was to introduce her to the public, whereupon she was to lay the wreath while the band played Ich hatt' einen Kameraden.

None of this worked out as arranged. On arrival the Kaiser stepped on the ramp. It was clear that he was in a state of acute nervous agitation. His movements were hurried and jerky. When the Zeremonienmeister went up to him to whisper something to him, he waved him aside with an impatient gesture with his good arm. The bandleader waited in vain for a signal to start. Not for a second did he take notice of the beautiful emissary of the Morgenland who was holding in her hand wreath that was about to become useless.

His Majesty cleared his throat.

"German men and women!" he began in the harsh metallic voice of the sergeants who had been drilling recruits on the parade grounds in the immediate proximity of the Lustgarten since the days of Friedrich Wilhelm I. "I herewith swear solemnly that, unless we can still stop our enemies from going through with their diabolical plans, in the days and weeks to come Germans will live up to the glorious example the brave General Helmut von Dansmarck set a hundred years ago. It was thanks to him and his fellow soldiers that Prussia recovered gloriously from the humiliation she had suffered when Napoleon Bonaparte crushed Frederick's army in the Battle of Jena. I herewith give you my sacred word of honour that if a war is indeed forced on us, I will avenge the even greater humiliation the world seems to be determined to inflict on us. If this should indeed occur, I assure you we will emerge from it as victoriously as we did on the battlefields of Leipzig and Waterloo."

For a moment it looked as though the Kaiser was about to lose his balance. There was no wall and no tree against which he could lean. One of his adjutants rushed forward to support him, but His Majesty gestured him aside impatiently, cleared his throat again and continued as though nothing had happened.

"The last word has not yet been spoken," he said, his voice hoarser than before. "Russian mobilization can still be reversed, whatever people are saying. I have made a final appeal to the Tsar. But if it is too late, then one thing becomes crystal clear. England, Russia and France have agreed among themselves to use the local, easily soluble Austro-Serbian conflict as pretext to wage a war of annihilation against us. So, unless there is a last-minute miracle, in spite of all the efforts our politicians have made to prevent it, the encirclement of Germany has finally become an accomplished fact. Let me herewith tell this to the world. Come what may, we will keep faith with the old and honourable

Emperor of Austria. If our adversaries expect us at this last minute to betray our allies and leave them to the tender mercy of Russia, then they don't know who we are and what we stand for."

When he stepped down from the ramp the Kaiser nearly stumbled. This time he accepted the arm of Professor von Kosenburg while the crowd once again shouted Hurra! and the band played Fridericus Rex, Unser König und Herr.

Why Was His Majesty in Such a Good Mood?

This is the question, my revered Master, that I am asking you to answer tonight. By now you know Wilhelm well, you know what pleases him and what displeases him, you know with what courage and zest he has overcome the many misfortunes he has had to suffer. And you know how frustrated — no, worse, how suicidal he feels — whenever he feels betrayed.

The year 1913 was his Silver Jubilee, marking twenty-five years on the throne. The date of this story was Tuesday, July 8, 1913, the place the port of Hamburg and the occasion the launching of the mighty Imperator, the 54,000-ton luxury superliner belonging to his friend Albert Ballin, the master of the Hamburg-Amerika Line, by now the largest shipping company in the world. To Wilhelm and to much of the German public, this ship was triumphant proof of Germany's commercial and technological prowess, although there were plenty of people who mumbled that it was actually a manifestation of effete snobbishness and vulgarity.

This sort of occasion, of course, is inherently pleasant, but this does not in itself explain the exuberantly high spirits Wilhelm displayed. In the evening he sat in the smoking room with a few of the most powerful industrialists and bankers in Germany, among them Walther Rathenau, whom I have mentioned to you before. I will have more to say about him in a few minutes. They talked about the war — the Second Balkan War — certainly not a subject of merriment. On the contrary, everybody understood it may well turn out to be the prelude to something infinitely more horrible. The Kaiser also did what he often does when he is in a particularly jovial mood — he told daring jokes that cannot be told in the presence of ladies, jokes of the kind that schoolboys and lonely soldiers in infidel Europe, cut off from their wives and girlfriends, tell each other at night in the barracks and roar with laughter. He told some of them in English with an Irish accent. Of course such jokes embarrassed the exalted gentlemen present, even though they were used to the Kaiser's frequent lapses of this sort, and occasionally even found them lovable, but on this occasion none of them knew how to signal to the All Highest that he should please cease and desist. As Your Majesty knows, Muslims are also often equally tasteless.

Your Majesty, I regret that I cannot repeat any of the jokes to you. No one has conveyed them to me. All I can tell you for sure is that one of them was about a Swedish countess who each time her husband made love to her had twins. Frankly, I don't see what is funny about that. Do you?

Perhaps a little more significant was what Wilhelm had to say about the situation in the Balkans. In the First Balkan War, an alliance between the Bulgarians, Serbs, Montenegrans and Greeks, following a Russian initiative, scored decisive victories over Turkey. It required delicate diplomatic efforts by the Great Powers, especially England and Germany, to prevent a conflagration. Before it was over, in November 1912, Russia, France and Austria had all mobilized. Finally, in the Treaty of London of May 1913, Turkey ceded to the victorious allies large parts of the Ottoman Balkan Empire, but left a number of claims unsettled. The treaty was followed by a number of bitter disputes over various regions of Macedonia that Greece, Bulgaria, Serbia, Bulgaria and Rumania each coveted. The Tsar proposed arbitration, but on June 15, less than a month before the Imperator was launched, Ferdinand, King of Bulgaria, without consulting his national assembly, attacked Serbian and Greek positions. He had been a Prince of Saxe Coburg Gotha and was therefore a relative of the Kaiser, who, however, together with the rest of the world, was appalled by this shameless assault.

Now, it so happened that Wilhelm had a strong dislike of his aggressive relative. In January 1910, Ferdinand had visited Berlin and, in a moment of jovial familiarity, Wilhelm slapped him hard on the behind. The Monarch was so furious that he left Germany immediately and, once back home in Sofia, showed his anger by switching his orders for munitions from Krupp to a French firm.

In the smoking room of the Imperator, apart from telling dubious stories that amused nobody but himself, Wilhelm spoke freely about the situation created by Ferdinand. Now he had the total undivided attention of his audience. He had very little sympathy for the Turks, he said. He blamed them for not making concessions in good time. In any case, he had no use for the revolutionary government in Constantinople and he thought the days of Turkish rule in Europe were definitely over. He had refused to become a party to any action that might prevent the formerly Ottoman Balkan states from obtaining the independence he thought they deserved, and he would do nothing to help his Austrian allies who felt threatened by their newly strengthened and revitalized eastern neighbours. He knew that the Austrians and Hungarians were particularly worried about the Serbs, who everybody knew were close to the Russians. However, the terms of the German alliance with Austria-Hungary required German assistance only if Russia attacked without provocation, and that was not likely to happen. Not this time, anyway. If, on the other hand, Austria-Hungary provoked a Russian attack, the terms of the alliance certainly did not require Germany to come to their assistance. Still, obviously the situation was extremely dangerous and could easily involve Germany in a war against Russia and Russia's allies, the French. Fortunately, the Russians persuaded the Serbs not to make any demands on Vienna affecting interests they knew Vienna considered vital, and German diplomats had successfully exercised a moderating influence on the Austro-Hungarians. But, whatever was happening in the Balkans, His Majesty felt that in the last few months a hostile coalition was being formed to encircle Germany, ready to strike.

So, in short, there was no reason at all for the Kaiser to be in such a good mood. His generals thought the sooner war broke out the better, and they often said behind his back — he always heard about it afterwards, he said — that in 1905 and in 1911, when Germany should have fought, he caved in. No Supreme War Lord, even if he is not a Prussian, wants to be called a coward. Why then was the Kaiser so cheerful?

It was certainly not because of anything the intensely serious Walther Rathenau said. Wilhelm had great respect for the son and heir of the self-made Emil Rathenau, the founder of the A.E.G., die Allgemeine Elektrizitäts Gesellschaft, Germany's leading electricity company. Walther Rathenau was an electrical engineer with huge ambition who sat on seventy boards and knew everybody of importance all over Europe. He was one of the Kaiser-Juden, the wealthy, patriotic, well-connected Jews whose Jewishness His Majesty was prepared to overlook. On one occasion, the Kaiser said he would make him a lieutenant if he got himself baptized, but Rathenau proudly refused. He thought of himself, and was regarded by many, as a monarch in his own right, in the world of high finance, high intellect and high culture. He wrote books on many important subjects. His erudition seemed to be so phenomenal that even those close to him — no one was very close — were sometimes not quite sure whether he did not make up some of the things he said and wrote.

Now, did this impeccably dressed, bald-headed great thinker, with his high forehead, piercing eyes, well-trimmed goatee and famous velvety baritone voice, who was never angry and who spoke so magnificently that every word could be printed and preserved for posterity, say anything that might have put His Majesty in such high spirits?

Certainly not. Rathenau's purpose, in any case, was always to fascinate and enlighten others, never to make them feel better. This time he certainly did not say anything memorable about anything. Not even about the concept of "The Realm of the Soul," of which he wrote extensively. He was a solid capitalist who believed in limiting the acquisitiveness of his fellow capitalists in favour of the public good. He was prepared to tolerate the common people provided he did not have to associate with anybody outside his admittedly enormous circle of acquaintances. He was a Jew who wished he was not an "oriental" (a word he often used to describe qualities in himself of which he was not proud), who preferred blond people to dark people and who was remote from — and sometimes even distinctly cool towards — other Jews. He had little interest in Jewish beliefs and traditions, though he knew a good deal about them. He thought for a long time Captain Dreyfus was guilty and Émile Zola merely a man with romantic illusions. He was a liberal who believed in a disciplined, authoritarian, an almost socialist Prussian monarchy. He hated war, but would welcome it if he thought it would serve the Fatherland. He longed for fame and power and relished the company of poets, painters, playwrights and actors. He was a great traveller who had been to Africa twice. He was a bachelor who, as far as anybody could tell, only seemed to have platonic affairs, who led a life crowded with business meetings and elegant dinners, but who relished the time he spent alone, or with a few carefully chosen people, in his spacious villa — it was actually a castle — in Freienwalde, an hour by car out of Berlin. The villa was an architectural gem built for Queen Friederike

Luise in 1798, the widow of the Prussian king Friedrich Wilhelm II, the successor to Frederick the Great. Rathenau acquired it in 1909 and had it restored. It contained a spinet that — so we were told — used to belong to Beethoven.

The Kaiser was familiar with Rathenau's views on Weltpolitik. He remembered well that two days after Lord Haldane departed from Berlin in February 1912 he described to Rathenau his plan for a "United States of Europe" — against America and Japan. Such an arrangement should include France, he said. He thought the British might well be attracted to such a plan as well. In any case, it would get the idea across to them that they had more important rivals than Germany.

Rathenau's ideas on this subject, which he had submitted to Bethmann Hollweg in writing in 1911, were a little more modest. He thought of a customs union with Austria, Switzerland, Italy, Belgium and the Netherlands, and also advocated closer political ties with these countries. The political unification of Europe — under German leadership, that was understood — was far more feasible, he thought, than disarmament, which he considered utopian. In the end he, too, hoped for an alliance with England, with the objective, among other things, of obtaining for Germany a stronger presence in Central Africa and in the Near East.

Your Majesty, I have not been fair with you. I have asked you to solve the puzzle why Wilhelm was in such a good mood on July 8, 1913, at the launching of the Imperator. I have not given you any clues at all. Or hardly any. All I have done was to give you reasons why he should be deeply depressed and frightened of the future.

All right. I will tell you why he was in such a good mood. Wilhelm had just heard that his detested relative, King Ferdinand of Bulgaria, who had unleashed the Second Balkan War, had suffered serious defeats on the battlefield. Wilhelm had every reason to be pleased with himself for having rejected Austria's request to support Bulgaria.

He did not know as yet that at the end of the month, after Rumania and Turkey had joined Serbia and Greece in their coalition against Bulgaria, Ferdinand would have to capitulate and, at the forthcoming peace settlement, hand back to Turkey three territories he had seized in the First Balkan War.

Would Your Majesty not also be in a good mood if events proved you right in such a spectacular way?

Chapter 19

Friday, July 31

After the debacle in the Potsdam Lustgarten, during which Zade had not even succeeded in making eye contact with the Kaiser, there was one last chance for an encounter before it was too late — the meeting His Majesty had requested through the Crown Prince with the author of the stories. It went without saying that at this time of ultimate stress, when the All Highest held the world's fate in his hand, the chances for such a meeting were less than negligible. Zade and Ali Hassan would have given up hope altogether had not Manfred von Kosenburg phoned them repeatedly during the last few days to tell them that His Majesty ordered the immediate distribution of the stories abroad and therefore had to make final arrangements with Zade or her representatives immediately. The meeting would not take longer than two or three minutes, he said. Such propaganda he thought was absolutely critical at a time when his enemies were burning him in effigy. Manfred asked Zade and Ali to come to his office at the back of the Schloss in Berlin — not the Neue Palais in Potsdam — at six forty-five p.m. on Saturday, August 1st, to be presented to the Kaiser at seven. This was her last chance, Zade thought, making a determined effort to retain her conviction that in the end Allah would not permit her to fail.

Jointly and separately, Alois Penner, Alphonse Picard and Jonathan Lind reported to Ali and Zade the momentous events that were shaking the world throughout the day. They described how millions of men on both sides, including socialists, had quickly returned from their summer holidays, whipped up by waves of hectic patriotism, and prepared for tearful farewell scenes on Europe's major railway platforms.

Penner reported that Vienna ordered general mobilization. Picard told them that the entente powers could mobilize more than twice the number of men than the Germans and Austrians, and added that therefore for the Germans and Austrians only the utmost speed could compensate for the discrepancy in relative manpower. He had also heard that the French Ministerial Council had decided to order mobilization tomorrow, Saturday. Lind could not get over his amazement that Bethmann Hollweg was still not giving up and strongly urged the Austrians to have last-minute talks with Saint Petersburg. To refuse to have such talks, the Chancellor desperately pleaded, would amount to a provocation that would remove the last chance for peace. Lind had also heard that at two that afternoon the Kaiser sent a final message to his cousin the Tsar.

> From Kaiser Wilhelm to Tsar Nicholas: No one is threatening the honour or might of Russia, which presumably is in a position to await the results of my efforts to mediate. You can still preserve the peace of Europe if you call a halt to the military measures that are directed against Austria-Hungary and us.

This communication, Lind had heard, crossed one from the Tsar to the Kaiser saying that it was technically impossible to put a stop to the mobilization. But he was giving the Kaiser his solemn word of honour that his troops would not commit any provocative acts while negotiations with Austria about Serbia were continuing.

But it was clear to one and all that no such negotiations were continuing.

The rest of the day's developments reached the Ouda Embassy in bits and pieces. It soon became clear that Helmuth von Moltke and his Austrian counterpart, Conrad von Hötzendorf, had decided that Bethmann Hollweg's policy of keeping the Balkan war localized and splitting the entente had finally collapsed. So they took matters into their own hands. At noon, it was officially confirmed in Berlin that Russia had mobilized. One hour later, the Kaiser proclaimed a "state of imminent war." He was not quite ready yet to order general mobilization. In Germany, such a move was the equivalent of a declaration of war.

At four, the Kaiser summoned Moltke to the Schloss. During the following six hours an incredible drama unfolded. In the presence of Bethmann Hollweg, whose knees literally trembled, of Erich von Falkenhayn, the Minister of War, and of General Hans von Plessen, one of the Kaiser's aide-de-camps, and of a few others, the highly agitated Kaiser raised strong objections to what he had heard were Moltke's immediate intentions. He had received excellent news from King George, he said, that changed the situation entirely. England would not only remain neutral but would also prevent France from coming to Russia's assistance. Under these circumstances, it was logical to throw the whole weight of the German army against Russia alone. No, said Moltke. He insisted the General Staff's existing plan be carried out in the East and in the West, to avoid the greatest conceivable catastrophe. He did not believe in the report from London and would not tolerate any change, insisting on immediate mobilization. The Kaiser saw no reason not to sign that, and did so. Now, Moltke said he would act in accordance with the procedures previously adopted, meaning mobilization east and west. The signed mobilization order in hand, he left the room, leaving the others behind in a state of utter confusion. His car was waiting for him.

Those assembled in the Ouda Embassy could not believe what they had heard — the Kaiser of Germany deciding that he was actually the All Highest and therefore entitled to act against his own General Staff. This was absolutely unprecedented. It simply could not be true. But they soon decided it was true.

So where did Moltke go after he left the Schloss? Ali and Zade wanted to know. The answer — to the offices of the General Staff. But he did not reach them. His car was stopped en route by one of the Kaiser's cars. He was summoned back. Even more excited than before, the Kaiser showed him a new telegram from England and said he interpreted it with absolute certainty as meaning that England and France would remain neutral. The army had to be ordered immediately not to proceed in the West. Moltke replied that one could not put before any army the alternative between a command and a countercommand, clearly meaning such an order could not be given. The Kaiser ignored him and turned to his military adjutant and ordered him to convey to the headquarters of the Sixteenth Division in Trier not to march into Luxembourg. Moltke proceeded to his home once again, paralyzed. He sat down at his desk and declared to his second-in-command he could not for the moment give any orders of any kind. After a few minutes, a messenger arrived from the Kaiser, with the order to Trier to be signed. Moltke refused to sign. At eleven o'clock, after having retired to bed, the Kaiser personally phoned him and summon him back to the Schloss. Now, in a dressing gown, he announced everything had changed again. Disaster was at hand. He had received another telegram from King George. The previous information, the King stated, had been based on a misunderstanding. He had not given any undertaking whatsoever, either in his own name or in the name of France.

"Now," the royal message concluded, "you can do whatever you want."

✦

"It is my view that the truth is at last coming out," Jonathan

Lind declared, at the end of the memorable day. "Wilhelm II of Germany is being sent to purgatory as the scapegoat for Bismarck's crime."

The two Oudanians did not understand.

"The crime was to create a state to suit him, and him alone, out of tune with the spirit of the times. He knew it, and he knew that his successors would have to take the blame for it. Wilhelm's father, Kaiser Friedrich III, quite rightly called Bismarck's creation 'organized chaos.' Since Bismarck's dismissal, there has been a universal feeling, under the surface, that nothing could be done to hold up the approaching Götterdämmerung."

"The what?" Zade asked.

"Collapse. Total collapse. With fire and brimstone."

"Aren't you a being a trifle over-dramatic?" Ali smiled. "Remember you are a cricket-playing Englishman."

"Not a bit of it," Lind replied. "If the events that are taking place aren't dramatic, what is? Listen to what I think. For all we know, war has already been declared. If not, this is likely to happen tomorrow. Whether or not the Kaiser's Germany wins, it cannot survive. This is not the Kaiser's fault. He does the best he can. It is Bismarck's fault for having created a soldier-state, a semi-absolutist militarist monster-state, after successfully provoking and winning three wars, a state with a constitution custom-made for himself and an emperor who did not want to be emperor, who wanted to remain King of Prussia and had to be dragged along. Old Wilhelm no doubt had premonitions of disaster. He probably thought that by 1870 Prussia had conquered enough territory and did not need to conquer the rest of Germany as well to enable him to head a new, second Reich. Now, it seems to me to be perfectly clear that what is happening at this moment will bring it to an end, one way or another, whether they win this war nor not. According to Bismarck's self-serving blueprint, it is supposed to be run by a monarch and his chancellor, and nobody else. Unless the chancellor is a Bismarck, and thank God there's only one of them every five hundred years, no wonder the monarch's personal friends fill the vacuum and take over. The Reich is no more workable in the twentieth century than the Ottoman Empire, where the Sultan also works solely on the advice of a Grand Vizier."

Lind did not know that Zade was the daughter of Ouda's Grand Vizier. There was no reason for her to point it out.

"Are you saying Bismarck's successors are now following his example and provoking another war?" Ali asked.

"No doubt the generals would like to. In a soldier-state generals usually have, let us say, a certain importance. 'Now or never,' they have been saying for years. And the Kaiser is in their hands. But not entirely. In the end, he has the last word. He is the Supreme Commander-in-Chief. I've been saying for years that if English politicians had been a little more flexible and far-sighted, they could easily have managed him. There was never anything difficult about understanding him! The Indians are far more difficult to understand, and so are the Burmese, and the Sudanese, and the Egyptians — the whole lot.

And the German generals are also quite easy to understand. They are behaving the way generals do everywhere. Of course, they are happy that it's the Austrians who are doing the provoking for them. The Germans have been egging them along. For the Tsar, it's war or revolution. I don't know what it is for the French. I have never understood them. If I were the Kaiser, I would give them Alsace and Lorraine and have it done with, once and for all. Most of their inhabitants prefer the French anyway. It's cheaper than a war."

Lind had a sudden coughing spell. Zade gave him a glass of water.

"Well, as I say, Bismarck needed a scapegoat for the disaster he saw coming, sooner or later. Wilhelm was the obvious candidate. He despised him from the moment he first set eyes on him. Much too soft, he thought, and far too English. So Bismarck made as much trouble as he could between him and his English mother. And once Wilhelm was on the throne, Bismarck watched as — predictably, he thought — Wilhelm covered up his almost feminine softness with tough talk and sabre-rattling and surrounded himself with the wrong kind of friends and — horror of horrors! — wanted to be Emperor of the Poor, opening the doors, my God! to Social Democrats! By then it was clear to Bismarck that Wilhelm had to be destroyed, whatever the consequences. Après moi le déluge. That is what so-called Great Men usually say at the end of their lives.

"Don't forget, Bismarck was one of history's great haters. He could not forgive the young Kaiser for dismissing him. First he only despised him. After being dismissed, he hated him — and he lived for another seven years. He decided to destroy Wilhelm through his friends."

Lind sneezed. He took a handkerchief out of his left sleeve. The two Oudanians had never before seen that strange English custom. He blew his nose, loudly.

"Yes," he said, "it is through them that he took his revenge. He knew a lot of newspapermen. He had mastered the art of influencing the press — mostly by flattery, often by bribery. Enormous prestige, superior intelligence, grand style, vast experience, contempt for almost everybody and congenital malice gave him an unsurpassable power over people. He chose as his instrument a clever, courageous, idealistic young journalist by the name of Maximilian Harden, who worshipped him and deeply regretted that Wilhelm did not live up to his idol Bismarck's lofty standards. Harden was an assimilated, patriotic Jew. A right-wing Jew, not, like most others — unless they were rich — a left-wing Jew. He was originally an actor whose real name was Ernst

Witkowski."

"A Jew?" Ali frowned. "Isn't that rather surprising?"

"Not at all. Bismarck understood that Harden wanted to compensate for being a Jew by being more German than the Germans. He was exactly the type who would work relentlessly and loyally to serve Bismarck's purposes. Harden identified with the Kaiser, and thought he could help him do better. Bismarck suggested to him that, to achieve this, he should launch a crusade to get rid of those dreadful friends of his. The technical term he and others used for them was the 'Camarilla.' That exotic word gave it just the right operatic overtones. The Camarilla he thought was a group composed of the wrong kind of people, and was dominated by one of them, the Kaiser's closest friend, his only friend, his bosom friend."

"Prince Philipp von Eulenburg," Zade volunteered.

Jonathan Lind opened his eyes wide.

"How did you know?"

"We Oudanians are well informed," she replied, inspecting her fingernails.

"That is indeed splendid. One day in 1892, two years after Bismarck's retirement, Harden made a pilgrimage to Friedrichsruh, Bismarck's estate near Hamburg. On that occasion the crusade was launched. In an attempt of reconciliation with the Great Man, the Kaiser had sent him a rare bottle of wine, Steinberger Kabinett 1862. Malice made Bismarck supremely inventive. To give Harden's crusade special significance, and of course to flatter the young crusader, they drank the bottle together. Harden later quoted Bismarck as saying on that occasion that 'it would be great misfortune for the monarchy and for our unity if we now had to endure absolutist relapses, such as rule by Camarilla, or even worse, by "The Eternal Feminine."'"

That stumped the Oudanians.

"Oh, I'm sorry." Lind blew his nose again. "That is a quote from

Goethe's Faust. I expect you don't learn that in school in Ouda. The last line of Part One, to be precise, when Faust, who was solely responsible for the death of his lady and their child, was welcomed into Heaven where he was to be entertained by 'The Eternal Feminine' for eternity. The Germans have spent nearly a hundred years trying to figure out what Goethe meant. But it is crystal clear what Bismarck meant. He wanted Harden to tell the world in a series of article to be published in his journal Die Zukunft [The Future] that there was something feminine about the Kaiser's bosom friend Philipp von Eulenburg, creating the impression — though he never said so — that the Kaiser himself was in some way suspect. If I may stop beating around the bush, Bismarck had evidence in his pocket that Eulenburg was an offender against Paragraph 175 of the German Criminal Code."

"What, if I may ask, does Paragraph 175 say?" Zade asked.

"The paragraph declares homosexual practices criminal acts."

She opened her mouth but was unable to utter a word. Homosexuality was as taboo in the Muslim world as in the infidel world. And the idea that the Kaiser himself ...

"Oh no!" Ali groaned.

Lind had never before heard Ali groan.

"You seem to be a little surprised, my friend."

"I certainly am. I read about that scandal but didn't really understand what it was about. So I paid no attention and then forgot all about it. That is why I did not include it when I prepared the packages I sent to Zade for her stories."

"I don't know what you're talking about," Lind said grumpily. There was no reason for him to be aware of Zade's thousand and one nights with King Shahriyar.

Zade was still speechless. She knew, of course, what the Koran said about homosexuals, and she had heard that they were men who seemed to be perfectly normal but who preferred men to women. She also knew about the curious ways they had to express their feelings for each other, but she could not remember ever coming across any. And now, what was this Englishman saying? That the Kaiser himself...?

"What is wrong, may I ask?" Lind asked her. "Are you shocked?"

"Oh no, not at all," she responded, perhaps a bit too quickly. "But you're a little too fast for me. Did you say the Kaiser himself offended against that, what was it? Paragraph hundred and —"

"Seventy-five. No, no, I didn't say that. Bismarck never pointed the finger at the Kaiser himself. He asked Harden to destroy the Kaiser through his friends, mainly Eulenburg. In the years after 1892 Harden went into this matter systematically, like a terrier, collecting evidence against Eulenburg, and found plenty — especially in connection with relationships with members of the lower classes. Now, since you ask, I have to tell you that Harden thought, rightly or wrongly, that he had enough evidence against the Kaiser himself to force him to abdicate, but he never used it, and I don't know of anybody who has seen it. I myself have no opinion at all on the subject. What do I know? In England not so very long ago, there was a lot of fuss about Oscar Wilde. I never got excited about that either. There's always a great amount of hysteria and hypocrisy connected with that sort of thing. At Eton boys get a good caning if they are discovered fooling around with other boys. That always seemed to me a very sensible way of dealing with it. Clean and honest. And possibly even effective — who knows? I must add that to Bismarck and all others who were running a society that worshipped masculine, martial virtues, homosexuality was the number one crime. Compared to it, murder was innocent child's play. Even though in a country run by soldiers that excluded women from having anything to do with anything important other than raising children homosexuality is bound to be very common. As a matter of fact, Maximilian Harden was more tolerant about it than most people. He was acquainted with the scientific literature and took the view that homosexuals were by no means vile persons but that homosexuality was an illness, an illness that by its nature disqualified men from having sound political judgement. Therefore those afflicted should be prevented from exercising political power. Since homosexuals had to conceal their true nature, he thought, dishonesty was built into their habits of thinking and acting. It was on that basis that he launched an eventually successful campaign in the Zukunft to have Eulenburg indicted. But, of course, nobody ever doubted that the real target was the Kaiser."

There was silence.

"So what did the Kaiser say when he heard about the campaign against his friend?" Ali asked at last.

"That was a very tricky problem, how to break the news to him. In the end, the Crown Prince was chosen as the man to show him the articles in Zukunft written by Maximilian Harden. It must have been quite a scene. Poor Wilhelm, Bismarck's sacrificial lamb! His Majesty was furious that nobody had told him before. Blow followed blow. One could not help grieving for him. He lost that old bounce of his for ever."

Lind uttered a deep sigh.

"Let me tell you more. You have heard of Holstein?"

"The Grey Eminence."

"Exactly, madame. You amaze me. Two years earlier Harden and Holstein had joined forces in their campaign against Eulenburg. Though Harden knew that there had already been distinct cooling off in the friendship between Eulenburg and the Kaiser, he took the view that Eulenburg and his friends continued to exercise a disastrous influence over him. He thought the Kaiser should have gone to war against the entente over Morocco, and would have done so if he had not received the opposite advice from his soft, feminine friends. These friends were dangerous to the Fatherland, he declared. In 1907, on April 6, at the height of his campaign, Harden wrote an editorial with the caption 'Wilhelm the Peace Lover,' and called him a timid pacifist, unqualified to rule.

Can you imagine what that meant? Newspapers of all kinds joined the battle, all over the country. There is relative freedom of the press in Germany, you know, rather surprising in a militarist state. The satirical magazines had a heyday, comparing Wilhelm's Germany with the last days of decadent Rome. The political excitement reminded those in the know of the Dreyfus affair in France a few years ago, with the vast difference that homosexuality, unlike anti-Semitism, is a subject that is rarely discussed openly. But the whole thing became wide open when the lawsuits against Eulenburg began. Between 1906 and 1909, there were six of them altogether, criminal and civil. At the height of the scandal some journalists thought it would lead either to the Kaiser's abdication or to a trumped-up war. A homosexual French friend of Eulenburg's, Raymond Lecomte, was drawn into the affair, spicing the story with an agreeable element of espionage. At the time, Lecomte was counsellor at the French embassy in Berlin. Incidentally, Lecomte is an uncle of Jean Cocteau, the young playwright who is now making a name for himself in Paris. In 1906, in Liebenberg, Eulenburg had introduced Lecomte to the Kaiser. Lecomte accompanied His Majesty on a walk through the woods. Our talkative Wilhelm told him he had no intention of going to war over Morocco. Lecomte promptly passed this on to his chief. If the public ever demanded proof of the danger that cesspool Liebenberg posed to the Fatherland, there it was. There was obviously a direct line between homosexuality and high treason."

"Was Eulenburg convicted?" Ali asked.

"Never. His health broke down. He had to be carried into the court-room on a stretcher. He now lives quietly in Liebenberg, in seclusion."

"And Harden?"

"He lost some proceedings and won some. In the end, he came through the ordeal, severely bruised but with his honour intact."

"And the Kaiser?"

"Ah, the poor Kaiser," Lind sighed deeply. "He must have sensed that he was the scapegoat for other people's sins. His popularity sank to the bottom. That was the only reason why the otherwise insignificant Daily Telegraph affair in the same year assumed such gigantic proportions."

"But he did not abdicate," Zade remembered, her mind firmly fixed on the fateful appointment with the All Highest tomorrow.

Chapter 20

Saturday, August 1

Ali had not said his morning prayers at the mosque in Neukölln since Tuesday, July 7, the day after Zade had arrived, more than three weeks ago. Today, the day in which the object of her journey from Ouda was to be achieved, they went again, at seven in the morning. After the prayers the mullah, the bearded old man from Cyprus, joined them once again for coffee, smoking his pipe, in the small open-air café in the Hermannstrasse where Zade was waiting for Ali. At the other two tables excited men in work clothes were conducting a heated argument. They seemed unhappy.

"This isn't Potsdam," the mullah said with wry amusement. "I fail to see much enthusiasm here. I wonder whether in Constantinople they're more cheerful this morning."

"Probably," Ali smiled. "If you don't know what to do to prevent going under, war is always a good idea. What's the latest?"

"Too early for the morning papers," the old man said. "But you can guess. The Russian generals will proceed with their mobilization. Never mind what the Tsar says. Which means war in the east is a certainty. And the French won't promise to remain neutral. So war with them is a certainty, too. It's just a question of time at what moment the Germans will march. The sooner the better, they say. This is what they have been waiting for. War — first against the French, then against the Russians. They'll be home by Christmas, they hope. The Austrians and the Serbs have been duly forgotten. And England is waiting to see whether the King of Belgium will let the Germans go through. If he won't and the Belgians defy him, the English will join in. But first, the Germans will be at war with France. That will be a good start."

"Unless somebody stops them," Ali Hassan said.

"Who?" The mullah blew smoke rings in the air. "Their Pope?"

•

Having written One Thousand and One Stories about the Kaiser, Zade knew him — almost — intimately. But now a new element had been added, the homosexuality element, an element outside her direct experience.

"It seems," she said to Ali in the horse-drawn Droschke on the way back to the Ouda Embassy in the Luisenstrasse, "that when that man Harden went after Eulenburg he thought he also had evidence against Wilhelm. What do you make of that?"

"I would ignore it," Ali responded. "Why do you ask? Are you worried? For Heaven's sake, the man fathered six sons and one daughter!"

"Yes, but a great emperor is supposed to have mistresses. I know he doesn't have any. Hasn't had any since he came on the throne. Yes, frankly, I am worried."

"No need," Ali assured her. "On the contrary. Suppose Harden was right. Suppose Wilhelm suspects that he was drawn to Eulenburg and the Liebenberg circle because, deep down, he, too, was just a little bit effeminate. He may think that this is also the reason why he feels so much more at home with tall, strong, clean-looking Prussian soldiers than with anybody else. If he suspects such a thing, he would fight it tooth and nail. As a matter of fact, he would be scared to death. It's the one thing a virile Prussian king must not be — homosexual — even if he knows that his great hero, Frederick the Great, was definitely homosexual. But that was long ago, at another time. For him, the Supreme Commander of a modern soldier-state, being homosexual would be even worse than being a Frenchman, or a Jew. So he would have to use every opportunity to prove to himself that he likes women better than men."

This argument was put with such conviction, and seemed so logical, that Zade banished all doubts from her mind.

The next thing to do was to telephone Baron Edgar von Toplitz, one of the Berlin bankers most actively engaged in financing Germany's economic expansion in the Near East. There had never been any doubt in Ali's mind that the ideal place where the All Highest and Zade would save the world was the Villa Suleika near the Tiergarten. The Baron had built it to celebrate Germany's profound affinity with Muslim culture. (Suleika was Hatem's beloved in Goethe's Westöstliche Diwan, Germany's poetic miniature version of A Thousand and One Nights.) The Baron, who was not married, was famous in Berlin for his wit and much admired for the generous presents of precious jewellery he gave to Berlin society's most elegant beauties, to reward them for keeping him agreeable company during the day and night. It was also known that he was fearless in expressing criticism, openly and frequently, of the Kaiser's "highly dangerous" submission to the generals.

Ali felt that he knew him well enough to take him into his confidence. He did not misjudge him. If there was any chance at all that war could be avoided, even now, the baron exclaimed enthusiastically, this was it. It was nothing less than his sacred patriotic duty to do all he could to help. His staff would be given appropriate instructions immediately. Ali said that, if everything went according to plan, the Kaiser should be expected between seven and eight tonight.

The Villa Suleika contained elements of the famous az-Zahra pleasure palace in Andalusia, built in the tenth century during the reign of Abd-ur-Rahman III. The villa was constructed in accordance with the basic principles of Islamic architecture. Its most striking feature was the beauty of its interior space, above all the magnificent courtyard, very different from the bare, windowless, undecorated high exterior walls. It was primarily this covered courtyard that made the Villa Suleika remarkable.

Baron von Toplitz never tired of talking about the Andalusian pleasure palace that was his model. He had all the figures in his head. Four hundred camels belonging to the Sultan were used to carry to Andalusia more than four thousand columns from four places — from Rome, from what is now France, from Constantinople, and from the ruins of Carthage — yes, Carthage! — came one thousand thirteen blocks of marble, mostly coloured green and rose. One of the wonders of the pleasure palace, the Baron often told his guests, was the Hall of Caliphs, with its world-famous golden roof. Unfortunately, he was not quite rich enough to replicate it in his Villa Suleika. But he enjoyed showing the pictures, and usually could not help pointing out that in his house, contrary to those inhabited by actual Muslims, male and female guests were not necessarily entertained separately.

Ali had often been invited to the Baron's receptions, major social events in Berlin's diplomatic and social worlds and often attended by the Kaiser himself. The last time he was there — the Kaiser was not — the outspoken banker said to anyone who was interested he was convinced that, even if Germany beat France and Russia while England remained neutral, England and the United States would never allow the Kaiser to enjoy his victories for long. Since the Anglo-Saxon powers had mastery of the sea, the German navy being no match to them, the Kaiser's days were numbered. A war would seal the Kaiser's — and Germany's — fate.

Shortly after nine in the morning Manfred von Kosenburg called Ali from his office at the back the Neue Schloss in Potsdam.

"I am afraid I have to disappoint Your Excellency." His voice was business-like. "The meeting with His Majesty for this afternoon has had to be cancelled."

"Oh." Ali felt a dark pain at the pit of his stomach. "Herr von Kosenburg," — he was being deliberately formal to underline the gravity of what he was about to say — "this is indeed bad news. Not for the reason why I originally approached you. To tell you the truth, all along I had something else in mind." He paused. "Something which, under these desperate circumstances, I am compelled to tell you."

"I see," said Manfred. Ali thought he detected an unusual hesitation in his voice. "I think Your Excellency and I know each other well enough to be frank with one another. If you give me your word of honour that you will observe a confidence, I will tell you the reason for the cancellation. It may have a bearing on your situation. It is not what I assume you think, that His Majesty has more important things to do. It is something else."

"I give you my word of honour."

"His Majesty is not well. My brother and a number of his colleagues are seeing him in the late afternoon, at the time I had set aside for you."

Oh thank you, Allah! Ali exclaimed in silent prayer. Once again, you have performed a miracle! You have done more than half of our work! His heart began pounding with excitement. What extraordinary good fortune! What amazing good luck! If they declare the All Highest incompetent and he is forced to vacate the throne, even if only temporarily, all Zade had to do is to persuade him not have the Crown Prince step into his shoes but somebody else.

Ali remembered that Manfred's brother, the eminent neurologist Professor Dr. Hermann von Kosenburg, was one of the Kaiser's doctors. He and Zade had seen him last on Thursday, at the ceremony in the Lustgarten, in the uniform of the Lützow Grenadiers. Was he there professionally, to keep an eye on the Kaiser? Like most people, Ali knew questions had been asked from time to time about His Majesty's mental condition. He also knew that in Germany the functions of neurologists and psychiatrists overlapped.

Ali's mind was racing.

"May I ask whether your brother considers the Kaiser's condition disabling?"

"He will make his diagnosis after examining him at noon."

"I understand. Herr von Kosenburg, you have done me the honour to take me into your confidence. May I now do the same for you?"

"Please go ahead."

"Many of us have been aware for a long time that the Kaiser's mental condition is — how shall I put it ? — fragile. He has already suffered one breakdown, after the Daily Telegraph affair. At the time, let's see, some six years ago, there was even talk of abdication. You are now telling me that under the current pressures he may be suffering another collapse."

"We will know more later this afternoon."

"But I am sure you and a few of your colleagues have already had to give the matter intensive thought. If by any chance a regency or even an abdication is again being considered, one assumes it would be in favour of the Crown Prince. I remember from our conversation after Albert Ballin's return from London that you take a critical view of the ever-growing influence of the military on the government's decision-making."

"I do indeed."

"So one would think the generals would be delighted if the somewhat unpredictable Kaiser was superseded by his more predictable son."

"One can be sure of that. Why are you telling me these things, if I may ask?"

"Because we have an alternative solution. My friend and I would like to put it to you and your brother before your brother's encounter with the Kaiser this afternoon. It is a solution I have not the slightest doubt you would welcome. And from the impression I have of your brother — I have only seen him once, at a ceremony in Potsdam — I can tell that he, too, will have no reason to regret listening to us."

Manfred von Kosenburg said he would do his best to arrange a meeting as soon as possible in his brother's office.

✦

The eminent Professor Dr. Hermann von Kosenburg had a spacious clinic in the Neurological Department in the Universitätsklinik, on the north side of the River Spree, not far from the Schloss. He turned out to be exactly as Ali remembered him, amiable, sympathetic, human, quite handsome with his white goatee. This time he wore a pince-nez with a gold chain, which he had not worn in the Lustgarten in Potsdam. He smoked a cigar.

Manfred introduced his visitors.

Vast experience with men and women did not prevent the great man from being completely tongue-tied by Zade's beauty. This time she wore a maroon dress.

The doctor invited his brother and the two Oudanians to take their seats on comfortable leather armchairs near the window. Ali Hassan accepted a cigar.

"To save time," Hermann von Kosenburg opened the conversation, "and on the firm understanding that this conversation will remain confidential, I must tell you I have already come to the conclusion, on the basis of my close observations of His Majesty over a period of seven years, but especially during the last week, that I will not take the responsibility of allowing him to lead this nation into a war. He is simply not well enough. My colleagues concur with me. His precarious mental illness would be serious enough for us to take immediate action even without the situation created this morning by an action of the General Staff that has — I am trying to find the right word — paralysed His Majesty."

The doctor's cigar had gone out. His brother found a match to light it again.

Manfred frowned. He had not heard anything about this, he said.

"Nor has anybody else, outside the immediate entourage. However, it was widely known that throughout the last three weeks there has been a great deal of resentment by the General Staff of what they consider His Majesty's interference. This resentment became more acute after His Majesty returned to Potsdam from his cruise last Monday. The Chief of Staff, General Helmuth von Moltke, who has for many years entertained a close personal friendship with His Majesty, developed grave doubts about His Majesty's command of the situation when, on the basis of the flimsiest evidence — to be precise, an ambiguous message from King George of England, a message that was quickly corrected — he endangered the projected military operations in the West by suddenly, in what they describe as an irresponsible, impetuous, capricious manner, trying to put a halt to them. Therefore, in the name of the General Staff, General von Moltke made a personal appeal this morning to His Majesty to abdicate in favour of his son, the Crown Prince, for reasons of health.

The thinking behind this is clear. At a time like this, the Kaiser is considered too soft and too volatile to be in charge."

"One would have thought," Ali said, "since they mention 'reasons of health,' the generals might have solicited your opinion before making their move."

"They did not." The doctor made a slightly impatient gesture meaning 'you're absolutely right, but that would be out of character, so let's not waste time on it.' "Quite independently from the generals, my colleagues have appointed me their spokesman. In their name and mine I shall recommend to His Majesty, later this afternoon, to abdicate. In the meantime I am told that steps are being taken to convene a Crown Council consisting of representatives from the twenty-five states that comprise the Reich, the Chancellor, and the Speaker of the Reichstag, for tomorrow morning. A temporary regency under His Imperial Highness, the Crown Prince, will be announced as soon as His Majesty has given his consent. He will be in no position to withhold it. No doubt later in the day the Crown Prince will declare war on Russia and France." He turned to Ali. "I assume that all this will radically alter the plan Your Excellency wishes to discuss with me."

"Oh, by no means," Ali responded. "But before I speak, may I ask how you would describe the Kaiser's illness?"

"Of course. That is an entirely reasonable request. He is suffering from a maniac depressive psychosis. Laymen call it 'periodic disturbedness.' This is not a new discovery. His increasingly frequent rages, his irrational and violent abuse of people often showing symptoms of megalomania and acute paranoia, his many flights from reality generally, have been the subject of innumerable conversations in and outside our profession. In England, I understand, questions about His Majesty's sanity have been raised privately for many years. Moreover, there is no question that the events of 1908 have taken a particularly heavy toll.

His Majesty has never fully recovered. So we were not entirely unprepared for this contingency. I might add that many of my colleagues believe that during his traumatic birth process he not only suffered the well-known injury to his left arm, but also considerable brain damage. You may not know that in 1896 he had an operation of the inner ear, leaving him deaf in the right ear. The inner ear is close to the brain. Moreover, you may already be familiar with the exercises His Majesty had to perform as a child, to compensate him for his physical infirmity, which, however well intentioned, no doubt caused permanent damage."

The doctor looked at Zade, clearly inviting a comment.

"The poor man," she said.

"Indeed, madame."

He turned expectantly to Ali.

"Professor von Kosenburg," Ali began, "the proposal I want to put to you is simple. Putting it to you will take no time at all. But before I do so, please permit me to ask you another question that you may at first consider off the point. I am trying not to waste time. It is a political question. I think you will agree that the Kaiser is immensely popular in Germany, even though many people, especially in the intelligentsia, enjoy criticizing him and complain that he gets on their nerves. Is that not so?"

Dr. Kosenburg wondered what was on the Ambassador's mind.

"Absolutely. So…?"

"I think you will agree, doctor, that without the German people's overwhelming consent, His Majesty would not have been able to stay in power for longer than a month."

"I would agree with that."

"I might even go further," Ali said, feeling encouraged by the doctor's positive responses, "and state that the Kaiser's upbeat and flamboyant performance and dynamic, virile personality correspond in many ways to the German mood at present and to the picture Germans have of themselves. It should not surprise us if in future our age will be called the Wilhelmian Age."

"Your Excellency, what are you driving at?"

"So if he is mad," Ali lowered his voice, "are the German people also mad?"

"Ah," Dr. Kosenburg said, without a semblance of a smile, "I wish our science was sufficiently advanced to answer this all-important question. Any unscientific reply would be, shall we say, mere journalism. You must have a good reason for asking it, at this time."

"I do. So far war has not been declared. Whatever they say, the Russian mobilization can be stopped, if there is a will to stop it. The last word has not been spoken. Only the Kaiser can speak it — before tomorrow morning. It seems to me that, if there is an honourable alternative, the Germans, if you think of them as individuals and not as a collectivity, are not mad enough to wish to go to war, even if most of their generals do and if thousands of young people, no doubt suffering from I am sure you would call mass hysteria, apparently can't wait to sacrifice their lives for Kaiser Wilhelm. After all, ordinary people in your country know that Germany is already the largest, richest, the most dynamic and best armed nation on the continent of Europe without a war."

"Your Excellency assumes," Manfred observed before his brother was ready, "that, other things being equal, individuals prefer to act rationally to acting irrationally."

"So do I, most firmly," the doctor agreed. "Of course, I speak as an individual German and not as a scientist. Many of us have heard of a colleague of ours in Vienna who does consider himself a scientist and who takes the view that we are all guided primarily by irrational impulses. There have always been philosophers who share that view. But at this moment let us feel free to err on the side of shallow optimism and assume that man is, if there is time to reflect, in all truly important, serious, existential matters, guided by reason. All right. Tell us what you propose."

"I propose that my friend" — he bowed gently to Zade — "be given the opportunity to persuade His Majesty to abdicate in favour, not of the Crown Prince, but of the Crown Prince's youngest son Friedrich. As you know, he is three years old. We have ideas on the composition of a civilian regency that would be established immediately but I don't think it would be right for us outsiders to tell Germans now who we think should be the head of the new Regency. The only thing that is important for you to know is that the new Regency would immediately cancel all plans to engage in any military action against Russia and France in the near future and tell the world that it has done so. Of course, firm precautions would have to be taken to prevent the generals from unleashing a civil war."

Dr. von Kosenburg took a deep breath and turned to Zade.

"Madame, if I understand this rightly, you are asking me to make arrangements for you to make this proposal to His Majesty personally. Have you met him?"

"He is well acquainted with me as the author of the One Thousand and One Stories. They are about him and he admires them greatly. As you know" — she said this to Manfred — "His Majesty has told the Crown Prince that he wished to meet me. That wish I am now prepared to grant."

"It is assumed," Ali explained without waiting for their next question, "that the two will be able to be alone together and converse, off and on, throughout the entire night. Baron von Toplitz, whom you know well, has kindly made his Villa Suleika available for the purpose. He has instructed his staff to expect His Majesty between seven and eight. My friend will be there to receive him. It could easily be suggested to His Majesty that the Villa would be suitable place for him to discuss the modalities for tomorrow's Crown Council and perhaps sign the necessary papers. He is to go there alone, of course. If he insists, as he often does, that at least one adjutant accompany him, it must be explained to him that there is only one precedent for this situation in Prussian history, the abdication, for similar reasons, of his great uncle Friedrich Wilhelm IV in 1857 to be replaced by his brother, His Majesty's revered grandfather Wilhelm I, and that he, too, had to face a similar situation alone. Never mind whether that is true or not. No one must know about the location. Least of all the Empress."

"I don't think," the doctor smiled at last, "even Clausewitz could have invented a more ingenious strategy."

◆

Nothing was easier for Manfred von Kosenburg, as the senior official in the Hausmarschall's office in charge of His Majesty's agenda, than to liberate himself from his other duties and drive His Majesty, accompanied only by the Emperor's senior physician who happened to be his brother, to the Villa Suleika at quarter to eight o'clock. They had to bypass the excited crowds assembled outside the Schloss to applaud him vigorously for cutting the ropes about to strangle the encircled Fatherland. The war that he would declare tomorrow would prove to the world what Germany was made of, demonstrate to one and all Germany's superior Kultur and give Germany's aimless youth a noble purpose to live for, and, far more important, to die for.

Another war, of which these crowds knew nothing, had already begun and, alas, been lost. It was also a war on two flanks, although not coordinated, conducted by the Kaiser's generals on one front and his doctors on the other, with the same objective, to force him to abdicate. The outmanoeuvred, overpowered Kaiser would have no choice but to agree to surrender tomorrow, Sunday, morning, August 2.

So this was to be his last night as the All Highest.

His mood alternated between paroxysms of rage directed at his rebellious son, at the generals who had betrayed him, at the English and the Jews, especially that "loathsome, dirty, Jewish fiend" Maximilian Harden, and lacerating self-pity, for having to suffer this horrendous fate without a single friend and without any weapons to defend himself. His only bosom friend and his former crisis manager, Philipp von Eulenburg, now old, sick and broken, with whom he could no longer communicate, at least had had a trial and could speak up. During the last two or three days he had not been able to eat and sleep normally and had mercilessly snapped at the helpless Empress whenever she tried to talk to him.

The emotional upheaval was too devastating for him to ask himself why he was not even allowed to wave to the crowds from the balcony of the Schloss — that would have done his spirits some good — and why, of all places, the Villa Suleika had been chosen for the formality that was to precede the session his executioners were planning for tomorrow morning. Whenever he had been in the villa, he had admired its gorgeous oriental courtyard with its beautiful fountain at the centre, the sculptures and the countless, multi-coloured columns arranged around it in symmetrical patterns. Why he should be taken here, on this of all occasions, was beyond understanding.

The brothers Kosenburg dropped His Majesty, wearing the uniform of the Scharnhorst Hussars, at the door and respectfully took their leave. A dark-skinned Egyptian butler let him into the villa, took his cape, his cane and pigskin gloves, and, walking briskly, guided him through the large central hall with its magnificent Persian carpets and furnishings directly to the courtyard. The butler politely pointed to an ornate bench near the fountain, next to a table covered with an array of exotic bottles and two crystal glasses, and trays of candied dates and figs. He said His Majesty should feel free to help himself, bowed and excused himself.

What was this? Why was there nobody here to receive him? A spasm of anger — for the first time combined with acute fear — seized him. What kind of honeyed trap had they laid for him? Why had the most idyllic spot in all Berlin been chosen for this occasion? He had been in total command of every situation ever since he cut loose from his oppressive tutor Georg Hinzpeter, and he hated surprises. How did Louis XVI spend the last night before they led him to the guillotine? And what indignities did Charles I of England have to suffer before they took him to the scaffold?

The Kaiser looked around. Not a soul to be seen. Not a sound. Total silence. He had the feeling that behind the hundreds of columns and sculptures people were hiding, watching him. Could it be that the doctors were right that he was paranoid?

He got up and walked around. No, there was nobody there. He sat down again on the bench and drummed his fingers on the wooden arms. Suddenly, unseen musicians began playing a sweet, sad, soothing melody in a minor key, very softly — violins, flutes and oboes. In recent years, he had rarely been touched by music. It must have been due to the emotional upheaval he was going through that, to his amazement, tears came to his eyes. Yes, the generals may be right — he was too soft for the job to be done. He took out a handkerchief and wiped his eyes. It seemed he had not heard anything as beautiful since the evenings with his friends in Liebenberg, long, long ago.

He closed his eyes and listened.

When he opened his eyes Zade was standing in front of him, carrying her Stories in her right hand.

He rose, stumbled slightly, regained his balance, looked at her, inhaling her perfume. It had the same effect on him as the perfume her predecessors used on their sultans for the last ten centuries.

"May I ask" — his throat was dry — "who are you? Why am I here?"

"Your Majesty is here because those who care for you have decided that you should spend the last night of your reign with me. I know you well. You wanted to see me. I am from Ouda and I am the author of these stories."

She handed the book to him. He glanced at them.

"Oh yes," he remembered, adding in the manner of a Prussian schoolmaster, "First-class work."

"Thank you, Your Majesty."

Zade took a bottle and poured dark red Anatolian wine in one of the crystal glasses on the table and handed it to him. Then she poured one for herself.

They touched glasses. He looked at her again and felt a pleasant tightening in the lower part of his abdomen, a delicious sensation he had not enjoyed since the days when he was left alone with those young ladies, sometimes two at a time, whom Frau Wolf in Vienna had procured for him, and never, in the same way, with his straightforward, business-like and serviceable wife before embracing her. Oh, what had he missed in the last twenty-six years, ever since he became Kaiser and allowed his duties to deprive him of these life-enhancing, life-justifying pleasures! He remembered with a shudder of delight that while in the thrall of this future-oriented stiffening, the burdens of rational thinking are lifted and the usual considerations and inhibitions suspended. No need to hide his withered left arm. The sensation took complete command of him, to the exclusion of everything else.

Zade sat down on the bench with the Kaiser. They slowly drank the wine. He helped himself to a candied fig. The sweet melancholy music continued.

She took his good, strong hand and caressed it.

"We are alone, Your Majesty," she said, feeling with her fingers the four rings on his. "We have the whole night. We will make love, gently, we take our time. We will eat and we will drink. We will sleep. For one night we belong together. I come from another world and I can say things to you no one has ever said to you. The musicians and servants have been amply paid and will be discreet. Baron von Toplitz sends his greetings and has given his blessing."

The Kaiser was not used to following a lady, certainly not a lady without European rank or title, but this time he did as she led him to the Baron's bedroom to the right of the hall, in the original Islamic architectural model the men's guest-room, always the symbol of the economic status of the household and therefore the most decorated room in the house. The room was filled with flowers. The huge, eighteenth-century Turkish double bed the Baron had purchased two years ago in Smyrna, exquisitely ornamented with half-moons and allegedly one of a certain insatiable sultan's favourite, was covered with dark blue silken sheets and pillows. On a side table were golden bowls filled with grapes and pomegranates and other exotic fruit, and a little silver bell.

Zade allowed him to kiss her, but pulled away as soon as he became too passionate. Clearly, there was no need to worry about him liking men better than women. Also, his mustache tickled her. She remembered with amusement Alphonse Picard's abortive strategy.

She did not let him undress her, but, because of his physical handicap, she had to help him take off his uniform. She knew all

255

there was to know about the Kaiser's tempo, about his insecurities, his impatience and restlessness, about the way he gobbled his food. That is why she had just said, 'We have the whole night'. She also knew a great deal about the politics of the bedroom. After Sarajevo, she had come all the way from Ouda to curb him, to prevent him from doing what he probably thought was natural — to march with lightning speed and shoot. The important thing now was to do exactly that, to curb him, to control him. He was not likely to be in the mood to listen to what she had to say afterwards if she now allowed him to do what he thought was natural — one, two, three, shoot. To prepare him for the all-important talk to come, she had to guide him tenderly from one delight to another, in a slow accelerando followed by a gentle diminuendo, a slow crescendo followed by a gentle decrescendo, using parts of the body he had never known existed, taking their time, finding their rhythm, climbing the ladder, until the all-consuming, all-liberating, all-cobwebs-removing Hallelujah.

A few minutes of grateful silence followed.

She reached for a bunch of grapes and offered him one after another.

Never had they tasted so good.

"Remember Constantinople, Jerusalem and Damascus?" she asked. "You should have visited us in Ouda. Your Majesty loves the Orient. So many ancient treasures still buried under the sand, waiting for you to dig up. You said you preferred us Muslims to Christians."

He laughed. "I never said that! You made that up!"

"You would be surprised how much I know," she replied. "Don't forget I did not invent my stories. I studied Your Majesty."

"Why did you write them?"

"I want my King Shahriyar to be like Your Majesty. I wrote the stories for him. I want him to be modern king of a modern nation, educated and productive. But I want Ouda to be built on sound foundations, on foundations friendly to human beings, not on foundations laid by a gigantic egomaniac who believed in power for its own sake and had contempt for humanity, an old man who thought nothing could be achieved without the use of force, cunning and corruption."

"I dismissed Bismarck," the Kaiser whispered.

"Yes, Your Majesty, you did, and I admire you for it. It was a heroic act. It required true courage. But you did not do it because you disapproved of his principles and his system. You did it to be your own Bismarck, to be a modern Bismarck, a Bismarck whose political power did not only derive from that of the Junkers in East Prussia but also from the captains of industry all over Germany. To be popular, you even wanted to be Emperor of the Poor, but that did not last very long. Bismarck was a dictator. He, not you, was responsible for the failure of Germany to develop stable government through political parties. For thirty-five years he dominated German politics. He invented crises for him to solve. Crafty, deceitful and vindictive, he took revenge on anyone who opposed him. You were not like that. Bismarck had contempt for everybody, even those who supported him. When things did not go his own way, he would smash china and burst into fits of sobbing. Your Majesty was made of different material. You were not cut out to be a dictator. Your Majesty is too interested in too many other things."

Wilhelm was caressing the back of her neck.

"In any case, you did not know it was already too late. The old man had done his work. Bismarck had built a dictatorship designed only for himself. 'Organized chaos', your father called it. Dictatorships are not hereditary. Monarchies are. To enable your monarchy to survive you had to invent something new that would keep it going, at least for a little while."

The Kaiser opened his eyes wide. "I did?" he asked. "What did I invent?"

"You invented the modern ruler, the ruler who understands the politics and the technology of image-making. You invented the modern technique of becoming and remaining popular. You invented a theatrical personality that was in tune with its time. You understood you had to be an actor to do this right. But you were more than an actor. You had studied kingship in the ancient world and you created a modern equivalent. You even made yourself believe that Allah Himself made you Kaiser. That is how you could justify to yourself that you were Germany and Germany was you. Your concept of modern kingship demanded that you appeared confident and optimistic even when you were depressed and despondent, and you did it superbly. You made sure you were seen everywhere. You made speeches. No other monarch in this century ever made speeches. Your technique was to flatter your public. You read a book by your friend Houston Stewart Chamberlain designed to demonstrate that you so-called 'Aryans' belonged to a superior race. Very flattering. This you thought gave you the right to despise everybody who isn't German or English, even though in your heart you knew better. You kept more then twenty German sovereigns more or less loyal to you because they had no alternative. Your generals had the power. They all sensed, as you yourself sensed, and as even Bismarck sensed, that your days were numbered, that it was your job to stem, to hold back revolution, anarchy, terror. In Bismarck's day, Tsar Alexander II was assassinated. Franz Joseph's brother Maximilian was shot in Mexico. There was an attempt on your grandfather Wilhelm's life. And on your grandmother Queen Victoria. And on Napoleon III. In your own day, Empress Elisabeth of Austria was murdered. The King and Queen of Spain had been shot at by a demented waiter. The King and Queen of Serbia were thrown out of the window."

Wilhelm gently kissed her soft shoulders.

"And speaking of grandfathers, you always talk about your

grandfather Wilhelm, never about your other grandfather, Albert, the Prince Consort. He would have been a much better model for you." Zade deliberately made herself sound long-winded and professorial, even hectoring, in order to create suspense for what was to come. "Following closely the upheavals in Germany in 1848 and 1849 from his position next to Queen Victoria, he was on the side of the liberals who had assembled in the Saint Paul's Church in Frankfurt, determined to work towards a united Germany with a liberal, democratic constitution and responsible government, like England's. Your other grandfather was on the other side and crushed the revolution. Germany could have gone the way of either of your two grandfathers, Albert or Wilhelm. Germany went the wrong way, Wilhelm's way, your way, it chose the wrong grandfather. Or rather, it didn't choose it. Bismarck imposed it. He made sure that the elected assembly could always be persuaded to vote the necessary funds for the army and navy. And if some of its members turned ugly he saw to it they were undermined or ignored, or flattered into eventually agreeing, or, if that didn't work, bribed. In Bismarck day, everyone boasted that in Germany the rule of law prevailed, and so it did most of the time. But the police could always take care of independent critics on the grounds that the security of the state or the honour of the army was at stake. You must admit you always admired Bismarck for all the things he did. Instead of Your Majesty now taking the consequences for his so-called achievements I propose to you an infinitely more rewarding path. Let us order something to eat."

Zade shook the little silver bell.

The Egyptian butler appeared promptly, pushing a wagon of oriental delicacies. Zade and the Kaiser were, of course, decently covered. The butler named some of the dishes — egg and cheese soup, Circassian chicken, stuffed courgette, and dozens of cakes and buns to chose from, baba tatlisi and baked semonila among them. They listened politely and helped themselves. Before the Kaiser had a chance to ask what path, Zade resumed her monologue.

"Bismarck's system gave you no alternative to personal rule. Which meant rule by you and those few whom you allowed to consider themselves your personal friends. But what it actually meant, ultimately, was rule by the General Staff. In December 1912, you summoned the 'War Council' under circumstances very much like those of today. The Generals wanted to go to war. And so did you. Or at least so it seemed. You might very well have welcomed a face-saving way out, at the last minute, if an opportunity had arisen. You certainly appeared to be disappointed when Admiral von Tirpitz said to you, and to them, 'Wait till we are ready. The Navy won't be ready until the summer of 1914.' Which is now. And now, the immediate cause, the assassination by terrorists of Franz Ferdinand, has been forgotten. It has become irrelevant. For the generals and admirals, the moment has come, to prevent the enemy from striking first."

Had it not been for the humanizing after-effects of the all-therapeutic Hallelujah, the Kaiser would have flared up and shouted, 'And now they dare to cut me out! If only that double-crossing hypocritical weakling King George had not let me down at the last minute! He's worse than his father! In the end I was quite prepared to go along with the generals.'

But that is not what he said.

"Did you come all the way from Ouda to tell me all this?" he asked softly.

"No, not at all. I have a much more important objective. But before I tell you what it is, I have something else to say. Every person is born a Muslim. We are all created by the One Almighty God. Your Majesty strayed. I know I could easily help you revert to being a Muslim."

"Revert? You mean convert?"

"Your Majesty may call it what you like."

"Oh no," the Kaiser laughed. "I am a Christian through and through!"

"Give me a chance and we will see about that," Zade replied. "Your Majesty is a student of history and archeology. You have always shown curiosity about other cultures. It will not be hard for you to learn that there is no essential difference between Allah and your god. Much of your Bible is our Koran. All you have to do is substitute Muhammad for Jesus Christ and bear witness that Muhammad is Allah's Messenger and you will cease being an infidel."

The Kaiser gently shook his head. "I promise nothing," he declared. "But I admit I never thought for a moment that I would find the idea tempting."

"I knew Your Majesty would. This, as you know, is your night of destiny. I am now ready to tell you what my real purpose was in coming from Ouda to Berlin. I wish to propose to Your Majesty a way to go down in History as the Saviour of Mankind."

The Kaiser sat up.

"The doctors and the generals have made my work easy. They are forcing you to abdicate tomorrow morning in favour of the Crown Prince. He would, of course, carry on the war and you would have had no choice but to give him your blessing. I offer you something better. I propose you go down in history as the greatest benefactors of mankind the world has known since the beginning of time. I offer you the opportunity to spare the world a war that undoubtedly would cost millions of lives. Only you can prevent it from breaking out. No one else can. It is an illusion to think it would be quick and easy. Even your Chief of the General Staff General Helmuth von Moltke is profoundly pessimistic and thinks it would be long and make the world, after it is over, unrecognizable."

The Kaiser was still the All Highest.

"Explain yourself," he commanded

"We have been talking about grandfathers. Let us talk about grandsons. I propose you abdicate in favour of your grandson, the Crown Prince's youngest son, Fritz, who is three. Do you want to save the monarchy? This is the way. I propose you establish a civilian regency that will immediate call off the war."

The Kaiser laughed.

"The generals will ignore me and march anyway."

"Oh no, they won't," Zade retorted. "They have sworn an oath to Your Majesty. German officers don't break their oath to their Sovereign. But let us assume Your Majesty is right and they defy the legitimate, constitutionally established Regency. It will then issue a proclamation to the governments of Russia, Belgium and France. It will appeal to them not to resist the invading German troops, even if they fire. 'Let them come in if they want to,' the proclamation will ask them to say. 'Don't resist the invader if, by threatening the use of force, they occupy buildings, loot and destroy. They will soon go home. The conscience of the individual men, if not their officers, will demand it.'"

The Kaiser tried to speak but no words came.

"'And so will their wives, mothers, and girlfriends at home.'" Zade concluded.

At last His Majesty managed to ask another question.

"And who is to be the head of the Civilian Regency you propose?"

"Professor Albert Einstein, of your Kaiser Wilhelm Institute."

•

Wilhelm II followed Zade's advice. Events unfolded exactly as she had prescribed and, as the whole world knows, everybody lived happily ever after.